TERESA MEDEIROS

The Vampire Who Loved Me

AVON BOOKS
An Imprint of HarperCollins*Publishers*

This is a work of fiction. Names, characters, places, and incidents are products of the author's imagination or are used fictitiously and are not to be construed as real. Any resemblance to actual events, locales, organizations, or persons, living or dead, is entirely coincidental.

AVON BOOKS
An Imprint of HarperCollins*Publishers*
10 East 53rd Street
New York, New York 10022-5299

ISBN-13: 978-0-06-076303-9
ISBN-10: 0-06-076303-5
www.avonromance.com

First Avon Books paperback printing: October 2006

Printed in the U.S.A.

10 9 8 7 6 5 4 3 2 1

"If you have a passion for fiction, try . . .

TERESA MEDEIROS."

Philadelphia Inquirer

"I'm not leaving until I get what I came here for. You owe me and I've come to collect."

For one fleeting second, Julian was almost thankful he was a vampire, because it took a supernatural effort to keep his features schooled in indifference. She was, beyond the shadow of a doubt, the most beautiful woman he had ever seen.

He swirled the last of the port around the bottom of the glass before bringing it to his lips. "You can't be one of my creditors, because I'm sure I'd remember being *dunned* by someone as lovely as you," he said, giving the word an inflection that was impossible to ignore. "And if you're not one of my creditors, then I suggest you step out of my way because I don't owe you so much as the time of day."

"That's where you're wrong, Mr. Kane." Her fingers steady, she reached up and jerked down on her velvet choker.

Julian froze, mesmerized by the sight of that graceful throat. A throat that should have been as creamy and flawless as the rest of her, but was instead marred by the faded scars of two distinct puncture wounds.

As Julian lifted his disbelieving gaze to meet the defiant blue of Portia Cabot's eyes, he knew his luck had finally run out . . .

By Teresa Medeiros

THE VAMPIRE WHO LOVED ME
AFTER MIDNIGHT
YOURS UNTIL DAWN
ONE NIGHT OF SCANDAL
A KISS TO REMEMBER
THE BRIDE AND THE BEAST
CHARMING THE BEAST
NOBODY'S DARLING
TOUCH OF ENCHANTMENT
BREATH OF MAGIC
FAIREST OF THEM ALL
THIEF OF HEARTS
A WHISPER OF ROSES
ONCE AN ANGEL
HEATHER AND VELVET
SHADOWS AND LACE
LADY OF CONQUEST

For Elizabeth Bevarly, Connie Brockway, Christina Dodd, Eloisa James, Lisa Kleypas and all of my other dear friends at www.squawkradio.com for giving me a reason to smile every single day.

For Doris Knight, Joann Ashby and Pat Dougherty—my beloved trio of aunties. I thank God every day for giving me such incredible women to learn from and love.

And for my Michael. A lifetime will never be long enough to love you.

Prologue

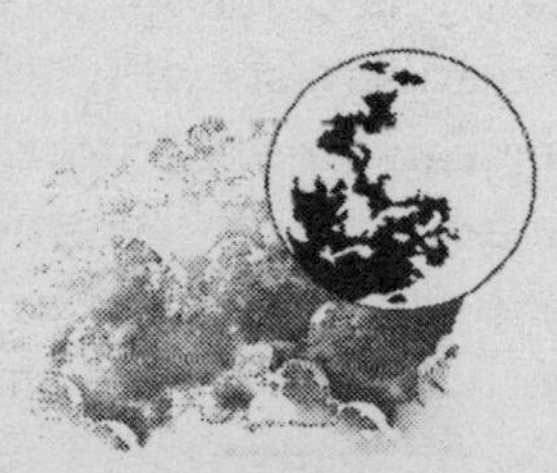

London
1826

It was a lovely night to die.

As twilight waned, plump feathers of snow began to drift down from the starless sky. Soon everything that was coarse and ugly and dirty about the teeming streets of Whitechapel was buried beneath a downy blanket of white. The flakes danced and swirled around the streetlamps, reducing their glow to a hazy halo.

Jenny O'Flaherty drew her shawl up over her fine, black hair, ducked her head, and quickened her steps. The snow's dazzling beauty didn't stop the wind from biting through her threadbare shawl with icy teeth. She had never been more eager to reach the dreary flat she shared with three other girls. Soon she would be hunkered down in front of her own hearth with a bowl of porridge to warm both her hands and her belly.

As a sneering footman elbowed her off the walk so his lady could sweep past, Jenny cast the woman's elegant kid gloves a longing glance. Working fifteen hours a day as a seamstress left her fingertips stinging and raw. On nights like this, they sometimes cracked and bled, leaving her to cry herself to sleep.

She lifted her chin, refusing to feel sorry for herself. Her dear old mother, God rest her soul, had always encouraged her to count her blessings. No gentleman was ever going to hire an uneducated Irish lass to teach his children or serve as a companion to his wife, but at least she hadn't had to take to the streets like so many girls who had come off that same boat from Dublin three years ago. The thought of selling her body to every man with a bone in his pants and two shillings to rub together chilled her to the soul.

As she approached the darkened mouth of the next alley, her steps slowed. By cutting through the winding lane, she could shave nearly three blocks from her journey. She wouldn't normally take such a risk, but surely there would be no one to accost her on such a bitterly cold night. She had no purse for a thief to cut, and with her shoulders hunched against the wind and her shawl drawn up to hide her rosy cheeks, any man intent upon mischief could easily mistake her for a toothless crone.

Thinking yearningly of the crackling fire and steaming bowl of porridge that awaited her at the end of her journey, she cast one last look at the bustling throngs behind her, then ducked into the alley.

She hurried through the shifting shadows, growing more uneasy with each step. The wind swooped through the tunnel created by the ramshackle buildings that loomed over her on either side, moaning like a betrayed lover. She stole a look over her shoulder, already beginning to wish she'd stayed on the congested streets and walked the extra blocks to her flat. Although the snow that had blown into the alley was unmarked by any prints but hers, she would have almost sworn she heard a muffled footfall behind her.

Determined to reach the end of the alley before she had true cause to regret her decision, she broke into a trot. She was almost to the mouth of the alley when the toe of her boot caught on a jutting cobblestone, sending her sprawling to her hands and knees.

A shadow fell over her. She slowly lifted her head, terrified of what she might find. But her gasp of shock was quickly swallowed by a sob of relief. No cutpurse would be arrayed in such handsome finery.

As the stranger looming over her gently cupped her elbow and lifted her to her feet, she found herself gazing up into a pair of eyes that almost seemed to glow in the dim light.

"You poor lamb," her rescuer crooned. "You took quite a nasty tumble. Do you have a name, child?"

"Jenny," she whispered, mesmerized by those extraordinary eyes. "My name is Jenny."

The stranger smiled, obviously detecting the telltale lilt in her speech. " 'Tis a bonny name for a bonny lass." The smile faded. "Why look at that! Your hands are bleeding!"

Jenny curled her fingers into her torn palms, suddenly embarrassed by the roughness of her skin and her grubby fingernails. "It's nothing really. Just a scratch."

"Why don't you let me have a look at them?"

Although she tried to resist, the stranger's grip was surprisingly strong. Before she knew it, one of her palms was exposed to that glowing gaze. She thought she might be offered a clean handkerchief to bind the wound. But to her keen shock, the stranger bent back her fingers and began to lap at the fresh droplets of blood with a greedy tongue.

Trembling with horror, Jenny snatched back her hand and wheeled around to run, already beginning to suspect that there would be no cozy fire or bowl of porridge in her future. Before she could take two steps, the stranger had seized her in a merciless grip. She flailed and kicked, her hands curled into desperate claws, but her strength was no match for her assailant's.

"Good night, sweet Jenny," whispered the singsong voice in her ear just before everything went red, then black.

One

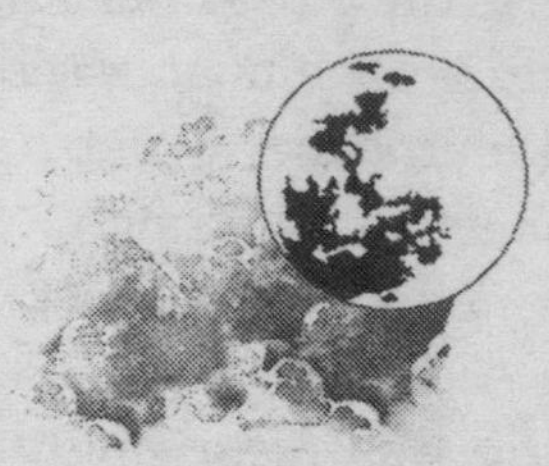

It was a lovely day to die.

Feathers of snow drifted out of the dawn sky, blanketing the park meadow in white. It wasn't difficult for Julian Kane to imagine how that pristine counterpane would look spattered with his blood.

His shout of laughter profaned the hush of the falling flakes. "What say you, Cubby, my man? Shall we sing a few rousing choruses of 'The Girl I Left Behind Me' to spur us onward to glory?" He stumbled as a contrary hillock snagged his foot, forcing him to drape his arm even more heavily over the ample shoulders of his friend.

"Perhaps 'Blow the Man Down' would be more fitting."

Cuthbert listed to the right, struggling to balance both Julian and the mahogany box tucked beneath his free arm. "I'd rather not, Jules. My head is aching something fierce. I can't believe I let you talk me into this. What sort of second allows his first to stay out all night getting foxed before a duel? You should have let me put you on that ferry back to the Continent while there was still time."

Julian wagged a chiding finger at him. "Don't scold. If I'd have wanted a nag, I'd have married one."

Cuthbert gave a doleful snort. "If you'd have had the good sense to fall in love and marry some unfortunate chit, Wallingford wouldn't have caught you nuzzling his fiancée's ear at their betrothal supper and I'd be tucked in my cozy bed right now, dreaming about opera dancers and toasting my feet on a warm brick."

"You insult me, Cubby! I never met a woman I didn't love."

"On the contrary, you love every woman you meet. There is a distinction, however subtle." Cuthbert grunted as his friend trod upon the side of his foot. He had imbibed nearly as many bottles of cheap port as Julian had, but at least he could still stand without assistance. For now.

"Shhhhhhh!" His friend's exaggerated plea for silence startled a flock of starlings from the branches of a nearby alder. Julian pointed one elegant gloved finger. "There they are now, lurking beneath that copse of firs."

From what Cuthbert could ascertain, the gentlemen waiting beside the crested town coach on the far side of the meadow were making no attempt to lurk. Miles Devonforth, the marquess of Wallingford, was pacing a shallow trench in the snow. His tautly controlled strides never varied, not even when he jerked his watch from its fob pocket to glower at its face. A trio of companions hovered behind him—two gentlemen in voluminous box coats and a dour figure garbed all in black. Probably some disreputable surgeon who dabbled in undertaking, Cuthbert thought grimly, summoned to treat the loser of this illegal contest.

Or to measure him for his coffin.

A shiver of dread coursed down his spine. He raked a sandy lock of hair out of his hazel eyes and tugged Julian to a halt, his desperation mounting. "Beg off, Jules. It's not too late. What are they going to do? Run us down in their carriage and shoot you in the back? Why, I'll even go back to the Continent with you! We'll sail the Rhine and climb the Carpathians and conquer Rome. My father will forgive me in time. He's already cut off my allowance because I bought that diamond brooch for that delicious little actress you introduced me to in Florence. What more can he do? I know my father. He'll never disinherit his only son."

Julian stifled his blathering with a reproachful look. "Bite your tongue, Cubby. Surely you're not suggesting that I prove myself to be that most despised of all creatures—a man without honor."

Beneath the sable fringe of his lashes, Julian's soulful dark eyes fixed him with a gaze rife with wounded pride and wry self-mockery. Most women found the combination irresistible. Cuthbert was equally devastated.

Who was he to deny his friend this moment? He was only the slow-witted son of a crotchety old earl, destined to inherit a title and fortune he hadn't earned and die of comfortable old age in his bed. He wouldn't even have survived his Grand Tour if Julian hadn't rescued him from the clutches of a furious creditor at their very first meeting in a moonlit alley in Florence. Julian was a war hero, knighted by the Crown after he and his regiment had defeated sixty-thousand bloodthirsty Burmese soldiers on the outskirts of Rangoon a little over a year ago. This was hardly the first time he had faced his own mortality with such effortless grace.

Cuthbert groaned his defeat.

Julian gave his shoulder a consoling pat, then sought to drag himself erect. "Unhand me, Cubby, my man. I'm determined to march forward and meet the enemy on my own two feet." Shaking his shoulder-length mane of dark hair out of his eyes, he called out, "Devonforth!"

The marquess and his somber party turned as one. Julian had just added injury to insult by addressing the nobleman by his surname instead of his title. Cuthbert fancied he could hear the hiss of the marquess's indrawn breath, but perhaps it was only the bitter January wind rushing past his frozen ears.

Struggling valiantly against the billowing snow, Julian marched forward to bisect Wallingford's path. Cuthbert hugged the wooden box to his chest, a twinge of pride piercing his anxiety as Julian paused at the crest of a knoll to throw back his broad shoulders. He might have been preparing to brave the blinding wind and torrential rains of Burma's monsoon season. No one would have guessed he'd resigned his military commission right after the battle for Rangoon and had spent the past year and a half drinking and gambling his way across Europe.

Cuthbert's pride changed to alarm as the adjustment in Julian's bearing caused him to topple slowly backward, like a felled oak. Dropping the box, Cuthbert scrambled forward to catch him beneath the armpits before he could sprawl full-length in the snow.

Julian righted himself, chuckling beneath his breath. "Had I known the wind was so gusty, I'd not have unfurled my sails."

"Christ, Kane, you reek of spirits!"

Cuthbert looked up to find the marquess sneering down his long, equine nose at them.

Julian's lips quirked in an angelic smile. "Are you certain it's not your fiancée's perfume?"

Wallingford's face darkened to a dangerous hue. "Miss Englewood is no longer my fiancée."

Julian turned his smile on Cuthbert. "Remind me to call on the young lady this evening to offer her my heartfelt congratulations."

"I doubt you'll have the chance. She'll probably be offering your friend here her condolences." Wallingford pulled off his kid gloves and slapped them against his palm, much as he had slapped them across Julian's cheek at the supper the night before. "Let's get on with this, shall we? You've already wasted quite enough of my valuable time."

Cuthbert stuttered a protest, but Julian interrupted. "I do believe the gentleman is right. I've wasted quite enough of everyone's time."

Robbed of the opportunity for further argument, Cuthbert retrieved the box and fumbled with its clasp. The lid sprang open to reveal a gleaming pair of dueling pistols. As he reached for one of the weapons, his hand began to shake with a palsy that had nothing to do with the cold.

Julian cupped a hand over his to steady it and said softly, "There's no need. I checked them myself."

"But I'm supposed to check the charge. As your second, it's my duty to . . ."

Julian shook his head and gently pried the gun from his grasp. As their gazes met, Cuthbert caught an elusive glimpse of something odd in his friend's eyes—a bleak resignation that made a lump of premature sorrow swell in his own throat. But Julian banished it with one of his devilish winks before Cuthbert could convince himself it wasn't simply an illusion caused by too much liquor and too little sleep.

Terse details cluttered Cuthbert's mind as they argued the rules of the contest with Wallingford and his second. The two combatants were to start out back to back before each took ten paces. Their pistols were to be held muzzles up, pointed at the sky, and only a single volley was to be allowed. Cuthbert eyed the gaunt specter of Wallingford's undertaker. Considering how deep in his cups Julian was, a second volley shouldn't be necessary.

Too soon, Julian and the lankier Wallingford had taken their positions, standing back to back like a pair of mismatched bookends.

"Gentlemen, are you ready?" called out the neutral party provided by the marquess. When they both nodded, he began to count. "One . . . two . . . three . . ."

Cuthbert wanted to wail a protest, to hurl himself between the two men. But honor demanded that he remain frozen into place by the icy wind whipping out of the north.

". . . seven . . . eight . . . nine . . ."

Knowing himself to be the basest of cowards and an abominable second, yet unable to watch his friend die, Cuthbert squeezed his eyes shut.

"Ten!"

A pistol blast shattered the meadow's tranquillity. Cuthbert's nose twitched at the caustic stench of gunpowder. He slowly opened his eyes to find his worst fears realized.

Julian lay sprawled in the snow while Wallingford stood forty feet away, a smoking pistol in his hand. His face bore such a smirk of grim satisfaction that the good-natured Cuthbert felt a wave of murderous rage roll through his own veins.

As he dragged his gaze back to his friend's motionless form, icy flecks of snow stung his eyes. Bowing his head, he reached up with a trembling hand to draw off his hat.

"Bloody hell."

The sullen oath, bitten off in such familiar tones, jerked Cuthbert's head upright. Disbelief coursed through his veins, sobering him more thoroughly than a blast of arctic air.

As Julian sat up, blinking snow from his lashes, Wallingford's nasty smile faded. Cuthbert whooped with joy and stumbled to his friend's side, dropping to his knees in the snow. Julian's pistol was sprawled a foot away from his hand. Apparently, he hadn't even managed to get a shot off. Cuthbert shook his head, marveling at his friend's astonishing good fortune.

"I don't understand," the marquess spat. "I would have sworn my aim was true."

The man's second frowned, looking equally bewildered. "Perhaps it was a misfire, my lord, or perhaps he lost his footing in the moment before you fired."

Wallingford stalked over to glare down at them, his aristocratic upper lip curled in a snarl. His second peered nervously over his shoulder, plainly fearing he would somehow be blamed for this debacle.

Julian's lips curved in a sheepish smile. "Sorry, mates. I've always held my women better than I hold my port."

Cuthbert's blood froze anew as Wallingford

snatched his remaining pistol from his second and pointed it straight at Julian's heart. Julian surveyed him with lazy amusement, refusing to yield so much as a flinch for his enemy's gratification. Cuthbert knew instinctively that if Julian betrayed a hint of fear, if he uttered a single plea for mercy, Wallingford would shoot them both without a qualm, and bribe the undertaker to say that Cuthbert had pulled a weapon on him after the marquess had killed his friend.

Wallingford slowly lowered the weapon; Cuthbert heaved a sigh of relief.

The marquess's velvety voice crackled with contempt. "You'll wish you were dead by the time I'm through with you, you scurrilous bastard. Assuming you wouldn't even bother to make an appearance this morning, I took the liberty of buying off all of your gambling vowels." He drew a sheaf of IOUs three inches thick from his waistcoat pocket and leaned down to rattle them in front of Julian's nose. "I own you, Kane. Body *and* soul."

Julian's chuckle swelled into a full-fledged laugh. "I'm afraid you're too late. The devil beat you to that particular vowel a long time ago."

His mirth only enraged the marquess further. "Then I can only pray he comes to collect very soon because I'd like nothing more than to see you spend eternity rotting in hell!"

Wallingford spun on his heel and marched toward the coach. His companions trailed after him, the undertaker visibly sulking at being deprived of the opportunity to practice his trade.

"A rather ill-natured fellow, isn't he?" Cuthbert murmured. "Do you suppose he suffers from gout or dyspepsia?"

As the angry jingling of the carriage harnesses subsided, Cuthbert and Julian were left alone in the hazy stillness of the meadow. Julian just sat there with one arm propped on his knee, gazing up at the sky. His uncharacteristic silence unnerved Cuthbert more than all of the morning's events combined. He had come to rely on his friend's repartee, the cutting edge of his wit. It had always been too much of a strain for him to think of anything clever to say.

He was about to clear his throat and try anyway when a bleak shadow of a smile crossed Julian's face. "Despite my best efforts, it seems I'm just not destined to die on a dueling field with the taste of another man's woman still on my lips."

Cuthbert replaced the pistol in its case and tucked the case beneath his arm before tugging Julian to his feet. "Don't give up all hope. Perhaps you can still expire in debtor's prison from a lingering bout of consumption."

Cuthbert was swinging him around to get him pointed in the right direction when he noticed the tear in the front of Julian's black greatcoat.

"What's this?" he asked, knowing his friend was far more fastidious about his attire than he was about his numerous affairs of the heart.

He brushed his fingers over the finely woven wool, puzzled by the jagged rip. It was well over an inch wide and the threads rimming its edge were twisted and blackened, almost as if they'd been scorched.

He'd already started to work one finger through the hole when Julian caught his hand in a grip that was both gentle and intractable. "The marquess's pistol ball must have grazed my coat as I fell. Curse the man! Had I realized it sooner, I'd have made him tear up one of those IOUs. This coat was tailored by old Weston himself," he said, referring to the king's favorite tailor. "It set me back nearly five pounds."

Cuthbert slowly withdrew his hand, the warning gleam in his friend's dark eyes giving him no choice.

Julian clapped him on the arm, a grin softening his expression. "Come, Cubby, my good man, my toes are nearly frozen. Why don't we share a nice warm bottle of port for breakfast?"

As he turned and started across the meadow, Cuthbert gazed after him, doubting his own senses. He would have almost sworn . . .

Julian suddenly stopped and swung around, his eyes narrowing. He turned his piercing dark gaze toward an ancient yew tree that squatted at the edge of the meadow a few yards away, its gnarled arms frosted with snow. His elegant nostrils twitched, then flared, as if he'd scented something particularly enticing. His lips drew back from his teeth and, for an elusive instant, there was something almost feral in his expression, something that made Cuthbert take a step away from him.

"What is it?" Cuthbert whispered. "Has the marquess doubled back to finish us off?"

Julian hesitated for a moment, then shook his head, the predatory glow in his eyes fading. "It's nothing at all, I suppose. Just a ghost from my past."

Giving the yew one last look through narrowed eyes, he continued across the meadow. As Cuthbert fell into step behind him, Julian launched into the chorus of "The Girl I Left Behind Me" in a baritone so pure it could have made the angels weep with envy.

The woman huddled behind the yew tree slumped against its broad trunk, her knees going weak. The notes of the song slowly faded, leaving her alone with the murmur of the falling snow and the unsteady throb of her heart in her ears. She couldn't have said whether her heart was pounding with terror or excitement. She only knew she hadn't felt this alive in almost six years.

She had slipped out of the house at dawn and instructed her driver to follow the marquess and his entourage to the park, torn between hoping the gossip was true and praying it wasn't. But all it had taken was one peek around that tree and she was once again a bright-eyed seventeen-year-old, basking in the first awkward flush of infatuation.

She had counted off each step the duelists took as if she was marking the final moments of her own life. When the marquess had turned, pistol at the ready, it had been all she could do not to leap out from behind the tree and scream a warning. When the pistol shot rang out and she watched the marquess's opponent crumple to the ground, she had clutched her chest, certain her own heart had stopped.

But it had started beating again the moment he sat up, shaking the curling dark mane of hair from his face. Drunk with relief, she had forgotten her own danger until it was nearly too late.

She had been gazing after him, her heart in her eyes, when he had suddenly stopped and turned, his body taut with the tensile grace she remembered only too well.

She had ducked back behind the tree, holding her breath. Even with the sheltering trunk of the yew between them, she could feel his gaze penetrate her defenses, its probing caress leaving her as vulnerable as the kiss he had brushed across her brow the last time they had met. Pressing her eyes tightly shut, she had touched one hand to the velvet choker that circled the slender column of her throat.

Then he was gone, his voice fading to an echo, then a memory. She slipped out from behind the tree. Fat snowflakes drifted from the sky, filling the scattering of footprints and the hollow where his body had lain. Soon there would be no proof that the misbegotten duel had ever taken place.

She almost pitied his sandy-haired companion for his ignorance. She'd had nearly six years to learn how to embrace the impossible, but she'd still had to bite back a stunned gasp when that lean form had risen from its grave of snow. If his companion's hand hadn't been stayed, she knew exactly what the man would have found. That plump finger would have wiggled its way through greatcoat, coat, waistcoat, and shirt, not stopping until it brushed the unblemished skin over a heart that should have been shattered by the marquess's pistol ball.

Portia Cabot adjusted the veil on the sweeping brim of her hat, a faint smile curving her lush lips. She didn't regret one moment of her reckless jaunt. She had proved the rumors were more than just idle gossip.

Julian Kane had come home. And if the devil wanted his soul, then the old rascal would just have to beat her to it.

Two

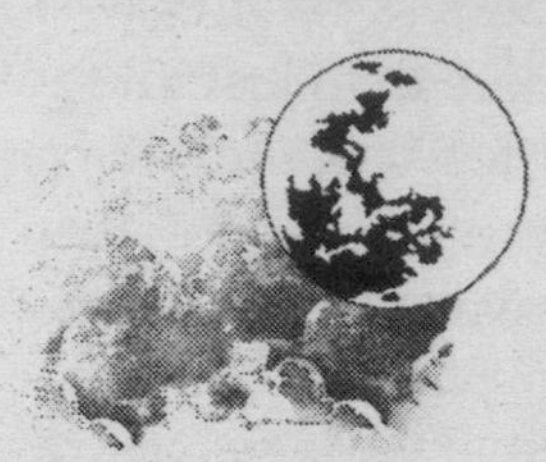

"Have you completely lost your wits?"

A more delicate soul might have quailed at having such a question directed at them—especially when uttered in a near roar by such an impressive specimen of a man—but Portia refused to take offense. After all, it wasn't as if her brother-in-law made a regular habit of questioning her sanity. He'd only done it twice before. Once when she had cornered a hissing six-hundred-year-old vampire during the bassoon interlude at Lady Quattlebaum's midsummer musicale, holding him at bay with a violin bow until Adrian could arrive with his crossbow. And only last month when she'd turned down not one, but two, handsome, wealthy young noblemen eager to make her their bride.

Had he been bellowing at her out of spite instead of concern, Portia might have been more alarmed. But she knew that Adrian could have adored her no more had she been born *his* sister instead of his wife's.

It was that steadfast certainty that allowed her to serenely blink up at him from the wing-chair in front of the hearth as he paced the drawing room of his Mayfair mansion, scowling like an ogre and dragging his fingers through his honey-colored hair until it bristled like a lion's mane.

He spun around on the heel of one polished boot and stabbed a finger in her direction. "You may be in danger of losing your mind, but I'm still in full possession of all of my faculties. And if you believe for one minute that I'm going to allow you to put yourself in such grave peril, then you're sorely mistaken."

"I don't plan on putting myself in any peril at all," she replied. "Now that I've found him, I simply want to have a civilized conversation with your brother."

Her eldest sister Caroline rose from the brocaded sofa to slip her arm through her husband's. With her belly just beginning to swell with their second child and her pale blond hair sleeked back into a crisp chignon, she should have resembled a placid Madonna. But the sparkle of humor and intelligence in her gray eyes made her look less than serene. "Adrian's right, pet. It's far too risky. Don't you remember what happened the last time you tried to help him? You nearly died."

"*He* nearly died," Portia reminded her. "I saved him."

Adrian and Caroline exchanged a glance, but Portia simply set her lips in a firm line. She had never told anyone exactly what had happened in that crypt nearly six years ago. And she had no intention of doing so now.

"I know you've spent many a sleepless night worrying about Julian," Caroline said. "We *all* have. But you still have to think about the danger to yourself."

"A little danger didn't keep you away from Adrian when everybody believed *he* was a vampire."

"In case you've forgotten, there was one

significant difference. And Julian may not even be the vampire you remember. He's been gone for almost six years and we've heard absolutely nothing from him for over three of those years. Not a letter, not a word, not a whisper. He didn't even contact us after we sent word that Eloisa had been born." Caroline stole an indulgent look at the rosy-cheeked, honey-haired toddler who was cheerfully gnawing at the gold tassels on one of the sofa cushions. "Nor did he respond after Adrian wrote to inform him that their mother had finally succumbed to consumption in Italy. He and Adrian were once as close as two brothers could be. Why would he sever all ties to us if he hadn't decided to turn his back on the search for his soul?"

"I don't know," Portia admitted. "But the only way to find out is to ask him."

"And just why would he confide in you?" Adrian asked, cocking one tawny eyebrow. "Because he's always had an eye for a pretty girl? Because there's still some streak of sentimentality left in him after all of these years of living as a monster? Some spark of humanity?"

Portia held her tongue. There were no words to explain the bond she'd felt tugging at her heart since their time in the crypt. Even if there had been, she knew they would just accuse her of clinging to a young girl's romantic fancy.

Adrian dropped to one knee in front of the chair, bringing himself eye to eye with her. Portia's parents had been killed in a carriage accident when she was only nine. After he and Caroline had wed, Adrian had eagerly welcomed her into their home, never once suggesting that they shuffle her off to some horrid relative like their lecherous cousin Cecil or their vapid Aunt Marietta.

He covered both of her hands with one of his own, his blue-green eyes darkened by worry. "I'm not completely blind. I know you've been hoarding weapons and secretly training to help me fight vampires for years. But this isn't your battle, child. It's mine."

She tugged her hands from his. "I'm nearly three-and-twenty years old, Adrian. I'm no longer a child."

"Then perhaps it's time you listened to reason and stopped behaving like one."

Portia would have much preferred bellowing to his measured, rational tones. She rose, drawing herself up to her full five-feet-two inches and wishing for one of the elaborate hats she favored to add height to her stature. "Very well," she said coolly. "If I'm going to stop behaving like a child, then I no longer require your permission or your approval to seek out your brother's company."

Adrian straightened and gently seized her shoulders, the pleading note in his voice more unsettling than any roar. "Have you forgotten that four women have died in the last fortnight? That their bodies were drained of every last drop of blood, then left to rot in the alleys of Charing Cross and Whitechapel? I've spent the last five years driving nearly every vampire from the borders of this city. Do you believe in your heart that it could be pure happenstance that these murders took place just as Julian was rumored to have returned to London?"

She met his gaze squarely. "Do you believe in your heart that your own brother is capable of committing such atrocities?"

Adrian's hands fell away from her, fisting helplessly at his sides. "I no longer know what he might be capable of. I no longer know him at all. But he is *my* brother. And *my* responsibility. If anyone is to confront him about these murders, it will be me." He exchanged another guarded look with Caroline. "I'll go first thing in the morning."

"In the morning?" Portia echoed. "While he slumbers? When he's at his weakest and most vulnerable?"

Caroline made a small sound of distress, but Portia couldn't seem to stop.

"I know *exactly* what happens to vampires when you come calling in the morning, Adrian. So which weapons will you take with you? The crucifix? The stakes? Your crossbow? You've dispatched many a savage fiend with that particular weapon. I suppose it was inevitable that Julian would someday feel its sting."

Adrian touched his fingertips to the burgundy velvet choker that adorned her slender throat, the regret in his eyes making him look far older than his thirty-five years. "Better that he would feel my sting than that you—or any other woman—would feel his."

As he strode from the room, Portia turned to Caroline, desperately hoping to find an ally in her sister. After all, hadn't she once helped Caroline prove that Adrian wasn't the villain everyone believed him to be?

But Caroline simply shook her head. "Oh, Portia, why must you make this more difficult for him than it already is? If Adrian hadn't been forced to destroy Duvalier to protect me," she said, referring to the ruthless vampire who had turned Julian into a vampire by sucking his soul out of him at the moment of his death, "then Julian might have retrieved his soul a long time ago. He never would have had to go searching for the vampire who sired Duvalier. Adrian fought so hard and so long to save his brother. How do you think he feels now, knowing that he may very well have failed? Knowing that innocent women may have suffered and died because of that failure?" She scooped her daughter into her arms and followed her husband from the room, shooting Portia one last reproachful look. Eloisa peered over her mother's shoulder, her own big gray eyes bewildered.

Portia blew out a beleaguered sigh. She supposed it had been naïve of her to expect her family to open their arms and their hearts to welcome home the prodigal vampire. For all she knew, Julian might be every bit as lost as they feared him to be.

But some small corner of her heart rejected

that notion, refused to believe that the man who had once tweaked her nose and called her his "Bright Eyes" could have drained the life from those women and tossed them into the alley like so much rotting garbage.

She went to the window, drawing aside the heavy velvet drapes. The scant daylight was already beginning to fade, leaving the broad street bathed in the luminous glow of the snow. Although a few flakes still spun on the wind, the clouds had scattered, exposing the pale crescent of the rising moon. She glanced at the marble clock on the mantel, her sense of urgency growing. Julian's time was running out and so was hers.

If she was going to prove them all wrong, she would have to do it before the sun came up and Adrian went in search of his brother—perhaps for the very last time.

At the moment Julian Kane didn't mind being soulless nearly as much as he minded being sober. His stagger had steadied to a swagger and even that was being robbed of its usual grace by exhaustion and hunger.

He turned his coat pockets inside out only to find them woefully empty. Perhaps he shouldn't have been so quick to abandon Cuthbert on the steps of his father's Cavendish Square town house.

Cubby had been quietly casting up his accounts on the earl's beloved azalea bushes when the old man had poked his head out of an upstairs window, his nightcap askew, and bellowed, "What have you done to my lad now, Kane? My Cuthbert was a good boy until he started running with the likes of you. Satan's spawn!"

Julian had gently yielded Cubby's floundering bulk to a footman before tipping his beaver hat to the earl. "And a good evening to you, too, my lord."

The old man had shaken his gnarled fist at him with such vigor that Julian had feared he was going to topple out the window and crack his fool skull.

Julian was shaking his head at the memory when his gloved fingers slipped through a hole in the silk lining of his coat pocket. He withdrew a single dull shilling and held it aloft.

"Adrian always did say I had the very luck of the devil," he murmured.

But it was the devil who had been unlucky on this day, he thought ruefully. Had circumstances been different, the old goat would have been standing at the gates of Hell, tapping his cloven hoof with anticipation at the exact moment Wallingford had fired his pistol.

How odd that the moment had brought with it not the stench of brimstone, but a whiff of heaven. It wasn't the first time he'd been haunted by that particular scent. The elusive fragrance had once stalked him down a narrow alley in Cairo, overpowering the exotic aromas of cumin and turmeric. It had wafted through the soot-stained window of a Paris garret, making his body burn with hunger. And on a rain-drenched battlefield in Burma while his nostrils were still choked with the smell of blood and smoke, he had scented it on the wind, the fragrance so dear and familiar it had made his gut clench with longing for a home he would never know.

It smelled nothing like the gardenia- and jasmine-drenched perfumes of the women who so frequently provided him with both solace and sustenance. This was the sweet soap-and-rosemary smell of a young woman's skin—innocence and allure mingled into an intoxicating brew. It was the scent of a girl's silky dark curls brushing his cheek as she leaned across him to turn the pages of his pianoforte music before favoring him with a mischievous smile.

As he had so many times before, Julian forced himself to ruthlessly banish the image. Flipping the coin to the opposite hand, he sauntered through the falling night. He might not be able to afford more than a single hand of cards, but perhaps he could coax some pretty bit of muslin into taking pity on him.

Turning up the collar of his greatcoat to ward off the icy flecks of snow, he crossed the street and ducked into one of the Covent Garden gambling hells disreputable enough to welcome even the likes of him.

Julian did have the very luck of the devil. Less than two hours later, he was sitting behind a fat pile of winnings at the brag table. Employing a lethal mix of charm, guile, and skill, he'd managed to parlay that single shilling into a shimmering heap of coins and pound notes. It might not be enough to stave off Wallingford and his threats of debtor's prison for more than a day, but it was enough to ensure that he wouldn't be spending the night alone.

Or hungry.

He gently rubbed the lower back of the dark-haired, sloe-eyed beauty perched on his knee, earning a jealous look from the golden-haired minx who had draped herself over his shoulders like an ermine stole. Every time he turned his head, he was nearly overcome by the stench of the cheap lavender water she had used to wash away the scent of the last gambler she had accompanied upstairs.

While the other three men at the table watched, unable to hide their hopeful expressions, his pale fingers flicked over the cards with negligent grace, fanning them out to reveal yet another winning hand.

One of the men groaned while another tossed down his cards in disgust. "Damn it all, Kane! Your luck is positively supernatural!"

"So they tell me," Julian murmured as the men snatched up their beaver top hats and walking sticks and quit the table, leaving more than a week's wages behind them.

Absently stroking the brunette's rounded hip, Julian settled back in his chair and stretched out his long legs. Peering through the haze of cigar and cheroot smoke, he searched for his next victims. Most of the club's patrons had exhausted their welcomes—and their credit—at the more reputable establishments like White's and Boodle's. A palpable air of desperation clung to them, similar to what Julian had witnessed in the hashish and opium dens of Istanbul and Bangkok. Their fingers twitched and their eyes gleamed as they waited for the next play. It shouldn't prove too difficult to lure a pair of overextended merchants and the bastard son of some impoverished nobleman into his snare.

"Why don't ye quit the cards and play with me for a while, guv'nor?" the brunette crooned, wiggling deeper into the cup of his lap.

The blonde leaned over his shoulder to pour him a fresh glass of port from the half-empty bottle on the table. She batted her fawn-colored lashes at him, pressing her ample breasts against the muscled contours of his upper arm. "If ye play yer cards right, luv, ye can win the both of us for the night."

Julian shifted in his chair. Their efforts were

undeniably . . . stirring, but he wasn't quite ready to abandon the table. "Patience, my sweets," he said. "At the moment luck is my only mistress, and I'll be damned if I'll leave her to a cold and empty bed when she's still warm and willing." While the blonde gave his earlobe a nip of protest, he soothed the brunette's pout by planting a lingering kiss on her rouged lips.

Someone cleared their throat.

There was such a stinging note of disapproval in the sound that Julian barely resisted the urge to jerk to attention like a guilty schoolboy caught at some mischief. He slowly lifted his head to find a woman standing just behind the chair directly across from him.

No, not a woman, but a *lady,* he corrected himself, his gaze sweeping from the burgundy of her mink-trimmed velvet pelisse to the feathered bonnet perched atop her upswept coils of gleaming sable hair. A bulging satin reticule dangled from her arm, the pouch's ribbons drawn tightly closed over its mouth. The exquisite cut and quality of her garments presented a startling contrast to the shabby finery of most of the club's patrons. A glowing halo seemed to surround her, separating her from the cigar smoke and raucous laughter that filled the room. From the corner of his eye, Julian could see her already garnering other glances—some curious, some wary, others openly predatory.

They'd seen her kind here before. Wealthy ladies with an insatiable appetite for deep play. Since the fair sex wasn't even allowed in the more reputable clubs that their husbands frequented, they were forced to seek their satisfaction in hells such as this. They were so in thrall to the thrill of the game that they were willing to risk their reputations and their fortunes on one fickle roll of the dice or turn of a card.

More often than not, a lady would play until every last coin of her blunt was gone, leaving her with only one way to pay off her debts. For some reason, Julian couldn't bear the thought of this woman being forced to accompany some gloating gambler to one of the rooms upstairs. Couldn't stomach the image of her being shoved to her knees and stripped of that ridiculous bonnet by his fumbling hands.

The net veil attached to its sweeping brim shadowed her eyes and gave her an irresistible aura of mystery. All he could see was the curve of a dimpled cheek, a pointed chin that boded a heart-shaped face, and a pair of lush lips perfectly fashioned for kissing and other even more illicit pleasures.

With some difficulty, he tugged his gaze away from her mouth only to have it settle on the burgundy velvet ribbon she wore around her throat as a choker; her long, graceful throat where a pulse, nearly invisible to the naked eye, danced to each throbbing beat of her heart. Julian jerked his hungry gaze away before he could betray himself. Bringing the glass to his lips, he took a deep swallow of the port, knowing it to be a pale substitute for what he craved.

"Might I have a word with you?" she asked, her voice low and rich.

He flicked a lazy glance her way, but before he could respond, the brunette snapped, "Ye ought to address 'im as 'sir'! 'Im's a knight, 'e is, knighted by the king 'isself. A real 'ero."

"*My* 'ero," the blonde purred, slipping a hand into the open throat of his shirt and raking her crimson nails through the crisp whorls of his chest hair.

Those lovely lips tightened with distaste. Or some other emotion Julian couldn't quite read.

"Very well . . . *sir.* I was wondering if I might have a word with you," she repeated, her scornful tone dismissing his companions. "In private."

It was the most intriguing proposition he'd received all night. She must be seeking more than just the thrill of the game. He'd encountered her kind before as well, in nearly every city around the world. Women possessed of a hunger as unholy as his own. Women who recognized and deliberately sought out creatures like him, courting danger and death as if they were the most accomplished of lovers.

Silently cursing the ghost of his scruples, he said, "I'm afraid I can't help you, miss. As you can see, my attentions are already"—he slid his hand from the brunette's hip to the rounded curve of her thigh—"occupied."

"Ye'd best scurry back to yer fine carriage, m'lady," the brunette said. "A great wolf like this one would gobble ye down in one bite."

The golden-haired wench looped her arms around his neck. " 'E needs a woman, not a lady."

"Or two women," the brunette countered,

earning a throaty laugh from her companion.

Taking another sip of the port to quench his regret, Julian waited for the woman to turn and flee into the night.

Instead those lush lips curved into the sweetest of smiles. "I hate to deprive you of such scintillating company, but I really must insist."

Julian glanced around the club, keenly aware that their exchange was beginning to garner more than casual interest. "This is no place for a woman like you. Why don't you go home before your husband wakes up and realizes you've crept out of his bed?" He arched the dark wing of one brow before leveling his iciest look at her, the one that had been known to freeze grown men in their tracks. "If you linger, I'm afraid you'll end up with nothing but regrets."

She lifted her chin, her smile fading. "Are you threatening me, sir?"

"If you'd like, you can take it as a warning."

"And if I don't choose to heed your warning?"

"Then you're a bloody little fool," he said, making no apology for his crude language.

"I'm not leaving until I get what I came here for. You owe me and I've come to collect." Revealing the tiniest crack in her composure, she reached up with trembling hands and drew off her bonnet.

For one fleeting second, Julian was almost thankful he was a vampire because it took a supernatural effort to keep his features schooled in indifference. She was, beyond the shadow of a doubt, the most beautiful woman he had ever seen. The sable curls piled atop her head were matched by the graceful arch of her brows and impossibly thick lashes that ringed eyes the same dark blue as the Aegean Sea at midnight. The delicate bones of her face were narrow at the chin and broad at the cheek. Those cheeks were blessed with a hint of natural color, as if someone had taken a rose petal and lightly dusted it over her satiny skin. She possessed a natural sophistication that all of the expensive powders and rouges in the world couldn't duplicate. Her mouth tilted upward slightly at the corners, just enough to make a man wonder if she was laughing with him or at him.

And all Julian could think as he faced this paragon of feminine beauty was that he wished she'd put her damned hat back on. Without the veil to hide her eyes, her gaze was too frank. Too challenging. Too blue. Desperate to escape her presence for reasons even he couldn't fathom, he surged to his feet, nearly dumping the sputtering brunette onto the floor.

He swirled the last of the port around the bottom of the glass before bringing it to his lips. "You can't be one of my creditors, my dear, because I'm sure I'd remember *dunning* someone as lovely as you," he said, giving the word an inflection that was impossible to ignore. "And if you're not one of my creditors, then I suggest you step out of my way because I don't owe you so much as the time of day."

Returning the glass to the table with a forceful thump, he claimed the brunette's hand and took a step toward the stairs.

"That's where you're wrong, Mr. Kane." Her fingers steady this time, she reached up, jerked off the velvet choker and tossed it on the table as if it were a wager he could never hope to answer.

Julian froze in his tracks, mesmerized by the sight of that graceful throat. A throat that should have been as creamy and flawless as the rest of her, but was instead marred by the faded scars of two distinct puncture wounds.

As Julian lifted his disbelieving gaze to meet the defiant blue of Portia Cabot's eyes, he knew his luck had finally run out.

Three

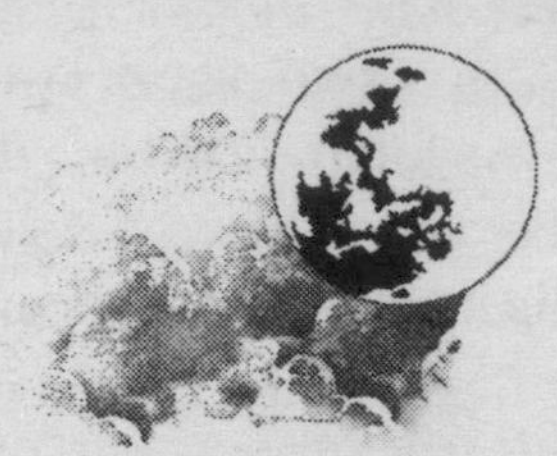

He hadn't recognized her.

Julian Kane had looked right at her with the same burning dark eyes that had haunted her dreams for the past five years and betrayed nothing more than the faintest flicker of interest. Or was it annoyance?

Apparently their time together had meant so little to him that he barely remembered her. And why should he? Portia thought. In the years since he'd been gone, he'd probably had dozens—she stole a bitter glance at the blowsy brunette still clinging to his hand—no, *hordes* of other women only too eager to help erase her from his memory. Why should he remember one awkward seventeen-year-old girl who had blushed and stammered and practically thrown herself at him every time he sauntered into a room?

As the initial rush of hurt passed, Portia had to fight the urge to fly into a towering rage. Despite her boast to Adrian that she was no longer a child, she wanted nothing more than to toss her lovely bonnet to the floor and jump up and down on it.

"Bright Eyes?" Julian whispered, his handsome face a gratifying study in shock and confusion.

"Don't call me that," she snapped, suddenly despising the endearment. If he tried to tweak her nose, she was going to bite his fingers.

He cast a desperate glance around them, as if becoming aware of the squalor of their surroundings for the very first time. "What in the name of God are you doing in a hell like this?"

"Where better to look for a missing devil?" she retorted.

They were beginning to attract an audience. Several of the seedier-looking men were already edging nearer, almost as if they scented blood in the air.

"If the lady's lookin' for a game," called out a hulking chap with a red-veined nose and hands as meaty as hams, "I'm ready to play."

"Big Jim is always ready," someone else shouted, nudging the man next to him. "That's 'ow 'e ended up with twelve brats and only two o' them on 'is poor wife."

Raucous laughter greeted his words, but there was no mistaking its ugly undertone. As Julian dropped the brunette's hand and advanced toward her, Portia took a step backward, feeling a tiny thrill of alarm.

It seemed she had finally succeeded in getting his attention.

His stride was as smooth and lethal as any predator's. Before she could protest, he had seized her hand in a crushing grip.

"Ow!" she muttered, trying to twist away.

"Sorry," he mumbled beneath his breath, gentling his grip but refusing to yield his claim on her hand. "Sometimes I forget my own strength."

That strength was in full evidence as he swung her around as gracefully as if they were waltzing across a ballroom floor and tucked her back against his broad chest.

As they faced the group of men who seemed to be rapidly devolving into a pack, Julian called out, "I'm afraid she's not looking for a game, lads. She's looking for me." He closed his hands gently over her shoulders and nuzzled her hair, his melodic baritone striking a pitch perfect note between rakish and sheepish. "And she's no lady. She's my wife."

Sympathetic groans rippled through the crowd. It obviously wasn't the first time an irate wife had marched into the club to drag her husband home. The men gazed at her with new respect, some of them even reaching up to doff their caps. But Portia was distracted from all of that by the disconcerting tickle of Julian's nose grazing her earlobe. She would have almost sworn he was sniffing her.

Determined to prove she wasn't quite as helpless—or as witless—as he believed her to be, she resisted the urge to stomp on his instep and twisted around to give him a dazzling smile instead. "When I awoke to find you gone from my bed, I couldn't help but worry, darling." She patted the ruffled shirtfront peeping out from the deep V of his waistcoat. "I know you promised me your French pox was all healed up, but you can never be too careful with those weeping sores."

The men's groans were even more sympathetic this time. The brunette gasped in outrage, then seized the sputtering blonde's hand. Both of the women went flouncing toward the stairs, shooting Julian disgusted looks over their shoulders.

Julian's eyes narrowed on her face even as he slid one arm around her waist, drawing the lower half of her body flush against his. Keenly aware of the dangerously snug cut of his trousers, she tried to wiggle an inch of distance between them, but her struggles only deepened his smirk.

"Your concern is most touching, my love," he said. "And how fortuitous that you should appear just as I was beginning to wonder where my next meal was coming from."

His lips parted, giving her a teasing glimpse of his fangs. Fangs that only lengthened and sharpened when he was hungry. Or aroused. Portia swallowed. Perhaps she had been unwise to bait him. If Adrian and Caroline were right and he had given up on the search for his soul, he was nothing more to her now than a dangerous stranger. And she was nothing more to him than a particularly juicy morsel.

She forced herself to give his chest another wifely pat, keenly aware of the rock-hard muscles beneath her gloved hand. "If you wish to play another hand of cards, sweeting, I'll hurry home and rouse the maid from her bed to fix you a midnight supper."

The corner of his mouth quirked upward in a knowing smile. "Nonsense, pet. I do believe you've roused an appetite that only you can satisfy." His long, sooty lashes swept downward as he leaned toward her. Too late, Portia realized that he had no intention of tweaking her nose.

She opened her mouth to protest but his lips were already there, sweeping over hers like molten velvet. The shock was so great that she might have jerked away were it not for the powerful hand that glided up her nape, the strong, sure fingers that wound their way through her upswept curls until she was as bound to him as any slave girl to her master.

Tugging her head gently backward, he laid waste to her inhibitions with devastating finesse. He brushed his lips back and forth across hers, then gently licked his way into her mouth, ravishing and seducing with each lazy stroke of his tongue. He kissed like a creature with an eternity to devote to her pleasure. He kissed like a vampire.

Portia clung to his waistcoat, but she could still feel herself falling, tumbling into some dark abyss where only he and the tantalizing promise of his kiss existed. She could barely hear the ribald hoots and catcalls of the hell's patrons through the roaring in her ears.

She might have been content to throw herself into that abyss, never to emerge, if not for the sudden sting on the inside of her bottom lip. She didn't realize she'd been nicked by one of Julian's fangs until she tasted the metallic tang of blood in her mouth. He tasted it, too. His sharply indrawn breath that wasn't actually a breath at all threatened to suck the remaining air from her lungs. He jerked away from her as if she had been the one to bite him.

His nostrils were flared, his pupils dilated. Although he didn't move a muscle, his entire body seemed to be vibrating with some sort of primitive hunger.

Portia touched a trembling hand to her lips. Her white glove came away smudged with a single droplet of blood. Julian closed his eyes briefly. When he opened them again, they were as hard and opaque as black quartz.

One of the men cleared his throat, then jerked a shoulder toward the stairs. "You and yer lady can rent one o' the rooms upstairs for a shilling or two."

"That won't be necessary," Julian said smoothly, gathering her back into his arms as if they were the most loving of spouses. "I've discovered that anything worth having, including your wife, is worth waiting for."

To the appreciative chuckles of the crowd, he laid claim to his winnings, including Portia's velvet choker, and wrapped his coat around her shoulders. Before she could utter so much as a token protest, he had swept her out of the gambling hell and into the night.

Driven forward by Julian's possessive grip on her elbow, Portia struggled to hold on to her bonnet and reticule and match his long strides.

His good-natured veneer of charm had vanished, leaving his jaw stern and his profile impenetrable. She could not stop stealing curious glances at that profile. Despite the excesses of wine and women she had witnessed in the gambling hell, dissipation hadn't left a single scar on his face. His strong aquiline nose, the sensual cut of his full lips, and his cleft chin possessed the same Byronic beauty she remembered only too well. Byron had been moldering in his Nottinghamshire crypt for nearly two years now, the victim of a mysterious fever and his own excesses, but thanks to the vampire who had stolen his soul Julian remained frozen forever in the first potent flush of manhood.

The snow had finally stopped. The muted glow of the streetlamps veiled his eyes and cast sinister shadows beneath his high cheekbones.

"Where are you taking me?" she demanded.

"To your carriage."

"I don't have a carriage. It was rented and the driver refused to linger in this neighborhood after dark."

"Which would make him far more intelligent than you, would it not?"

"You can insult me all you like, but I have no intention of storming off in a huff."

"Then I'll take you where you belong," he said shortly. "Home."

She dug in her heels, bringing them both to an abrupt halt. "I can't let you do that."

He swung around to face her. "Why not?"

She opened her mouth, but hesitated a heartbeat too long.

He held up a hand. "Wait. Let me guess. I'm probably no longer welcome in my brother's household. After all, what father in his right mind would want me lurking around his helpless child?" He snorted. "Adrian would probably run me through with one of Caroline's parasols before I could open my arms and croon, 'Come here, Eloisa, and meet your Uncle Julian. My, what a pretty little neck you have!' "

"So you *did* get the letter Caroline sent when Eloisa was born!" Portia said accusingly. "Why didn't you ever reply?"

He shrugged. "Perhaps I did. You know the post can be notoriously unreliable."

She narrowed her eyes, suspecting that it wasn't the post that was notorious or unreliable. "Well, it was quite thoughtless of you to leave us wondering about your whereabouts for so long. For all we knew, you could have been—"

"Undead?" he offered when she hesitated. In

response to her chiding glance, he sighed. "If you won't allow me to escort you home, then how would you suggest I dispose of you? Should I just drop you off at the next gambling hell we come to?"

Portia slipped on her bonnet and knotted its satin ribbons in a jaunty bow beneath her chin, knowing she would need all of the courage it could provide. "I was hoping I could accompany you to your lodgings."

All traces of humor vanished from Julian's face, leaving it as cool and polished as a mask. "I'm sorry, but I don't believe that would be advisable. Since you found your way here, I'm going to assume that you'll be equally adept at finding your way home." He sketched her a crisp bow. "Good night, Miss Cabot. Give my brother and his family my fondest regards."

He turned and started to stride away as if he had every intention of leaving her standing all alone on that street corner, still wrapped in the warm tobacco-and-spice scented folds of his coat.

"If you won't take me to your lodgings," she called after him, "I'll simply follow you."

Julian swung around. As he came striding

back toward her, his face set in ruthless lines, Portia had to resist the overwhelming urge to go stumbling backward.

He stopped a scant foot from her, his dark eyes blazing. "First you come barging into the seediest of gambling hells like you're bloody Queen Elizabeth. Then you volunteer to accompany a man like me—no, a *monster* like me—to his lodgings? Have you no care for your reputation, woman? For your very life?"

"It's not my life that concerns me at the moment. It's yours."

"I don't have a life, sweetheart. Only an existence."

"Which could be rapidly drawing to an end if you don't at least listen to what I have to say."

He swore in fluent French. Portia lifted her chin, refusing to blush. She had heard far more colorful oaths from Adrian's lips, most of those in English.

A man went stumbling past them, reeking of unwashed flesh and cheap gin. As the stranger's greedy gaze raked over the ample swell of Portia's breasts, Julian bared his teeth and growled, the primal sound lifting every hair on her nape. The man lurched into a clumsy trot, barely missing a lamppost as he cast a terrified glance over his shoulder.

"It appears I'm not the only beast prowling the streets of London tonight." Julian stroked his chin, visibly struggling with her demand. "Very well," he finally bit off. "If you insist, I'll take you to my lodgings. But only if you promise you'll leave me to rest in peace once you've had your way and your say." Without waiting for her pledge, he offered her his arm.

Still haunted by the echo of that growl, Portia hesitated for the briefest second before resting her gloved hand in the crook of his arm.

To Portia's surprise the rickety stairs leading to Julian's rented lodgings deep in the heart of the Strand led up instead of down. She had expected to find him inhabiting some luxurious cellar flat, much like his secret chamber in the dungeon of Trevelyan Castle, his and Adrian's boyhood home.

That chamber had been draped in cashmere and Chinese silk and adorned with Chippendale furniture, numerous busts and paintings, and a marble chess set where he could while away the daylight hours when he wasn't sleeping in the ornate wooden coffin that dominated the room. Julian had always been a vampire who prized his comforts, creature and otherwise.

Which was why it was such a shock to her sensibilities when he swept open the door at the top of the shadowy staircase to reveal a narrow, low-ceilinged room that was little more than a garret. The room was furnished with a battered armoire, a shabby wing-chair, and a scarred table flanked by two ladder-back chairs, all carved from the cheapest of pines. A lamp burned low on the table, sending shadows creeping over the peeling paint on the walls. If not for the sheets of thick black crepe draped over the dormer windows, no one would have guessed that there was a vampire in residence.

In lieu of a coffin, a sagging cast-iron bedstead slumped in one corner. Portia accepted Julian's unspoken invitation to precede him into the room, averting her eyes from its rumpled bedclothes.

As she turned to face him, he closed the door and leaned his back against it, surveying her through heavy-lidded eyes. "So little Portia Cabot is all grown up."

Warned by the wary edge in his voice that he was none too pleased by the notion, Portia shrugged. "It was bound to happen. I couldn't stay a naïve young girl besotted with Byron's poetry forever."

"More's the pity," Julian muttered.

Abandoning his post by the door, he brushed past her to get to the table. After blowing the dust out of a pair of mismatched goblets, he poured two drinks from the amber bottle resting next to them. He offered her one of them, his long, elegant fingers cradling the bowl of the goblet.

She took it and brought it to her nose, eyeing him suspiciously as she sniffed at the ruby red liquid.

"Don't worry, it's only port," he assured her, a spark of amusement lighting his eyes. "And cheap port at that. But it's all I can afford at the moment."

She took a tentative sip of the musky wine. "Just how much have you had to drink tonight?"

"Not nearly enough," he said, leaning against the table and draining his glass in one deep swig. He lifted the empty goblet to her in a mocking toast. "I do hope you'll forgive my ill temper. You interrupted my evening meal and I tend to get a bit cranky when I'm hungry."

Portia choked on the port, her eyes widening in horror. "Those women back there at the g-gambling hell? You were going to . . . eat them?"

He opened his mouth, then evidently thought better of what he was about to say and closed it again. "If you're asking me if I was going to kill them, the answer is no. I prefer to think of them as more of a tasty little snack."

When her eyes only widened further, he sighed. "There's only so much rare roast beef and butcher shop blood a vampire can stomach. As I was traveling the world in the past few years, I made a fascinating discovery. It seems that wherever I go, there are always women willing—no, eager—to offer me a little sip of themselves. I take just what I need to survive, and in return . . . I make sure they get what they need." His jaded gaze flicked over the pale scars on her throat. "Since you were the first woman I ever drank from, I suppose I have you to thank for teaching me that lesson."

Portia almost hated him in that moment. Hated him for taking an act born out of desperation and tenderness and trying to turn it into something sordid and dirty.

As if that wasn't enough of an affront, he took one step toward her, then another. "I'm not nearly so careless or clumsy as I was with you. I've even learned to drink from other places so the scars won't be so visible." He lifted one hand to her throat, his fingertips caressing the marks he had left on her with a seductive tenderness that made her shiver. "Did you know there's a particularly juicy little artery on the inside of a woman's thigh, just below—"

"Stop it!" Portia shouted, slapping his hand away. "Stop being so horrid! I know exactly what you're trying to do and it's not going to work!"

He backed away from her, holding up both hands in mocking surrender. "You never did scare easily, did you, Bright Eyes?"

He was wrong. She was terrified. Terrified of the way her pulse had raced beneath his fingertips. Terrified of the power his touch still had over her. Terrified she might be no better than those women who were willing and eager to satisfy his cravings as long as he satisfied theirs.

But he wasn't the only one who had learned

how to bluff in the past few years. She smiled at him, using her dimples to their best advantage. "I hate to wound your legendary vanity, but I have no intention of scurrying out the door just because you say 'Boo!' to me."

She shrugged off his coat and tossed it toward the bed, removed her bonnet and set it carefully on the table, then began to tug off her gloves one finger at a time. As she slipped out of her pelisse, one of Julian's eyebrows shot up, as if to inquire just what garment she might consider removing next.

Keeping the ribbons of her reticule looped around her wrist, she settled herself gingerly on the edge of the wing-chair and took another dainty sip of the port. "Your growling and posturing might impress the sort of women you're accustomed to consorting with, but quite frankly, I find them to be a bit of a bore."

The dark wing of Julian's eyebrow shot even higher. "I beg your pardon, Miss Cabot. I obviously mistook you for the enchanting child who used to hang on my every syllable with breathless delight."

"I'm afraid even the most enchanting of children must someday grow up. I hope it won't disappoint you to learn that I no longer believe in mermaids, leprechauns, or werewolves."

"But you still believe in me."

Portia barely managed to hide her start. Had he developed a talent for reading minds along with his other dark gifts?

"You still believe in the existence of vampires," he clarified to her keen relief.

"I haven't any choice, have I? Not when your brother has spent the last five years driving the worst of them out of London."

"Well, that would explain why they're overrunning the alleys of Florence and Madrid." Scowling, Julian poured himself another glass of port and settled one lean hip against the opposite corner of the table. "Adrian has obviously been neglecting his duties as your guardian. I would have thought he'd have you married off by now to some wealthy viscount or earl who could give you a half dozen babes to keep you in the nursery where you belong."

"I've been out of the nursery for several years now and I've no intention of going back. At least not for a very long while. So tell me," she said, blinking up at him, "while you were traveling the world learning how to enslave weak-willed women with your seductive powers, you didn't stumble across anything else of interest, did you? Like, for instance, your immortal soul?"

He rested the goblet on the table, then patted the pockets of his waistcoat, as if the one thing that held the power to restore him to humanity was of no more import than a lost riding glove or a misplaced cravat. "Damn thing's proved to be devilishly slippery. I haven't had a single vampire stroll up to me and offer to let me tear out their throat so I can suck my stolen soul out of them."

"So you never even found the vampire who sired Duvalier, the one who inherited your soul after Duvalier was destroyed?"

"I'm afraid not. Unless they're feeding, vampires are a notoriously close-mouthed lot, even amongst themselves."

Portia frowned. Something in his tone made her suspect that he wasn't being completely forthcoming. "So you didn't find your soul, but you did find time to prove yourself a hero on the battlefields of Burma?"

He lifted one shoulder in an indifferent shrug. "How difficult is it to be a hero when you can't die? Why shouldn't I volunteer to lead every charge? Sneak behind enemy lines and rescue every fallen soldier? I had nothing to lose."

"Unless the sun came out."

His lips slanted in a mocking smile. "It was monsoon season."

"Since he bestowed a knighthood upon you, I gather the king was more impressed with your efforts than you were."

"The dreamers of this world are always looking for a hero. I suppose the king is no different from any other man."

"Or woman," she remarked, meeting his gaze boldly.

He straightened, folding his arms over his chest. "Perhaps it's time you told me exactly what *you're* looking for, Portia. Because if it's a hero, you've come to the wrong place."

Unnerved by his unblinking stare, she rose from the chair and strolled over to the window. Easing aside the veil of crepe, she peered into the dimly lit alley below. Every shadow seemed to hide some faceless menace, yet none of them was more dangerous to her than the man waiting—not so patiently—for her reply.

She traded a bracing glance with her reflection in the glass, then let the crepe fall and turned to face him. "I'm looking for a murderer."

The grim words hung in the air between them until Julian threw back his head with a hearty laugh and said, "Then I suppose you have come to the right place after all, haven't you?"

Four

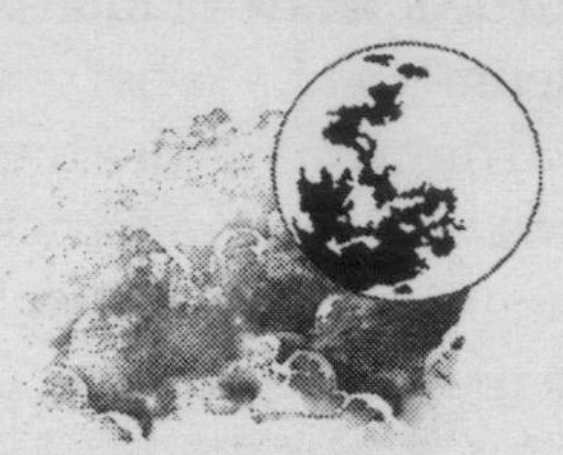

Portia felt the blood drain from her face. "So it's true," she breathed, her fingers biting into the sleek satin of her reticule.

"That I'm a murderer? That I've taken human life in order to survive? I hate to crush the last of your girlhood illusions about me, sweetheart, but in that respect I'm no different from any other soldier in His Majesty's Army."

She drew in a deep breath to steady her voice. "I wasn't talking about battle. I was talking about those women in Charing Cross and White-chapel."

The sparkle of amusement in his eyes faded. He frowned. "What women?"

"The four women who have died since you returned to London. The four women who were drained of every last drop of their blood by some merciless fiend."

Julian's frown deepened. He turned away from her, toward the brick fireplace. "Just when did these murders take place?"

"The first was a fortnight ago, just before Adrian received word that you'd been spotted in London. The next two followed shortly thereafter. Then just three nights ago, a fourth woman was found in an alley behind the Blessed Mary church, her corpse still warm."

He gazed into the cold hearth, locking his hands at the small of his back. "Are you absolutely certain they were killed by a vampire?"

"Beyond any shadow of a doubt," Portia informed him, her voice trembling with suppressed emotion. "And I can assure you that these women were not willing victims eager to surrender themselves to the vampire's kiss. Their hands were bloody, their fingernails torn. They all fought quite passionately and courageously for their lives." Although she knew it was madness, she could not seem to stop herself from creeping closer to him. "Did you do it, Julian? Did you slaughter those poor, helpless creatures?"

He turned and lifted his dark-lashed eyes to her. "You believe me capable of such a crime and yet you sought me out tonight? Why would you be so foolhardy?"

How could she explain her unshaken faith in him? Her unswerving belief that he would not harm her? Not even when she knew *exactly* what he was capable of. "I didn't believe you would hurt me."

"I've already hurt you." His heavy-lidded gaze flicked to her throat, avoiding her eyes. "You've still got the scars to prove it."

Portia touched her fingers to the faded marks to still their tingling, wishing she had never surrendered her choker on the gambling table. Without it, she felt exposed. Naked.

She forced herself to lower her hand and lift her chin, boldly meeting his gaze. "I came here tonight because I had to make sure that you didn't kill those women. I'm the one who kept you alive in that crypt all those years ago. If you take an innocent life now, then I'm just as responsible as you are."

He drew nearer, his shadow falling over her. His voice was a husky lullaby, perfectly pitched to lure a woman to either delight or doom. "But what if I did kill them? What if I stalked them through the night, haunted their every step, just waiting for them to hesitate or stumble so I could make them mine?" Bracing his hands against the window frame behind her, he lowered his head, brushing his cheek against hers. His flesh should have been cold, but it was warm, burning with an unnatural fever that threatened to incinerate her every defense. As his parted lips grazed the downy flesh behind her ear, a primal shiver that had little to do with fear raked through her. "What's to stop me from doing the same to you?"

"This," she whispered, pressing the sharp point of the stake she had just drawn out of her reticule against his heart.

He went as still as a statue. She expected him to jerk away from her so she could begin to think about breathing again. But he simply spread his arms in surrender, his smile as lethal a weapon as the stake in her hand. "If you've come here to finish me, then let's have done with it, shall we? My heart, as you well know, Bright Eyes, has always been yours for the asking. Or the staking."

As badly as she wanted to believe him, Portia suspected he'd offered that same heart to a multitude of women, only to yank it out of their hands as soon as they dared to reach for it—or the next morning after they'd awakened in his bed, dazed from blood loss but satisfied beyond their wildest dreams.

"If you were as eager for oblivion as you'd like me to believe," she replied, "you'd simply take a morning stroll in the sunshine."

Despite his crooked smile, Julian's eyes were oddly somber. "Would you mourn me after I was gone? Would you scorn every man who tried to win your heart and squander your youth weeping over my grave?"

"No," she retorted sweetly, "but if one of my more ardent suitors should ever give me a cat, I might consider naming it after you."

"Perhaps I should leave you with something else to remember me by." Ignoring the press of the stake against his vulnerable breastbone, he leaned even closer.

As the seductive scents of port and spice soap

and tobacco enveloped her, Portia felt her lips part and her eyes began to flutter shut against her will. That was all the distraction Julian needed. One dizzying blur of movement and he was holding both the stake and her reticule, leaving her empty-handed.

As he backed away from her, taking his seductive fragrance with him, Portia settled back against the windowsill, blowing a stray curl out of her eyes. "That was a bit unsporting of you, don't you think?"

Eyeing her disbelievingly, he held up the stake. "More unsporting than you threatening to impale me with a pointy stick?"

She shrugged, her delicate sniff less than penitent. "A lady has every right to defend herself against unsought advances. *And* creatures of the night."

Apparently, he had no argument for that because he simply rested the stake and reticule on the table and began to root around in the bulging purse. His hand emerged with one of the delicate scent bottles that had become so popular with the young ladies.

"Oh, I wouldn't bother with that," Portia quickly said as he withdrew the stopper and brought the bottle to his nose. "That's just my lavender—"

She winced as he recoiled from its contents, baring his teeth in an involuntary grimace.

He rammed the stopper back into the bottle, shooting her an accusing glare. "Nothing like a dab of holy water behind the ears to stir a young man's fancy."

He gingerly set the bottle aside before reaching back into the reticule. He was rewarded for his successive forays into its silken interior with a miniature stake no larger than a quill pen, a sheathed dagger, three leather garrotes of varying lengths, and an elegant pearl-handled flintlock pistol just large enough to hold a single pistol ball.

Studying the mini-arsenal displayed on the table, Julian shook his head. "Prepared for all eventualities, aren't you, my dear?"

Portia didn't even try to hide her smirk. "You should see what I can do with a hatpin."

"You *are* full of surprises, aren't you, pet?" His bemused gaze took a languorous journey from the snug bodice of her gown to her dainty little kid boots. "Just what other weapons do you have stashed under there?"

"Keep your distance and you won't have to find out."

"Am I to assume that my brother has recruited you for his vampire hunting enterprise?"

She lowered her eyes. "Not exactly. Well, at least not yet," she amended. "But I believe it's only a matter of time before he realizes what an asset I could be."

He surveyed her with grudging admiration. "And to think I was worried about what those rogues at the gambling hell might do to you. I should have been worried about what you might do to them." He trailed his hand down the length of the stake. "Or what you might do to me."

Portia jerked her gaze away from the long, elegant fingers wrapped around the smooth shaft of wood, flushing to the roots of her hair. "If I'd have come here tonight to stake you, you'd already be dust."

"Or I'd have had some dinner to go along with my wine." The mocking glitter in his eyes made it impossible to tell if he was teasing her or threatening her.

She gave him a cheery smile. "If you're hungry, I'd be more than glad to run down to the nearest butcher shop and fetch you some rare roast beef or a nice kidney pie."

"I had something a little fresher in mind." His gaze flirted with her throat again. "Something sweeter."

Her smile faded. "Is that what you were looking for when you murdered those women?"

"Is that what you believe?"

"I don't know," she confessed, turning back to the window and edging aside the crepe to escape his penetrating gaze.

A lone man was melting out of the shadows that draped the alley below.

"Oh, no," she breathed. "It can't be him. He swore he wasn't coming until morning."

"What is it?" Instantly alert, Julian glided up behind her, making the tiny hairs on the back of her neck shiver to life.

He peered over her head, both of them hanging back from the window just enough to remain invisible from the alley below. The imposing shoulders beneath the layered cape of the intruder's greatcoat were as distinctive as the walking stick gripped in his powerful hand. A walking stick that could be transformed into a deadly stake with nothing more than a deft flick of the wrist.

"My brother is nothing if not predictable," Julian murmured, his smoky voice very close to her ear. "I suspected it would only be a matter of time before he came calling."

"This might not be a social call," Portia ventured as Adrian was joined by the long, lanky, and damningly familiar shadow of a second man.

Alastair Larkin was a former constable who had been Adrian's best friend at Oxford. The two men had been estranged for years when Caroline came into their lives and brought them together to wreak revenge on Victor Duvalier, the vampire who had not only stolen Julian's soul but murdered Adrian's first love, Eloisa Markham. Larkin also just happened to be Adrian's partner in his vampire-hunting endeavor—and Portia's other brother-in-law, the doting father of her twin nephews.

As the two men briefly conferred, then proceeded toward the building, their shadows still hugging the wall, Portia spun around to face Julian, flattening a hand against his chest.

"There's no time to waste. We have to get you out of here right now!"

He covered her hand with his own, plainly bemused by her urgency. "I'm touched by your concern, darling, but there's really no need for such high drama. What's Adrian going to do? Give me a stern lecture for failing to write? He knows I've always been a wretched correspondent."

"I'm afraid he's not coming here to lecture you," she informed him grimly.

"Then what's he going to do—disown me? Cut me out from my inheritance? Can't you just see him marching in here in high dudgeon and announcing, 'You're no longer my brother! You're dead to me!'?"

When Portia failed to so much as crack a smile at his quip, he grew very still. Although his wry smile lingered, it no longer reached the glittering darkness of his eyes. "So my brother's common sense has finally overcome his sentimental devotion to brotherly duty." He lifted one shoulder in a careless shrug. "I can hardly blame him, you know. He should have driven a stake through my black heart all those years ago when Duvalier first stole my soul. It would have saved us both a great deal of bother."

Portia grabbed his arm and tried to tug him away from the window. "Don't you see? We have to go! Before it's too late!"

He appeared to be on the verge of tweaking her nose. "It's already too late for me, sweeting. So why don't you run along before you earn a lecture from Adrian, too? There's no need to fret about me. This is hardly the first torch-bearing mob I've faced."

Hearing a fresh ruckus, Portia turned back to the window and lifted the crepe again. "I suspect *that* would be the torch-bearing mob," she said, pointing toward the opposite end of the alley.

A tall man with a narrow nose and an upper lip perpetually curled into a sneer had just come striding into the alley, followed by at least a half dozen scraggly-looking henchmen, some of them actually bearing torches.

"Wallingford!" Julian exclaimed, adding an oath as his brother and Larkin moved to intercept the new arrivals. "I had hoped the bastard would at least allow me one more night of freedom before he had me cast into debtor's prison."

She gave his arm another sharp tug. "Perhaps if he hadn't caught you making love to his fiancée at their betrothal supper, he would have been in a more charitable frame of mind."

Julian shifted his accusing glare to her. "You *were* in the park this morning, weren't you? I knew I smelled you." He tugged a coil of hair from the mass of curls piled on top of her head and brought it to his nose. His nostrils flared as if he was once again drinking in some elusive scent.

The scent of his prey.

Muffled shouting rose from the alley as the men below gave up all pretense of stealth. To her disbelief, Julian strolled over and sank down in the wing-chair, crossing his long legs at the ankles as if he had no intention of budging for the next century or so.

"What do you mean to do?" she demanded. "Just sit there and wait for Adrian to march up here and stake you?"

He buffed his fingernails on the cuff of his shirt. "If that's his pleasure."

"And if Wallingford gets to you first?"

"Debtor's prison won't be so bad," he said cheerfully. "It's always dark and there should be plenty of food."

Portia's frustration finally spilled over into anger. "Is this why you returned to London? Because you're weary of provoking men who can't kill you into challenging you to duels? Because you knew Adrian would eventually find you and do what you haven't the nerve to do?"

In reply he simply gazed at her, as unblinking as an owl or some other far more dangerous nocturnal predator.

"Have you thought about what will happen to me if you stay?" she asked. "You may be destroyed but I'll be ruined as well."

A hint of unease flickered through his eyes. "What are you talking about?"

"If I'm found here in this rented flat with you," she replied, daring to give the rumpled bed a provocative glance, "my reputation will never survive."

His eyes narrowed. "You didn't seem to give a flying fig about your reputation when you came strolling into that gambling hell just a short while ago."

"No one knew me there. But the marquess

of Wallingford is a *very* powerful and influential man. Once he starts spreading the word that Viscount Trevelyan's sister-in-law has been consorting with the viscount's own brother, a shameless ne'er do well and a notorious libertine—"

"You forget bloodsucking fiend," he interjected.

She continued as if he hadn't spoken. "—there won't be any wealthy viscounts or earls lining up to ask for my hand. Or any half dozen babes to keep me in the nursery." She sighed, affecting the same air of tragic resignation she had once used to coax Caroline into buying her a pretty length of ribbon they couldn't truly afford. "I suppose I'll have no choice but to offer myself as a mistress to some man just like Wallingford. I'm sure he'll be a cruel and exacting master, but perhaps in time, I can learn to please him."

Julian crossed the room with stunning speed, seizing her by the hand. As he jerked her toward the door, he shot her a smoldering look over his shoulder. "I'm perfectly willing to answer to God for my sins, but I'll be damned if I'll allow you to be punished for a crime I haven't had the pleasure of committing tonight."

As Julian plunged down the darkened stairwell, his grip on her hand unrelenting, Portia struggled to keep pace with him. Before they could reach the first landing, a loud thump sounded from below. He jerked to a halt, reaching back to steady her before she could slam into him. Over the panicked rasp of her breathing she heard the unmistakable clatter of booted feet on the stairs. They'd dallied too long. Their only escape route had been cut off.

Julian whirled around, all but dragging her back up the narrow winding staircase and past the door of his rented room. Up, up, up they went until they finally burst through a sagging wooden door and onto the roof.

A blast of icy air whipped the heavy coils of Portia's hair from its pins, reminding her that she'd left her bonnet, pelisse, and all of her weapons in Julian's room, leaving her at the mercy of both the elements and him. Yet instead of fear, a strange rush of exhilaration coursed through her veins.

A thin blanket of snow clung to the chimney pots and gables. Glittering flakes danced in the fitful moonlight, tossed about by the whims of the wind. Although she had sworn to him that she'd forsaken all of her childhood fancies, Portia could not help but feel as if she'd stumbled onto some enchanted fairy kingdom, both beautiful and dangerous.

When she was a child, she had believed such a kingdom would be ruled by a golden-haired prince who would rescue her from every threat. Yet here she was racing hand in hand through the night with a dark prince who was just as likely to bring destruction as deliverance.

They stumbled to a halt at the very edge of the roof. With the snow cloaking the grime and soot, the city stretched out before them like the frosted parapets of a vast castle, the next rooftop an impossible leap away.

The furious shouts and thunder of footsteps swelled. In a matter of seconds, Julian's pursuers would be upon them.

Teetering in his arms on the edge of that yawning precipice, a nervous chuckle bubbled up in Portia's throat. "For years Adrian has been hearing rumors about vampires who possess the concentration to turn themselves into bats. It's a pity you're not one of them."

As a helpless shiver wracked her, Julian drew her into his arms, using his body to shelter her from the wind. He smoothed her hair out of her eyes, his gaze fierce. "Tell them you came looking for me, but I was already gone. That I fled London to avoid Wallingford's wrath and I'll not trouble any of them again. Tell them you came here to convince me to come home. Because you knew how my estrangement from Adrian was affecting your sister and the rest of the family. You won't be able to fool Adrian but Wallingford will believe you. You can be a very convincing little actress when you want to be."

Portia opened her mouth to protest, then closed it, realizing there was no point. "But where will you go? How . . ." She trailed off, gesturing toward the starry expanse of the night sky.

The corner of his mouth quirked upward in a rueful smile. "Before Adrian destroyed him, Duvalier gave me one sound piece of advice. He told me I'd be a fool not to embrace my dark gifts."

As if to share the darkest and most priceless

of those gifts, he bent his head to hers. There, with the snow and starlight swirling around them, with disaster bearing down upon them on booted feet, he kissed her.

This was no seductive foray artfully designed to maximize her pleasure. This time he took what *he* wanted, what *he* craved. His tongue swept through her mouth, claiming it, claiming *her,* with a passion and power that threatened to rip the soul right out of her. Even if she'd had a stake in one hand and a pistol in the other, she couldn't have defended herself against such an onslaught of passion. Nor would she have wanted to.

Julian groaned and she clung to the front of his waistcoat, answering that siren call with a deep-throated moan in a voice she no longer recognized as her own. That moan turned to one of helpless dismay as he dragged his mouth from hers and gently set her away from him.

Her eyes fluttered open just in time to see him turn and dive straight over the side of the roof. Before the scream caught in her throat could erupt, he had vanished into thin air. A dark shape went soaring past the roof, hurtling into the night sky. Portia stood there with her mouth hanging open, watching as it wheeled in a graceful circle, then went flapping away toward the sickle-thin crescent of the moon.

Shaking off her shock, she cupped her hands around her mouth and shouted, "Don't eat anyone!"

It might have been nothing more than a trick of the wind but she would have almost sworn she heard Julian's rich baritone float back to her on a note ripe with laughter. "Don't nag!"

Then the door behind her came crashing open and there was nothing left for her to do but turn around and face the torch-bearing mob and her brother-in-law's thunderous brow.

Five

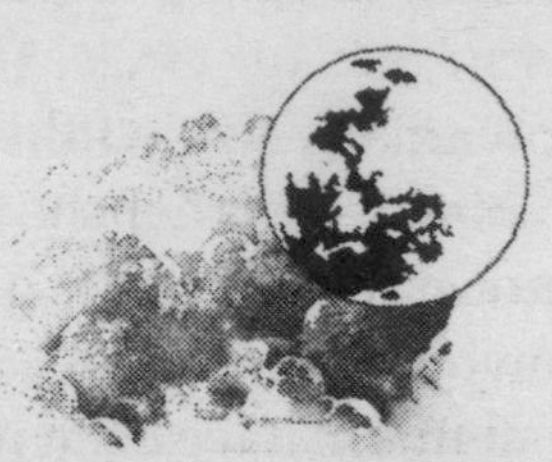

"What do I have to do to keep you safe from him? Lock you away in a convent? At least he wouldn't be able to set foot on holy ground." Adrian was once again wearing a fresh path in the elegant Aubusson carpet that ran the length of his drawing room. Judging from the shadows beneath his eyes and the fact that he still wore his rumpled trousers, shirt, and waistcoat from the night before, he didn't appear to have slept so much as a wink since bringing Portia home.

"Perhaps we should see if Cousin Cecil is still in the market for a bride," Caroline offered, referring to the toadlike lech who had once offered to beat the spirit out of Portia with his fists.

Both Adrian and Portia turned to gape at her in horror. When she blinked innocently at them and added, "Or Aunt Marietta might be in need of a companion," they realized she was only jesting. She sat on the brocaded sofa with Eloisa perched on her knee. The honey-haired toddler appeared to be in imminent danger of swallowing the wildly expensive pearls Adrian had given Caroline for their third anniversary.

Watery afternoon sunlight sifted through the tall arched windows of the spacious room. Portia had managed to postpone this discussion for several hours, first by feigning a swoon in the carriage on the way home, then by pleading tearful exhaustion when Adrian had delivered her to Caroline's waiting arms. Unfortunately, her strategy had backfired. The delay had only given Adrian time to summon the rest of the family to witness her disgrace.

Portia's other sister, Vivienne, sat in the leather wing-chair near the hearth, keeping one watchful eye on the four-year-old towheaded twins playing at wooden soldiers before the cozy fire. Not even giving birth to two budding hellions at once had seemed to ruffle her legendary composure. According to family legend, when the midwife had handed her the second baby, she had simply murmured, "Oh, my! Would you look at that?" while her stoic husband had crumpled to the carpet in a dead faint.

Alastair Larkin, whom they all tended to address as simply "Larkin" in a nod to his former career as a constable, perched on the arm of his wife's chair. Every few minutes, he would reach over to absently stroke her golden hair. Given his stern lips and hawk nose, there were some who might have wondered how such a plain man had managed to capture the heart of a beauty like Vivienne Cabot. Until they saw the way his shrewd brown eyes lit up every time he looked at her.

Portia had dressed for her dressing down in a somber green morning gown that she hoped would make her look suitably penitent. A matching velvet choker adorned her throat. She sat on her favorite ottoman with her hands folded demurely in her lap, watching Adrian resume his pacing.

"Julian is *my* brother," he reminded her. "You

should have trusted me to take care of the situation, not gone off on some misbegotten mission of your own."

"I did trust you to take care of the situation. That's precisely what I was worried about."

He swung around to face her. "Did you really believe I was going to stake my baby brother through the heart without so much as a polite by-your-leave?"

"Adrian . . . the children," Caroline reminded him, touching a finger to her lips.

Shooting her a frustrated glance, Adrian strode over to the tasseled bellpull in the corner and gave it a hard yank. After what seemed like an eternity, their elderly butler Wilbury came shuffling into the drawing room. With his sunken cheeks, hunched back, and startling shock of white hair, he appeared to be at least 275 years old.

"Wilbury, my dear," Caroline said, "would you mind taking the children and keeping them occupied for a bit?"

" 'Twould be the high point of my golden years, my lady," he replied with frigid politeness. "The culmination of a lifelong dream I had nearly abandoned in favor of waiting peacefully for the Grim Reaper to come and relieve me of my earthly duties."

Immune to his sarcasm, Caroline beamed fondly at him. "Thank you, Wilbury. I thought that's what you would say."

Shuffling toward the hearth, the butler muttered beneath his breath, "I just love children, you know. I simply dote upon the overindulged little darlings with their grasping little hands and their sticky little fingers that foul up every freshly polished surface in the house." As he leaned toward the hearth, the twins paused in their play to gape up at him. Baring his pointed, yellowing teeth in a grimace of a smile, he rasped, "Come now, lads. I'll take you to the kitchen for some nice hot cocoa."

Eyes widening in terror, the two boys leapt to their feet and ran shrieking from the room. Wilbury straightened as much as his hunched back would allow, rolling his eyes.

"Wilbuwy!" Eloisa crowed, scrambling down from her mother's lap and toddling across the room. Wrapping her arms around one of the butler's scrawny legs, she looked up and batted her long lashes at him. "Me want cocoa!"

With a long-suffering sigh, he scooped the plump child into his arms, every one of his ancient bones creaking in protest. She joyfully tugged on his misshapen ears as he carried her toward the door. His curdled expression never varied, but as he passed Portia he gave her a nearly imperceptible wink.

She bit back a smile, heartened to know she had at least one ally in this house. Wilbury had always been partial to Julian. After Duvalier had turned Julian into a vampire, Wilbury had been the only one to share the brothers' dark secret, helping Adrian turn Julian's crypt in the dungeon of their ancestral castle into a chamber fit for a prince. He had forever endeared himself to Portia by guarding the door of the mansion's ballroom while she practiced wielding a stake and firing a crossbow instead of dancing and conjugating French verbs. He had also swept up the shards of the numerous vases and busts she had broken with only a mutter of reproach.

Adrian waited until his daughter was safely out of earshot before returning his attention to Portia. "I suppose I have only myself to blame. I should have known that no good would ever come of this infatuation of yours."

"There's no longer any need for you to worry about that," Portia replied primly even as the memory of Julian's kisses made both her throat and her lips tingle. "You were right all along. Julian is neither the man—or the vampire—I remembered." She lowered her head, deliberately avoiding Caroline's sharp-eyed gaze. Although she and Vivienne were closer in age, it was Caroline who had always been able to read her heart.

"What exactly did he say when you confronted him about the murders?" Larkin leaned forward, no longer able to keep his natural curiosity in check. "Did he deny any knowledge of them or did he confess?"

He had done neither, Portia remembered grimly. Which meant that he was deliberately hiding something. But who was he trying to protect? Himself? Or someone else?

Although she loathed lying to her family, she met Larkin's clear-eyed gaze with one of her own. "I never had the chance to ask him. I'm afraid your impromptu little witch hunt interrupted my interrogation."

Larkin settled back on the chair arm, his disappointment palpable. Vivienne patted his knee and smiled at her little sister. "I really don't see what all the fuss is about. The only thing that matters is that our Portia is back with us—safe and sound."

"I'd like for her to stay that way," Adrian countered. "But I can't count on that as long as Julian is lurking about."

"He told me he was leaving London," Portia said softly. "That he wouldn't . . . trouble any of us again."

A shadow of grief passed over Adrian's face, making her own heart clutch with regret. She had no way of knowing if Julian had spoken the truth or if his words had just been a clever ruse to throw them off of his scent. She hadn't even dared to tell Adrian how he had made his escape, preferring to let them all believe he had used his superior strength to climb down one of the roof's drain spouts. In all of their battles, none of them had ever encountered a vampire who could actually focus his power long enough to shape shift into a bat. If Adrian knew his brother possessed that rare gift, he might consider him even more of a threat.

Adrian surprised her by sinking down heavily on the edge of the ottoman and running a hand over his unshaven jaw. "I know you probably think I'm overreacting, but when I saw you standing on the edge of that roof with your face so pale and your hair all atumble . . ."

"You believed the worst," she finished for him.

He nodded. "I was afraid he'd drank from you again. That he'd come one step closer to killing you, or worse yet, stealing your soul."

Knowing that it wasn't her soul in jeopardy, but her heart, Portia looped an arm through his and gave it a squeeze. "I'm sorry I gave you such a fright. What I told Wallingford was partially true. I just wanted to bring him home. For you." There was no guile in the gaze she swept over her family. "For all of us."

Adrian stood, tugging her to her feet and pressing a gentle kiss to her brow. "Vivienne is right. For now the only thing that matters is that you're home and safe. We'll worry about the rest of it later."

As he moved toward the door, Vivienne rose with a graceful swish of her skirts. "Come darling," she told her husband. "We'd best go rescue the boys from Wilbury's clutches before we find them in a cookpot somewhere."

"Didn't they lock poor Wilbury in the cupboard the last time we left them alone with him?" Larkin asked.

"No, that was the time before. The last time he locked *them* in the broom closet," she replied as they followed Adrian from the drawing room.

Only Caroline remained seated, gazing thoughtfully into the dancing flames of the fire. Portia was inching toward the door when her sister said, "Not so fast, pet."

Portia widened her eyes in a look of studied innocence. "Did you say something?"

Caroline patted the sofa next to her, her smile equally innocent. "Why don't you join me for a little chat?"

Portia reluctantly complied, sinking down on the sofa but maintaining her stony silence.

"You know," Caroline said, toying with the monogrammed handkerchief in her lap, "I've been dying of curiosity, but in all these years I never once pressed you to tell me what happened in that crypt with Julian."

Portia couldn't quite hide her guilty start. She had assumed her sister was going to question her about the events of last night, not the events of six years ago. "I always did admire your restraint. It was very unlike you."

"I suppose it was easier for all of us to just pretend it had never happened, wasn't it?" Caroline's candid gray eyes searched her face. "But I never stopped wondering if Julian took more from you in that crypt than just your blood. If that might not explain your lingering feelings for him. Your obvious reluctance to marry."

Portia could keep her voice deliberately light but she couldn't stop the heavy rush of blood to her cheeks. She studied her own hands, wishing for a handkerchief to wring. "If that's what you suspected, why didn't you send for a physician to examine me?"

"Adrian suggested it, but I refused to subject you to such an indignity. In truth, we both believed you'd suffered enough at his brother's hands."

Before Portia could stop it, a brittle laugh bubbled from her lips. "I appreciate your concern, Caro, but I can assure you that no woman has ever suffered unduly at Julian Kane's hands."

"Even now?" Caroline countered, her gaze more probing than before.

Since she had no answer for that, Portia

simply rose and strode from the drawing room, her head held high and her secrets still her own.

Portia sat curled up in the window seat of her third-story bedchamber that night, watching the lights in the windows of the Georgian-style town houses that lined the other side of the Mayfair square wink out one by one. Just as a distant church bell tolled a single note, the last lamp in the square surrendered to the darkness, leaving her alone with the moon.

She pushed open the window, preferring the chill rush of air to the stifling warmth of the fire crackling on her brick hearth. Although carriages had carved muddy ruts through the broad cobbled streets below, snow still frosted the rooftops and the spindly arms of the tree branches, making them glow in the lambent light. A thin mist trailed ghostly fingers through the deserted streets.

She drew her woolen shawl tighter over her thin cotton night rail, her hungry gaze searching the night. The sleeping hush of the house made her feel as if she was the only one left awake in all the world. But she knew Julian was out there somewhere, a prisoner of the night with all of its dangers and temptations. For all she knew, he might already be in the arms of another woman who could never be anything more to him than his next meal.

She touched a finger to the plump swell of her bottom lip, remembering the demanding pressure of his mouth on hers. How he had kissed her as if she was both his salvation and his doom. How he had wrapped her in his arms so tightly that even the furious lash of the wind couldn't tear them apart.

But in the end, it had. She slowly lowered her hand. What if Julian's kiss truly had been a kiss of farewell? What if he went back to wandering the world, exiled from everyone who had ever loved him? What if she never saw him again? Somehow that prospect was even more unbearable than it had been before. In time, she might even come to believe that those moments in his arms had been nothing more than a dream, the feverish delusion of a woman destined to spend her life yearning for a man she could never have.

The wind moaned through the trees overhanging the courtyard below, sending a shiver dancing over her flesh. She reached to draw the window closed, but after a moment's hesitation, edged it open even wider.

"Come home, Julian," she whispered to the night. "Before it's too late."

Julian slipped through the window of Portia's bedchamber, landing on the balls of his feet with the soundless grace of a cat. He should have been halfway to France by now, sailing across the Channel with a clueless Cuthbert in tow.

Instead he'd spent the day huddled in an abandoned warehouse in Charing Cross, waiting for the pale winter sun to set. He had crept out just after moonrise, dodging the crowded thoroughfares of Fleet Street and the Strand where one of Wallingford's henchmen might still be lying in wait for him. Before he'd realized it, his aimless wandering had led him to the alley behind his brother's mansion.

He lingered in that alley, drawing back into the shadows when Larkin emerged to bundle Vivienne and a matched pair of chattering little lads into their waiting carriage. He watched through a lighted window while Caroline slipped into Adrian's study and then into Adrian's lap, seeking to ease his visible tension with a tender kiss. As the two of them strolled from the room, arm in arm, Julian studied his brother's handsome face, knowing he was responsible for the new lines of strain he found there. Adrian had always been willing to bear every burden that should have rightfully been Julian's.

As Wilbury made his customary rounds through the house, extinguishing the last of the lamps, Julian bided his time. It was easy to be patient when one had an eternity to waste.

Or so he thought until he crept around to the front of the house and saw Portia sitting in the window of her bedchamber. She was gazing up at the night sky with her chin cupped in her hand, looking as wistful as a child who had just been told that the man in the moon had departed for sunnier climes. Julian knew he should bid her a silent farewell and melt back into the shadows where he belonged.

He would leave London. The murders would stop. And if she spent the rest of her life believing the worst of him, wouldn't that be the best for her? He turned to go.

Come home, Julian. Before it's too late.

Julian froze, his keen hearing picking up the

echo of her whispered words. His gaze shot back to the window only to find it empty.

"Please tell me the little fool latched it," he muttered beneath his breath. But even from his vantage point, he could see that the window stood ajar.

He stood there for a very long time, but he doubted even his saintly brother could have resisted such a compelling invitation. One minute his feet were firmly planted on the snowy ground. The next he was slipping through her window like a thief intent upon stealing some priceless treasure.

He glided silently toward the bed. The canopy of the four-poster was draped in sheer gauze, giving it the appearance of a sultan's tent. As he parted that shimmering curtain, it wasn't difficult to imagine the woman he found sleeping within ruling over both a man's harem and his heart.

She'd made a valiant effort to contain her rioting curls in a neat pair of braids, but several silky, dark strands had escaped to frame her face. She slept on her back with one hand nestled against the sleep-flushed curve of her cheek. A rueful smile quirked Julian's lips when he saw the stake clutched in her other hand.

"That's my girl," he whispered as a delicate snore escaped her parted lips. Despite her fondness for whimsy, Portia had always possessed a practical streak.

Julian knew that if he chose to press his suit, the stake would be a feeble defense indeed. He could only be thankful that she hadn't yet realized she possessed other weapons that might be even more lethal to his heart.

It didn't take long for his overdeveloped sense of smell to betray him. His nostrils flared as he leaned closer, allowing himself the forbidden luxury of drinking in her scent. If not for the press of unwashed bodies and cigar smoke in the gambling hell, he might have smelled her coming and had time to flee out a back entrance. She still smelled exactly as he remembered—clean and sweet like wind-tossed sheets drying on a rope in the sunshine. Yet underlying that innocent fragrance of rosemary and soap was a woman's irresistible musk, the elusive perfume that had been driving men mad with longing for centuries.

He swallowed back his own longing, fighting the urge to bury his face against her throat.

He was dangerously hungry and her enticing scent made him ache to devour her in more ways than one.

In some ways, it had been easy to keep his distance from her as long as he could pretend she was still just a lovelorn little girl. He had put oceans and continents and scores of other women between them, content to let his memories of her both tantalize and torment him.

Was he the reason she had never wed? he wondered. He had certainly wasted enough of the lonely hours between dusk and dawn envisioning her in another man's arms, another man's bed. Yet here she was, still bearing the scars of his kiss on her throat like a burning brand. The irony did not escape him. She bore his mark, yet he could never again claim her for his own.

And why not?

Julian stiffened. He was no stranger to that sly voice or its dark insinuations. He wasn't even surprised to find its oily cadences identical to Victor Duvalier's. After all, it had been Duvalier who had turned him into a vampire. Duvalier who had taunted him, swearing that he would never know a moment's peace or satisfaction until he stopped trying to be a man and embraced being a monster. Duvalier who had hurled Portia into his arms in that crypt, encouraging him to slake both his hunger and his loneliness by ripping the soul right out of her and making her his eternal bride.

The temptation had lost none of its allure since that moment. If anything it had grown stronger, honed by endless nights of feeding without ever sating his appetites, touching but never truly feeling.

No longer able to resist touching her, he brushed his fingertips across the pale scars on her throat. A frown flickered across her face. Her lips parted in a soft moan that could have indicated either pleasure or pain.

A savage wave of heat flooded his groin and he felt his fangs lengthen and sharpen in reckless anticipation. Portia turned her face toward his, murmuring a sleepy protest as he gently tugged the stake from her hand.

Surrender.

The seductive whisper twined like silk through Portia's dreams, coaxing her to lower all of her defenses. To lay down the last of her weapons and welcome the swirling darkness with open arms.

She was no longer alone in the darkness. *He* was there. It was his voice she heard, urging her to confess all of her secret longings. She could feel herself getting lost in the hypnotic power of his whisper, feel her limbs growing heavier with each shallow breath, each languid beat of her heart. He had to have her. Without her, he would die. No longer able to resist his entreaty or his command, she drew back her hair with a trembling hand and offered him her throat.

Portia jerked awake, the dream still so real she half expected to find Julian looming over her, his fangs already bared. But the only thing looming over her was the bed's canopy. She touched a hand to the scars on her throat, a shaky sigh escaping her lungs. What sort of perverse creature was she? The dream should have terrified her, not left her breasts taut and her body aching with yearning.

She pressed her other hand to her pounding heart, realizing it was empty. The stake must have slipped from her grip while she was thrashing about in the bedclothes. She didn't know if she could ever bring herself to use it against Julian, but its familiar heft still gave her comfort.

She rolled to her side to search the sheets. That's when she saw the stake, propped up on the pillow next to her with the burgundy ribbon she had tossed atop Julian's winnings at the gambling hell tied around its length in a neat bow.

Wondering if she was still dreaming, she slowly sat up and brushed her trembling fingers across the velvet ribbon. Her gaze flew to the window.

Snatching up the stake, she tossed back the blankets and ran to the window. It was closed, but not latched, as if someone had pushed it shut from the outside. An impossible feat since there was no balcony, no ledge, and no tree within ten feet of her bedchamber. She shoved open the window, inviting a frigid rush of air into the toasty warmth of the room. Someone had not only closed the window, but stoked her fire with a fresh log.

She leaned over the sill, searching the shadows below for any hint of movement. But the night with its distant moon and glittering stars was no less lonely than before. Sinking down in the window seat, she turned the stake over in her hands. She could easily imagine Julian's deft fingers tying that ribbon around its deadly length before gently resting it on her pillow.

Was it meant to be an invitation or a parting gift? A promise or a warning?

Surrender, he had whispered in her dream. But what did he want her to surrender? Her heart? Her hopes? Her very soul? Drawing the stake to her chest, she turned her face to the moon and waited for dawn.

Portia shuffled into the breakfast room the next morning, smothering a yawn behind her hand. She had kept her vigil at the window for most of the night, finally nodding off just as the first rays of the sun had come peeping over the rooftops. She had awakened less than two hours later, her muscles aching and stiff, her cold fingers still wrapped around the stake.

She had slipped the beribboned weapon into the detachable pocket of her skirt before coming downstairs. She knew she would eventually have to show it to Adrian, but some small selfish corner of her heart wanted to keep it tucked safely out of sight for just a little while longer. It might be the last secret she and Julian would ever share.

Adrian sat on the far side of the circular table with Caroline by his side. Judging from the dark circles beneath both their eyes, they hadn't slept any more than she had. Their glum expressions were in direct contrast to the dazzling brightness of the sun winking off the snow that still blanketed the terrace outside the tall French windows. Little Eloisa, who usually entertained herself by hurling gobbets of porridge at Wilbury, was conspicuously absent. Larkin slouched in the chair across from Adrian, his cravat half untied and his light brown hair tousled as if he'd just blown in on a winter gale.

There wasn't a single footman in attendance and the plates they'd filled from the elegant walnut sideboard appeared to be untouched. As Portia watched, Caroline absently poked her coddled egg with a two-pronged fork but made no attempt to bring a bite to her mouth.

Her puzzled gaze swept the table. "What on earth is the matter with all of you? You look as if someone had died."

"Someone did," Larkin replied in a clipped tone, brushing a stray hank of hair out of his eyes. "There was another murder in Charing Cross last night, this one even more brutal than the others."

Portia groped blindly for the back of a chair, wishing for a footman. She no longer trusted her knees to support her.

Caroline reached over and squeezed Adrian's hand. "It couldn't have been your brother. You heard Portia. She promised us that he was leaving London."

Adrian shook his head, his eyes as bleak as his expression. "I might be able to take comfort in that if we knew for certain that he'd already gone."

"He hasn't." Portia's stark words fell into the void left by his, drawing every eye in the room to her ashen face. "He came to my room last night while I was sleeping. He left this for me." Reaching into the pocket of her skirt, she withdrew the stake and tossed it on the table. The bow unfurled against the starched white linen of the tablecloth like a ribbon of dried blood.

Adrian gazed at it in silence, a muscle in his jaw twitching.

"Darling," Caroline whispered helplessly, reaching for his arm.

Evading her grasp, he shoved his chair away from the table and surged to his feet. He started around the table but before he could reach the door, Portia was there, blocking his path.

"Don't!" he warned, stabbing a finger at her chest. "I love you as if you were my very own sister and I'd drag the moon down from the sky if I thought it would make you happy. But I can't allow you to stop me from doing what must be done."

"I don't want to stop you," she replied. An eerie calm had washed over her, leaving her mercifully numb. "I want to help you."

"How?" he asked warily.

"By offering him something he can't resist."

"And just what would that be?"

Portia felt her full lips tilt in their most seductive and dangerous smile. "Me."

Six

Tendrils of mist rose from the damp cobble-stones. Earlier in the day a chill rain had washed the last of the snow from the streets, leaving them gleaming beneath the moody glow of the streetlamps. Clouds still hung low over the rooftops and chimneys of the city, making it a moonless night, perfect for hunting.

Three figures came melting out of the mist—a woman flanked by two men. Despite her petite stature and the fact that both of her companions towered over her by nearly a foot, a casual observer might have judged the woman to be the most dangerous of the three. And in that moment, they would have been right.

Her dark blue eyes glittered with determination beneath the hood of her dove gray cloak. Her shapely hips rolled with each step in a gait perilously near to a swagger. The tilt of her head exuded both confidence and purpose. She might be willing to play the role of victim, but anyone foolish enough to take the bait she offered would clearly be trespassing at their own risk.

As they reached the outskirts of the rookery that had sprung up just behind the royal stables, Adrian touched a finger to his lips and motioned Portia and Larkin into a deserted alleyway. The three of them huddled in the shadows of an overhanging eave like any other ne'er-do-wells out for a bit of mischief on such a foggy and forbidding night.

This island of squalor between Charing Cross and the end of the Mall would perfectly suit the purposes of any villain, vampire or mortal. Winding alleys and narrow streets separated the ramshackle hovels from dingy courts bearing deceptively exotic names like Caribee Islands and the Bermudas. Many a poor woman had been dragged into one of those dark and deserted alleys, never to be seen again.

"Are you sure you can do this?" Adrian asked Portia, his brow furrowed in a worried frown.

"Just watch me," she replied, unfastening the top frog of her cloak so that the swansdown-lined garment hung loosely on her shoulders.

Beneath it she wore an evening dress woven from rich garnet velvet the color of blood, its slashed sleeves and deep, square-cut bodice better suited to a courtesan than the sister-in-law of a reputable viscount. She hooked her thumbs in the stiff whalebone corset sewn into the bodice and tugged it down to better expose the ample curves of her cleavage.

Adrian immediately reached to tug it back up. She smacked his hands away.

He sighed. "I can't believe I let you talk me into this. Your sister was dead set against it, you know. If I let any harm come to you, she'll have my head."

"And Vivienne will have my—" Larkin began, but stopped when Adrian barked out a cough. Clearing his throat, he finished with, "Well, she'll have my head as well."

Portia adjusted her hairpins and dragged a

few curls from the lustrous coils of hair piled on top of her head, knowing that even a mortal man couldn't resist a woman who looked as if she'd just tumbled out of bed.

Although her heart was beating so loudly she was afraid they would hear it, she fought to keep her hands steady. "There's no need for the two of you to fuss over me like a pair of nervous mother hens. I've been training to fight with you for years. We always knew this day would come."

"But not with Julian as our quarry," Adrian reminded her softly.

Portia gnawed on her lips to bring some color to them, hoping the brisk January wind would whip some roses into her bloodless cheeks. "Then we'll just have to stop thinking of him as Julian, won't we, and start thinking of him as the ruthless killer that he's become."

The two men exchanged a troubled glance over her head, but when Larkin opened his mouth to speak, Adrian shook his head in warning.

Adrian pointed to an abandoned warehouse down the street. "We'll be right across the way, Portia. If it looks like you're getting into any trouble at all, we'll come running."

He moved closer, opening his arms as if to embrace her, but Portia stepped away from them both. Her bones felt as brittle as Wilbury's. If one of them so much as patted her on the shoulder, she feared they would snap.

"Do you have everything you need?" he asked, awkwardly tucking his hands into the pockets of his greatcoat.

"I can only hope," she said, drawing the stake Julian had left on her pillow from the secret pocket Vivienne had sewn into her skirt. She slid the burgundy ribbon from the weapon before tucking it back into the pocket, then secured the length of velvet around the graceful column of her throat, making it an even more enticing target. "But I am confident that I have everything *he* needs."

Poking his head out of the alley to peer both ways down the deserted street, Larkin drew a small flintlock pistol from the pocket of his coat and passed it to her. "If anyone else accosts you, just fire this into the air."

"Or into them," Adrian said grimly.

They politely averted their eyes as she lifted the flounced hem of her skirt and tucked the pistol into her lace garter. She shivered at the bite of the cold steel against her bare skin.

"Once he recognizes you, he may suspect it's a trap," Adrian warned her.

"Doubtful," she replied. "Given his colossal arrogance, he'll probably think I just came to warn him you were coming or to read some of Byron's poetry by the fire."

She straightened, the steely glint in her eye informing them that she was ready. Adrian and Larkin exchanged a nod, then ushered her toward the mouth of the alley. As they reached the street, the three of them parted ways as if they'd just concluded some sordid assignation. Adrian and Larkin went stumbling toward one of the courts, their raucous laughter ringing through the night, while Portia meandered in the opposite direction, teetering slightly on the heels of her kid slippers to make herself appear more defenseless.

Although she knew it would only take a matter of minutes for the men to double back and slip into the warehouse across the street, she had never felt so utterly alone in her life.

For over five long years she had comforted herself with the notion that Julian was out there somewhere in the night, pining for her as she pined for him. Stripped of that illusion, the night felt as vast and cold as the moonless sky. She wanted nothing more than to huddle deeper into her cloak, but instead she shrugged the garment off of one shoulder and lifted her chin high, baring the vulnerable curve of her throat.

She strolled slowly along, not wanting to get too far from the warehouse. They had chosen this spot deliberately because it was only a block away from where two of the murdered women had been found. She jumped when a drunken sailor stumbled out of one of the alleys just ahead of her. But he spared her little more than a bleary glance, obviously more intent on finding his next tumbler of gin than his next woman.

The mist distorted every sound, making it impossible to tell if a ghostly echo of laughter or a furtive footfall was coming from a block away or from just behind her. An icy trickle of sweat eased down the back of her neck. Without warning she whirled around. The street behind her was empty. Now she was being haunted by the echo of her own footsteps.

Shaking her head at her own jumpiness, she resumed her leisurely stroll. But she'd only taken a few steps when she suddenly stopped in her tracks. Less than twenty feet away, a tall hooded figure in a black cloak stood haloed beneath the flickering glow of a streetlamp.

Portia knew there was still time to shout for help. Still time for Adrian and Larkin to come rushing to her rescue. But if she sounded the alarm too soon, Julian might flee. She cringed inwardly to realize that in some small pathetic corner of her heart, she almost wished he would.

She slipped her icy fingers into the pocket of her skirt, closing them around the stake. She knew now that he hadn't left it on her pillow as a parting gift, but as a challenge—a taunt.

She forced her feet into motion. The figure beneath the streetlamp stood watching . . . waiting, so still that one would have sworn he had never even felt the need to draw breath. Portia was almost upon him when he reached up and eased back his hood . . . to reveal a shimmering mane of white-gold curls.

Portia's relief was so keen that she gasped aloud. It wasn't a man, but a woman. And not just any woman, she quickly realized, but one of the most ravishing creatures she had ever laid eyes on. Her dazzling fall of blond hair was complimented by a pair of ripe ruby lips and hypnotic green eyes. Her fair skin was eerily unlined, making it impossible to judge her age. Her pale, slender fingers were adorned with jewels—a winking emerald, a teardrop ruby, an opal the size of a small egg. Portia wondered what on earth she was doing in the rookery. She might very well be a nobleman's pampered mistress, but such an uncommon beauty could never be mistaken for a common prostitute.

"You shouldn't be out here alone, madam," Portia warned her, stealing a glance over her shoulder. "The streets aren't safe tonight."

"Are they ever?" the woman replied, gazing down her long, patrician nose at Portia.

Portia detected a ripe ripple of amusement and the lilting hint of a French accent in her throaty voice. "Probably not in this neighborhood. Have you a carriage and driver somewhere nearby?"

"I have no need of a carriage." The woman gazed up and down the street, allowing Portia to admire the stunning elegance of her profile. "I am waiting for my lover."

Portia blinked, taken aback by both the woman's candor and her imperious air. "It's very late," she said tentatively. "Are you certain he's coming?"

The woman's full red lips curved in a smile. "Oh, he will come. I've made sure of that."

She turned that dazzling smile on Portia. Portia couldn't help staring, mesmerized by the feline slant of the woman's eyes. She was starting to feel a little like a cobra coiled in the basket of a master snake charmer. If the woman started to sway, she feared she would too.

"So why does an innocent little dove like you brave the streets tonight?" the woman asked. "Are you also waiting for a lover?"

Portia stiffened. "I'm afraid not. My love"—she stumbled over the word—"my *lover* betrayed me. He has been proven false."

To her surprise, the woman reached out a snow white hand tipped with crimson nails and gently stroked her cheek. "Poor little dove," she crooned. "A lover broke my heart once. The pain was as fierce as any I have ever known. I longed for death."

Portia felt her own bruised heart leap in sympathy. "You actually wanted to die?"

The woman's eyes widened. "Not *my* death,

little one. His. I felt much better after I'd cut out his heart and eaten it."

Portia's mouth fell open, but before her scream could escape, the woman's hand shot out and closed over her throat. She lifted Portia clear off her feet, sending the stake in her hand tumbling from her numb fingers to the ground.

The woman's ruby red lips parted to reveal a gleaming white pair of fangs. "If you will allow me, my dear, perhaps I can put an end to your suffering as well."

"You promised me we were leaving London," Cuthbert muttered, crouching down next to where Julian was kneeling and shooting him an accusing look. "You come knocking at my window in the dead of night and say, 'Abandon your nice toasty bed and come away with me, Cubby. Bring a handful of your father's jewels and we can spend the rest of the winter lazing on the sunny beaches of southern Spain with some delicious little opera dancer.'" Tugging down the brim of his beaver top hat to cover ears pink with cold, he eyed the shadowy loft of the abandoned warehouse with a mistrustful eye.

"Instead you drag me down to this miserable hellhole where some miscreant may very well cut my purse or, worse yet, my throat."

"If you don't stop whining," Julian said absently, peering through the jagged hole where a pane of glass had once resided, "I'm going to cut out your tongue."

Cuthbert snapped his mouth shut, but his breath continued to escape his nostrils in frigid little puffs, making him look like an indignant dragon.

Julian sighed and pivoted on one knee to face him. "I told you I had some unfinished business in London. As soon as it's settled, I swear I'll find you that sunny beach *and* your bloody opera dancer."

"Your unfinished business usually involves sneaking into a lady's bedchamber to return a missing undergarment before her husband gets home, not spending half the night huddled in Charing Cross freezing our tailcoats off." He leaned forward to survey the street below, forcing Julian to grab the tails of his coat to keep him from tumbling headfirst out the window. "Is this about Wallingford? Is the scoundrel up to no good? Have you found a way to blackmail him into tearing up your vowels?"

"This is about settling another debt I owe." Julian's wayward memory conjured up a vision of Portia nestled snugly in her bed. Only in this vision, she opened her eyes and her arms to welcome him. "And I won't leave London without seeing it paid."

"Well, I just hope this uncharacteristic attack of scruples doesn't prove fatal. For either one of us." Cuthbert settled back on his haunches. "What on earth have you been doing since you dropped me off at my father's town house the other night? Based on your impressive performance at the coffee house earlier, it certainly wasn't eating. I've never seen a man shovel down five rare beefsteaks at one sitting." He shook his head in grudging admiration. "But I have to admit that it improved your color. You were looking a trifle bit pasty."

Julian murmured something noncommittal. He was still so hungry that even Cubby's thick neck was starting to look a little tempting.

"Once we get to Madrid, perhaps we can—"

"Shhhhhh!" Julian raised a warning hand

as a shadowy figure came stumbling out of one of the alleys below.

But it was just a drunken sailor searching for another tavern. Somewhere in the distance, the bells of a church began to chime midnight, their high pure tones out of place in this dangerous corner of hell where wisps of fog drifted up from the cobblestones like brimstone-scented smoke. Julian narrowed his eyes as another figure came melting out of the fog that had just swallowed the sailor.

"It's a woman," Cuthbert said.

"I can see that," Julian snapped, his nerves frayed to the breaking point.

The cloaked woman meandered down the street as if she had no particular destination in mind. Julian might have thought she was drunk, but she was neither weaving or staggering. If she were a light-skirt trolling for coins, it should have been easy enough for her to coax the sailor into one of the nearby alleys for a quick coupling or a *ball-against-the-wall,* as it was known in cruder circles.

He felt some of the tension seep from his muscles as she drew abreast of the warehouse and he realized she was buxom and petite, not tall and willowy. But his relief was quickly replaced by a more discomfiting emotion. There was something distressingly familiar about the saucy roll of her hips, the glossy dark curls piled atop her head, the challenging tilt of her chin.

"What in the bloody hell . . ." he breathed.

He blinked rapidly, hoping hunger and fatigue would account for the sight of Portia Cabot gliding right out of his fantasies and down the damp, cobbled streets of Charing Cross.

Despite the seediness of her surroundings, she might have been taking a stroll through Hyde Park on a sunny Sunday afternoon. Her cloak had slipped off of one creamy shoulder, making her look even more vulnerable. As Julian's keen eyesight focused on the burgundy ribbon tied around the pale expanse of her throat, he felt his mouth go bone dry with longing.

"Not a very wholesome path for a young woman to take," Cubby whispered. "Should we intervene?"

Julian wanted nothing more than to do just that. He wanted to leap right down there and shake some sense into her foolish little head, something his brother was apparently unable to do. But some primitive survival instinct made him hesitate. She had defied Adrian and risked both her life and her reputation to seek him out in the gambling hell. But what if he'd played the role of villain too well? What if her allegiance had shifted? He could think of no sweeter bait for his brother to use to lure him out of hiding.

Cuthbert pointed to the streetlamp on the corner. "Ah, there's no need for worry after all. She must be meeting someone."

Someone who had miraculously appeared out of thin air. Someone whose willowy grace made her appear to float even when she wasn't in motion. Someone who was even now sweeping back the hood of her cloak to reveal the alabaster skin of an angel and a fall of silvery blond hair.

Julian felt the scant nourishment he'd derived from the beefsteaks turn to ice water in his veins. "Dear God," he whispered, invoking a name he no longer had the right to use.

He scrambled to his feet.

"Where are you going?" Cuthbert demanded, his side-whiskers quivering with alarm. "You're not going to leave me here all alone, are you?"

Julian seized his friend by the shoulders and hauled him effortlessly to his feet. "I need your help, Cubby. I wouldn't have asked you to accompany me tonight if I could have done this alone. But I was afraid we were walking into some sort of trap. I need you to do what you do best—watch my back."

He dragged Cuthbert to the edge of the loft and pointed to a pair of sandbags dangling from a nearby beam. They hung right over the splintery wooden doors that stood guard over the main entrance of the warehouse. Earlier in the day, Julian had looped the ropes holding them aloft over a nearby peg. "If anyone besides me tries to come through those doors, I want you to loosen the ropes and drop those sandbags on them. Do you understand?"

Cuthbert nodded mutely, his throat too swollen by panic for speech.

"Good man." Julian clapped him on the shoulder, sparing him a brief but fierce smile.

Then he was gone, moving so swiftly that Cuthbert would have sworn his feet never once touched the rungs of the ladder they'd climbed to reach the loft. Before Cuthbert could puzzle over what he'd seen, a faint shriek, quickly muffled, came from the street. He started back toward the window but a man's shout and the thunder of running footsteps drew him up short.

Remembering the charge with which Julian had entrusted him, he stumbled over to the peg where the rope was looped. He cocked his head to the side, frowning. The footsteps were coming from the wrong direction. They weren't coming from the street but from the ground floor of the warehouse. An icy band tightened around his chest as he realized they had been sharing their hiding place with someone else all along. Someone who was even now racing toward the very door Julian had ordered him to guard.

He reached for the rope, but hesitated, torn by indecision. Hadn't Julian told him to drop the sandbags on *anyone* who tried to come through that door? He hadn't specified in which direction. The footsteps were drawing nearer. In just a few more seconds, they would be at the door.

Before he could lose his nerve, Cuthbert gave the rope a decisive tug, loosing it from the peg and sending the sandbags plummeting to the floor below.

There were two loud thumps, muffled groans, and then dead silence.

Wincing in belated empathy, Cuthbert peered over the edge of the loft. In the dim light, he could barely make out two shadowy figures sprawled on the dirt floor below. Although he doubted the impact could have killed them, he was confident that they weren't going to be troubling Julian—or anyone else—any time soon. He smiled and dusted off his hands, rather pleased that he had managed to fell two such giants without Julian's help.

Portia deserved to be eaten.

She'd allowed herself to become totally consumed with the notion that Julian was both a murderer and a monster and now she was about to be consumed by some bloodsucking witch she should have recognized as a vampire at twenty paces. As she hung helpless in the creature's deadly grasp like a rag doll caught in the jaws of a snarling mastiff, she found it odd that in these, the last moments of her life, she would be feeling not terror but acute embarrassment at her own ineptitude and bittersweet relief that she had misjudged Julian so thoroughly.

The toes of her slippers scrambled for purchase on the damp cobblestones. The woman wrapped a handful of her curls around one ruthless fist and gave them a harsh yank, jerking her head to the side.

As she hooked one of her scarlet-tipped fingernails beneath Portia's choker and prepared to rip it away so she could better reach the soft, vulnerable flesh of her throat, Portia squeezed her eyes shut. She could not help but wonder if Julian would miss her "bright eyes" when they were forever closed.

She waited for those lethal fangs to descend, for that bright, piercing agony to paint her world the color of blood. But nothing happened. She opened her eyes. The woman still had her scarlet claw hooked in the choker. Her fangs were still gleaming only inches from Portia's throat. But her hungry gaze had been transfixed by something else. Something over Portia's right shoulder.

Portia took advantage of her inattention to twist around in her arms. Although that powerful hand was still splayed over her jaw, the pressure on her throat had eased a fraction.

A man was walking down the street toward them. No, not a man at all, Portia quickly realized, her heart lurching with hope.

Julian came sauntering out of the mist as if he had an eternity to rescue her, his every motion fluid with masculine grace. With the lamplight lovingly caressing the sculpted bones of his face and the wind stirring his dark mane of hair, he looked like some sort of doomed angel cast out of heaven for committing a sin he could not resist. He had never looked as dangerous—or as beautiful—as he did in that moment. Portia sagged against her captor, biting back a sob of relief.

"Hello darling," he said as he drew abreast of them, his voice low and silky.

Portia opened up her mouth to reply, but before she could, the woman purred, "Hello, my love. You're just in time to join me for a little snack."

Seven

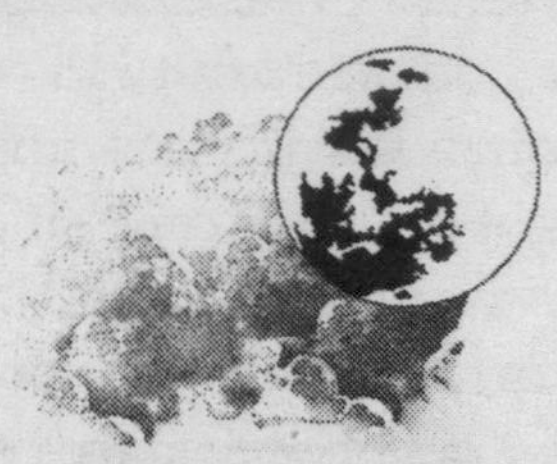

Although her mouth continued to hang open, Portia couldn't have choked out a word if her life had depended on it.

Julian raked a disparaging gaze over her. "*Little* indeed. A mouthful that small is hardly worth the bother. If I were you, I'd toss her back in the Thames."

"I was hoping we could keep her." Portia shuddered as the woman's tongue darted out to give her cheek an affectionate lick. "She's rather charming and I've always wanted a kitten."

Julian's laughter had a cruel edge she had

never before heard from his lips. "Why would you wish to keep her, Valentine? So you could drown her in a bucket when toying with her ceases to amuse you?"

Valentine.

It didn't seem fair to Portia that such a beautiful name would belong to such a cruel creature. But after all, it did rhyme with *mean.*

"Excuse me," she rasped, her throat still raw. "I hate to interrupt this touching little reunion but am I to assume—"

"Silence!" Julian hissed.

Portia hated herself for flinching, but the sparkling warmth she had always seen in his eyes whenever he looked at her had vanished, leaving them cold and flat. She pressed her lips tightly together to keep them from trembling, forced to satisfy herself with a defiant glare.

"I always knew you'd come back to me," Valentine said, the gloating note of triumph in her voice unmistakable.

"Come back to you?" Julian snorted. "You're the one who's been following me from one end of the world to the other."

"Only because I knew you'd come to your

senses someday and realize that we were destined to be together."

Portia's stomach was beginning to roil. It didn't help to know that she'd had countless fantasies about saying those exact same words to him, preferably while cradled in his arms and gazing deeply into his eyes.

"Then I suppose that day has finally come." Julian's contemptuous gaze skirted over her again. "So why don't you send the kitten scampering on its merry way so we can be alone?"

"Why waste such a succulent little morsel? I thought the two of us could share her to celebrate our new beginning."

Portia gritted her teeth against a wave of pain as Valentine trailed a blood red nail across the front of her throat, carving a shallow trench.

"No!" Julian barked. She felt a flare of hope but then he scowled, that beautiful mouth of his taking a sulky turn. "I'm not in the mood to share tonight. If I'm going to have her, then I want her all to myself. She can be your gift to me."

Valentine sounded genuinely surprised. "But you've always been so finicky about dining on humans, darling. Have you had a change of heart?"

"How can he change what he doesn't have?" Portia muttered, renewing her squirming efforts to escape the woman's vise-like grip.

Valentine shrugged. "Very well. If you want her, she's all yours. But only if you let me watch."

She gave Portia a harsh shove, sending her careening into Julian's arms much as Duvalier had done in the crypt all those years ago. But then Portia hadn't known he was a vampire. She had pressed her trembling body to his as if he was her salvation.

He wrapped his arms around her, dragging her flush against him. His body was burning with that peculiar fever she now recognized as hunger. Hunger for her.

She shuddered as her own body betrayed her with a perverse thrill at being back in his arms again. She began to fight in earnest, kicking with her feet and striking out with her fists until he was forced to twist both of her wrists behind her back to subdue her. Although she doubted his grip would leave so much as a bruise, there wasn't an ounce of mercy in it. She might as well have been a helpless fly twisting in the sticky strands of a spider's web.

"Struggle all you like, little one," he murmured, his seductive gentleness somehow crueler than all of Valentine's brutality. "It will only make your surrender all the sweeter when it comes."

Portia sagged against him, undone by her darkest fear. What if she succumbed to him? What if, in that moment when he pierced her flesh and made her his own once again, she felt not despair but exultation?

His lush dark lashes swept down to veil his eyes. He leaned over her, the lethal points of his fangs already visible. His warm mouth grazed her throat in the caress of a lover, not a monster, and Portia felt her resistance melting away, leaving only desire and shame. If she was going to die, then why shouldn't it be by his hand, in his arms?

His parted lips lingered against the pulse behind her ear, making his whisper little more than a vibration. "I may have to nibble you just a little, Bright Eyes, but when I shove you away from me I want you to run as if the devil himself were fast on your heels."

For a fevered moment, Portia almost thought she'd imagined his words. Especially when his strong fingers ruthlessly ripped away the choker and his fangs descended toward the tender flesh of her throat.

"Wait!" Valentine's shrill cry froze them both where they stood.

This time there was no mistaking the succinct oath Julian swore beneath his breath.

Slipping her wrists out of his suddenly lax grasp, Portia wiggled around in his arms until they were both facing Valentine. The woman was pointing at Portia's throat, her scarlet-tipped finger all aquiver.

"What is *that*?" she demanded.

Even though she knew it was too late, Portia clapped a hand to the scars on her throat. Valentine's accusing gaze glided to her face. "This isn't the first time you've tasted a vampire's kiss, is it?"

"Perhaps not," Julian growled. "But I can promise you it will be the last." To underscore his threat, he grabbed a handful of Portia's curls and gave them a rough yank.

"Ow!" she exclaimed, throwing him a glare over her shoulder.

Valentine began to prowl around them in a lazy half-circle, the hem of her cloak flowing behind her like the train of a queen's ermine-trimmed robes. Her gaze was still fixed on Portia's face. "Why didn't you tell me that you were no stranger to our ways?"

"Because you were too busy trying to rip out my throat," Portia retorted. She lowered her hand, brazenly exposing that throat and her scars.

The woman's hypnotic green eyes narrowed. "Ah, so the kitten has claws after all. You'd best watch your eyes, Julian."

But Julian was watching Valentine, his every muscle rigid with wariness.

Portia instinctively shrank against him as the woman reached out one hand and brushed her fingertips over the scars, her touch almost gentle. "Who left their mark on you? Who is your master, kitten?"

Having had just about enough of being bullied by vampires for one night, Portia boldly knocked the woman's hand away. "I don't have a master and my name isn't kitten. It's Portia. But that would be *Miss Cabot* to the likes of you."

Valentine's eyes widened. "Portia?" She spat the name from her mouth as if it were the foulest of poisons. *"You're* Portia?"

Julian groaned before muttering, "I knew I should have eaten you when I had the chance."

Portia ignored him, her attention now fixed on Valentine. "How do you know me?"

The female vampire threw her hands in the air with a dramatic flourish. "How could I not know you, what with Julian here constantly murmuring your name in his sleep?"

"Don't do this, Valentine!" Julian warned. "There's nothing to be gained from it."

The woman continued as if he hadn't spoken, her upper lip curled in a snarl. "*Darling* Portia. *Sweet* Portia. *Precious* Portia. And then there was that time when he was making love to me and he forgot my name but had no trouble remembering yours."

Portia gaped at her for a moment in stunned silence, then wheeled on Julian, torn between kissing him and kicking him. "You cried out *my* name? While you were making love to *her*?"

His face was so hard it might have been carved from a diamond. "She probably just misunderstood me. I barely spared you a thought while I was away. You were never anything more to me than a lovestruck child."

Valentine made a skeptical noise that sounded

distinctly like the French version of *"Ppphtl!"*

Although Portia knew she should be recoiling from the cruel lash of his words, she drew one step nearer to him, gazing up into his glittering eyes. "Is that why you stayed away so long? Because you couldn't bear the sight of me? The sound of my voice?" she asked softly. "My scent?"

He closed his eyes for an instant, his nostrils flaring involuntarily. "I stayed away because I was relieved to be free of your fawning adoration. I found it to be a burden and a dreadful bore."

"Good," Valentine said briskly from behind her. "Then you won't mind if I proceed with my plans to tear out her pretty little throat, will you?"

Before Portia could react to the woman's threat, Julian had swept her back into his arms. He held her against his broad chest, sheltering her behind the barricade of his well-muscled forearm. "I'd advise you to keep both your fangs and your claws sheathed, Valentine."

"Or you'll what?" the woman purred. "Stake me? Drench me in oil and set me on fire? Cut off my head and stuff it with garlic?"

"Don't tempt me," he snarled.

She pursed her lush red lips in a pretty pout. "You really shouldn't make idle threats, my darling boy, when we both know you'll do no such thing." She shifted her mocking gaze from Julian to Portia. "You may have his heart, kitten, but I'll always have his soul."

Eight

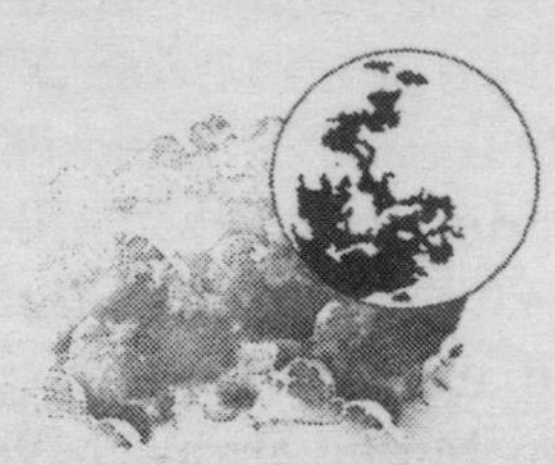

Julian had faced enemies of all sorts in his life—bloodthirsty vampires, ferocious soldiers, irate husbands—all willing to go to excessive lengths to put an end to his worthless existence. But he'd never known the depth of dread he felt as Portia calmly disengaged herself from his embrace and turned to face him. Even in heeled slippers she barely came up to his chin, but he still caught himself taking a step backward.

Her eyes were clear and bright, her expression amiable. Yet he knew that if she'd had a stake in her hand at that moment, there would have been nothing left of him but a film of dust on her slippers. "So you went in search of your soul and you found *her.*"

Although it was not a question, he slowly nodded.

"You left everyone who loved you waiting and worrying for over five years. While we were spending all of those sleepless nights praying for your safe return, you were cavorting in the bed of the vampire who possessed the one thing that could restore you to humanity."

"When I went looking for the vampire who sired Duvalier, the last thing I expected to find was a woman."

"Especially not such a beautiful one, I'll wager. If you'd have found some homely, bow-legged old crone with a hairy wart on her chin hoarding your soul, I'm sure you would have had no compunctions about ripping out her throat and retrieving it."

Gazing at him fondly, Valentine sighed. "My Julian has always been such a gentleman when it comes to the ladies. I've often feared it would be his downfall."

"For once, madam, you may just be right,"

Portia said softly, never once taking her eyes off of his face. "So why did you come here tonight, Julian? Did you come to rendezvous with your lover? Or to destroy her and claim your soul so that you could come home to us?" It was pure agony to watch her lift her chin and swallow the last bitter dregs of her pride. "To me?"

Although he owed her so much more, all he had to give her was the truth. "I wanted to make sure the murders were going to stop. So I came to tell her that I was leaving London. I knew she'd follow me, whether I wanted her to or not."

Julian felt a pang of unexpected grief as he watched all that had been spring turn to winter in Portia's eyes. Since he'd never deliberately sought her affection, he'd had no idea he would mourn it so keenly once it was gone. For the first time in a very long while, he felt like the monster he was.

"You suspected that she was the murderer all along, didn't you? Yet you let me believe it could have been you. Why would you do such a thing? To protect her?"

"To protect you. If you believed the worst of

me, I thought it might be easier for you to let me go."

A wealth of emotions played across Portia's expressive face before she finally nodded. "You were right. Because as far as I'm concerned, you and your soul-sucking mistress can both go straight to the devil."

Valentine clapped her hands like a child on Christmas morning. "She's giving us her blessing, darling! Isn't that quaint?"

Shaking her head in disgust, Portia turned and began to walk away from him, wobbling slightly on a loose heel.

Fighting an irrational flare of anger, Julian moved so swiftly that she could not quite hide her startled jump when he appeared directly in front of her. "I'm afraid I can't let you go."

"You already have," she said, unshed tears burning bright in her eyes. "So I would suggest you take your precious Valentine and flee London before Adrian puts a crossbow bolt through her shriveled little heart and some other bloodthirsty beauty inherits your miserable soul. I hope the two of you will live happily ever after. Oh wait—it's too late for that, isn't it?"

She neatly sidestepped him but before she could make her escape, he had blocked her path again. His desperation mounting, he reached for her arm. "Please, Bright Eyes, you have to listen to me."

Before he could react, she had hiked up the hem of her skirt, revealing a delicious froth of petticoat and silk stocking, whipped a pistol out of her garter, and pointed it straight at his heart. She cocked the hammer with a decisive flick of her thumb. "Don't *ever* call me that again!"

He rolled his eyes. "Oh, for heaven's sake, Portia, put that thing away! It's not as if you're going to shoot me."

"Oh, no?" Smiling sweetly, she pulled the trigger.

Julian staggered backward, the blast ringing in his ears. Gritting his teeth against a searing wave of pain, he gazed down at his chest in stunned disbelief. The wound was already healing, its ragged edges neatly folding in on themselves, but there would be no repairing the blackened hole in the expensive silk of his waistcoat.

Regaining his balance, he shifted his disbelieving gaze back to her. "You know, it's one thing to threaten to drive a stake through a man's heart, but ruining a perfectly fine waistcoat is just bloody rude!"

"You can send me your tailor bill." She blew on the mouth of the spent pistol before tucking it back into her garter, then pointed to Valentine, who had been watching their entire exchange with poorly concealed delight. "Or perhaps you can get the Duchess of Darkness over there to darn it with her teeth."

His chest and his temper still stinging, Julian growled at her, his fangs instinctively lengthening. This time she didn't yield an inch. Her blue eyes blazed up at him, all but daring him to do his worst.

"Step away from her, Julian!"

They both swung around as Adrian's commanding voice came ringing through the night. He was moving out of the mist toward them, his gaze locked on Julian and his powerful hands gripping a full-sized crossbow with a lethal bolt already slotted. Except for a few stray threads of silver woven through the honeyed gold of his hair, Adrian hadn't changed one whit since the last time he and Julian had come face-to-face. His hands were steady on the weapon, his blue-green eyes every bit as resolute as they'd been when the two of them had played at knights and soldiers as boys.

Alastair Larkin moved like a shadow behind him, sporting a shiny new lump on his brow and hauling a sheepish-looking Cuthbert by his starched collar.

"I tried to stop them, Jules," Cubby blurted out. "I dropped the sandbags on their noggins and knocked them out cold just like you said, but they came to before I could get them tied up. You always said I never could tie a decent knot in my cravat. I fear they may be madmen escaped from Bedlam. They keep blathering on and on with some nonsense about monsters and minions and vampires. When we heard the pistol shot, I feared the worst and—"

Larkin gave Cubby a sharp shake, startling him into silence.

Julian faced his brother without flinching, the night wind sifting its fingers through his hair. Ever since the day Duvalier had stolen his soul and turned him into a vampire, he'd known this moment would come. Perhaps Portia had been right all along. Perhaps he had returned to

London because he knew there was no longer any point in delaying the inevitable.

He fully expected her to bow out of the tragic scene, giving Adrian a clean shot. But to his keen surprise, she stepped in front of him, putting herself between his heart and that lethal bolt.

"He didn't murder those women, Adrian. It was *her*. She was the one who . . ." Portia turned to point an accusing finger, but her voice quickly trailed off.

The pool of light beneath the lamppost was empty. Valentine had vanished just as swiftly as she had appeared.

Portia blinked in astonishment but Julian wasn't the least bit surprised by her defection. Valentine would have never thrived for over two hundred years, even surviving a near fatal brush with the guillotine after the French revolution, without possessing a healthy instinct for self-preservation.

"But she was standing right there only a second ago," Portia said helplessly, turning back to Adrian. "Didn't you see her?" She shot Larkin a pleading glance. "*You* must have seen her, didn't you?"

The look Adrian gave her was both tender and pitying. "I know you have strong feelings for my brother, Portia, but you simply can't protect him any longer."

"You're absolutely right. I have very strong feelings for him." She ticked them off on her fingers. "There's loathing. Contempt. Revulsion."

"The lady doth protest too much, methinks," Julian murmured beneath his breath.

"Despite my *feelings*," she said crisply, tossing him a murderous glance of her own over her shoulder, "I won't see him executed for crimes he didn't commit."

Adrian shook his head. "You forget that I know you've always had a penchant for play-acting. How can I be sure this isn't just another ploy to help him make his escape?"

"Oh, she's sincere this time," Julian assured him. "She even shot me."

Adrian and Larkin exchanged an incredulous glance before saying in unison, *"She shot you?"*

"She shot you?" Cuthbert echoed weakly, blinking like a befuddled owl.

"Right through the heart," he said proudly. "If I was alive, I'd be dead right now instead of undead."

"I'm sure I'm not the first woman to shoot you," Portia said out of the corner of her mouth. "They're probably queuing up for the privilege down in Covent Garden even as we speak. As you can see," she told Adrian, "you no longer need to worry that sentimentality is clouding my good judgment."

Adrian took another step toward them, his eyes narrowing. "So despite all of the evidence to the contrary, you're asking me to believe that Julian is innocent?"

A bitter laugh escaped her lips. "Hardly! What I'm asking you to believe is that he's not the vampire who killed those women."

"Vampire?" Cuthbert repeated, his round face going so pale he might have easily been mistaken for one of the undead himself. His glazed eyes slowly rolled back in his head. He crumpled into a swoon, his dead weight sending Larkin staggering to his knees.

"I gather that you never found the time to tell your devoted friend that you were a bloodsucking fiend," Portia said.

"He never asked," Julian replied, sparing Cuthbert a worried glance. "He just thought I was a late sleeper."

"If Julian didn't kill those women," Adrian asked, "then just who did?"

"His lover," Portia replied, frost dripping from her every syllable.

"She's no longer my lover," Julian said, biting off the words with equal ferocity. "If she was, I wouldn't have purchased a commission in His Majesty's army and gone all the way to Burma just to escape her."

Turning her back on both Adrian and his deadly crossbow, Portia faced him, planting her hands on her shapely hips. "I suppose she simply found your charms so irresistible that she decided to pursue you to the ends of the earth."

"Is that so inconceivable?" He reached out to cup her cheek in his hand, softening his voice so that it would be audible only to her ears. "There was a time when you would have done the same."

He might have carelessly killed her love for him, but she couldn't completely hide the ghost of yearning in her eyes as he ran his thumb down the velvety softness of her cheek.

In that moment Julian made a startling discovery. He didn't want to end up as nothing more than dust on her slippers. In some sentimental corner of his heart he supposed he'd always believed that even if he perished without retrieving his soul and abandoned all hope of heaven, he would still live forever, if only in her heart. If he let Adrian destroy him now, she probably wouldn't even spit on his grave.

"I'm sorry," he whispered.

"For what?" Fresh tears sparkled in her eyes. "Breaking a young girl's foolish heart?"

"For this." Without giving himself time to ponder the consequences, he slid his hand from her cheek to her nape and jerked her into his arms. Wrapping his other arm around her slender waist, he dragged her around so that they were both facing Adrian. Using her vulnerable body as a shield was the only way he knew he could protect them both.

Adrian lunged toward them.

Forced to wield his only weapon, Julian dipped his head toward Portia's throat, baring his fangs.

Biting off an oath, Adrian froze in his tracks while Larkin glared daggers at him. Portia's warm body was trembling against his, but Julian suspected she was vibrating with rage, not fear.

"You should have listened to her," he said grimly. "There's a predator out there who's far more dangerous than I am. Her name is Valentine Cardew. She was the vampire who turned Duvalier that night in the hellfire club. When you destroyed him, she inherited all of the souls he'd stolen *and* all of his power. And now that she knows who Portia is, she won't rest until she sees her dead."

"Then give her to me," Adrian begged, his anguished gaze flickering over Portia's face. "Let me protect her."

Julian's temper finally erupted. "You've done a capital job so far, haven't you? Allowing her to travel unchaperoned through the city streets at night visiting gambling hells and men's lodgings! Using her as monster bait and sending her to parade up and down dark alleys like a common light-skirt! If you'd have protected her as you should have, she'd have been married to some nice young earl by now and forgotten my bloody name!"

"I should be so fortunate!" Portia bucked wildly against him, but only succeeded in wedging her lush bottom against his hips, a position that was undoubtedly far more painful for him than for her. "In case you've forgotten, Adrian is my brother-in-law, not my father. I'm perfectly capable of looking after myself!"

"Oh, yes, that's quite evident," he replied dryly, wincing as one of her flailing heels connected soundly with his shin.

"What do you want from me?" Adrian demanded of Julian.

"It's not about what I want. It's about what you need. And if you're going to have any hope at all of protecting Portia from Valentine, then you're going to need me."

"We've managed just fine without you for all these years," Portia choked out, cutting off her own breath by surging against the arm he had locked beneath the beguiling softness of her breasts. "I'm sure we'll find a way to carry on."

Adrian took another step toward them. "Why Portia, Julian? Why would this Valentine of yours have a particular vendetta against Portia?"

Portia went still in his arms, all of the fight draining out of her as she held her breath, awaiting his reply.

He gentled his grip to something dangerously near to an embrace. "Because Valentine is not only slightly insane, but insanely jealous. And somewhere along the way, she may have received the mistaken impression that I . . . that Portia and I . . . that we once were . . ." He faltered, his usual glib eloquence deserting him.

"Oh, for pity's sake," Portia wailed, "shoot him or shoot me but please put one of us out of our misery!"

His gaze traveling between her face and Julian's, Adrian slowly lowered the crossbow. Portia immediately jerked herself free of his grip and stumbled to Adrian's side. He wrapped an arm around her, drawing her into the shelter of his body.

Cuthbert let out a loud groan and began to stir, giving Julian no choice but to hasten over and help Larkin wrest him to his feet.

"Come now, Cubby," Julian said gently, dusting off Cuthbert's rumpled frock coat, "you've gone and knocked your poor cravat all askew."

The fog in his eyes clearing, Cuthbert slapped Julian's hands away and began to back away from him, trembling with genuine horror. "Get away from me, you devil!"

"I was going to tell you, Cubby. Truly I was. I was just waiting for the right time."

"And when would that have been? After you'd ripped out my throat in my sleep?"

Julian took an involuntary step toward him, his hands clenching into helpless fists at his sides. "I never would have hurt you. You're my friend."

"I can't be friends with a fiend! I should have listened to my father. He was right about you all along. You really *are* the spawn of Satan!"

With those damning words, Cuthbert wheeled around and took off down the street at a near lope, the fastest Julian had ever seen him move.

He shifted his beseeching gaze to Portia but she simply shook her head in disgust and turned away from him, stumbling when the heel of her slipper gave out altogether. Muttering beneath her breath, she hopped up and down just long enough to divest herself of both slippers, hurled them into an alley, then marched away from them all in her stocking feet.

"Where do you think you're going?" Julian called after her.

"Home," she said shortly. "Where I plan to accept the first proposal from the first man who can prove he still has possession of his soul. I hear the marquess of Wallingford just might be in the market for a new fiancée."

Julian gazed after her, swearing softly beneath his breath.

Adrian joined him, the crossbow now pointed at the ground instead of his heart. "I'm glad to see you haven't lost your touch with the ladies, little brother."

Fingering the fresh hole in the silk of his waistcoat, Julian shot him a dark look. "You won't be surprised to learn that I'm even more popular with my tailor."

A knock sounded on Portia's bedchamber door, polite but persistent.

Her only response was to huddle deeper into the window seat, drawing the down-filled counterpane she'd wrapped around her shoulders up to her chin. Outside the window the first pearly blush of dawn was just beginning to blur the edges of the night.

She heard a soft creak as the door swung open, then closed again.

Without turning around, she said, "Have I ever told you that there are times when I wish

•

you were a vampire so you couldn't come into my room without being invited?"

"Haven't you heard?" Caroline asked, crossing the room and easing herself down on the opposite end of the window seat. "Older sisters are far more powerful than vampires. Not even garlic or a crucifix will keep us away when we're determined to meddle in your affairs."

She drew a monogrammed handkerchief out of the bodice of her gown and offered it to Portia. It was the same handkerchief Adrian had given Caroline at their very first meeting. Portia accepted the offering and honked loudly into it. At the moment she had no patience for such sentimental tripe.

She dabbed at her tender nose. "Now that I've succeeded in bringing home the prodigal son, shouldn't you be out killing the fatted calf? Or did he volunteer to do that himself?"

"I don't believe he's had the opportunity. Adrian's been locked in the study with him for most of the night."

"So that's what all the shouting was about. I doubt there's any plaster left on the ceiling down there."

Caroline reached out and patted her knee through the counterpane. "Adrian told me what happened in Charing Cross."

"Oh, he did, did he? Did he also tell you that while I was mooning over his brother and making an utter cake of myself, Julian was rolling around in the bed of a female vamp who makes Lucretia Borgia look like the Virgin Mary? A vamp who just happens to have his missing soul tucked away in her reticule?"

Caroline nodded. "I believe he might have made mention of that. Larkin is coming back tonight after sunset so they can discuss what's to be done about her."

"Good," Portia said briskly. "The sooner she's gone, the sooner Julian can return to the life he's chosen."

Caroline sighed, plainly reluctant to continue. "I'm not trying to make excuses for him, pet, but when he left home to search for his soul, you were little more than a—"

"Don't!" Portia warned, stabbing a finger at her. "If you say 'child,' I'm going to throw a tantrum so loud Wilbury will have to lock me in the broom closet with the twins."

"Can you truly blame him for going away? What did he have to offer you but danger and heartache?"

"What are you trying to say?" Portia fought to blink back a rush of fresh tears. "That it was noble of him to sacrifice his body on the altar of dissolution and debauchery? That he did it all for me?"

"He knew he couldn't change what he was. Not even for you."

"Ah, but there's the rub, isn't it, Caro? Once he found *her,* he could have changed what he was. For me. But he didn't." She shook her head, dashing a tear from her cheek. "I've wasted all these years believing I was the only one who could save him when he never really wanted to be saved at all."

Caroline gently stroked a damp strand of hair from her cheek. "Perhaps he didn't believe he was worth saving."

Afraid she would crumble anew beneath the weight of her sister's sympathy, Portia drew the counterpane even more tightly around her shoulders and went back to gazing out the window. "Perhaps he was right."

As Caroline rose and slipped silently out of the room, Portia watched the shadows of the night steal away, taking the last of her girlhood dreams with them.

Nine

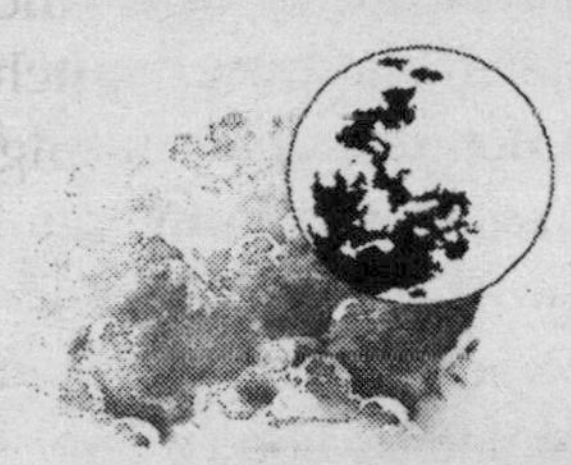

Portia lingered in her bedchamber until well after noon that day. She might have hidden out there indefinitely, but she didn't want her family to think she was sulking, or worse yet, nursing a broken heart. The sun had finally crept out as well and with it not due to set for several hours, she knew she wouldn't have to worry about running into Julian on some deserted landing. After over five years of waiting for him to come home, it was still difficult to believe that they were now residing beneath the same roof.

She glided gracefully down the long curving

staircase, one hand drifting lightly over the banister. It was pure happenstance that she'd chosen to don one of her most flattering gowns—a day dress woven from Spitalfields silk the exact rich blue shade of her eyes. Sashes had been creeping lower for nearly a decade and the deep V of her stomacher bodice only served to accentuate her slender waist and the generous swell of her not-so-slender bosoms. A delicate chemisette peeked out of her rounded neckline in a teasing hint of lace. She had eschewed her usual choker in favor of a scarf fashioned from white Japanese gauze, wrapping it around her throat twice so that its gossamer ends floated behind her like angel wings.

She touched a hand to her hair. It wasn't as if she'd instructed her maid to take excessive care with her coiffure. It had required less than thirty hairpins to coil the heavy mass on top of her head, leaving a shimmering cascade of curls to frame her face.

She passed the gilt-framed looking glass in the entrance hall, then stopped and backed up, unable to resist tweaking a bouquet of fresh roses into her cheeks. Why shouldn't she strive to look her best? After all, a young lady never knew when an eligible suitor might come calling.

She was tilting her chin this way and that to admire her reflection when a cadaverous figure garbed in black livery materialized just over her left shoulder.

"Wilbury!" she exclaimed, clapping a hand to her fluttering heart. "You simply must stop creeping up on me that way. If you didn't have a reflection, I'd have sworn you were a vampire!"

Although the butler's puckered face wore its customary scowl, there was an unmistakable twinkle of glee in his rheumy eyes. "Have you heard that Master Julian has come home?"

Portia turned around to glare at him directly. She knew that he knew that she knew very well that Julian was back in residence. Age hadn't dulled the crusty old snoop's eyesight, his hearing, or his wits. He probably also knew exactly what time she'd finally stopped weeping into her pillow last night and drifted into a dreamless sleep.

"I had heard a rumor to that effect," she said primly. "Am I to assume he's napping in the wine cellar?"

Without uttering a single word, Wilbury lifted his arm and pointed one long, bony finger at the library door. All he needed was a scythe and a hooded cloak and he could have passed for Death himself.

Swallowing a knot of dread, Portia gazed at the tall oak door as if it was the portal to her own crypt. She hadn't expected to be presented with such a temptation so early in the day. But perhaps it was just as well. After all, what better way to prove to both her family and herself that she was finally free of Julian's seductive spell?

She smiled at Wilbury as if she hadn't a care in the world. "Perhaps I should just peek in on him and make sure he's resting comfortably."

"That would be ever so considerate of you, miss." The butler bared his yellowed teeth at her in a death rictus of a smile.

Portia took two hesitant steps toward the door, then turned back, determined to inform Wilbury that she'd thought better of the notion and perhaps Master Julian should be left undisturbed for at least the next century or two.

The butler was gone. He'd somehow managed to slip away without as much as a creak of his ancient bones. Puffing out a sigh, Portia turned back to the door.

Swallowing her misgivings, she slipped into the library, easing the heavy door shut behind her. She could see why the room might be enticing to a vampire in dire need of a good day's rest. Rich dark mahogany paneled two of the walls while the remaining two were lined with floor-to-ceiling bookshelves. The room sported only a single narrow window and its opaque velvet drapes had not only been drawn, but painstakingly pinned shut—Wilbury's doing, no doubt. It would hardly do for little Eloisa to wander in and accidentally drag them open to the sunshine, leaving nothing of her uncle but a charred spot on the crimson and gold Turkish carpet.

As her eyes adjusted to the dim light, Portia could just make out a man's lean form sprawled on one of the burgundy fainting couches that flanked the cold hearth. She crept closer, her heart lurching into an all too familiar rhythm.

Julian had stripped down to shirtsleeves, trousers, and stockings. His lawn shirt hung open at the throat, revealing a teasing sprinkle of crisp dark hair. His head lolled against the couch's scrolled arm and his long, muscular legs were stretched out in front of him. His silky dark lashes rested flush against his cheeks. Despite the unnatural stillness of his chest, he appeared to be in the deepest of slumbers.

Portia felt her heart soften against her will. He was no longer a threat to anyone. His supernatural strength and predator's instincts might make him nearly invincible by night, yet it was those same instincts that betrayed him with the rising of the sun, leaving him as vulnerable as a child.

She wondered if he still dreamed. If he strolled through sunlit meadows or if the shadows of night cloaked his sleeping hours as well as his waking ones.

Before she could stop herself, she had reached to brush back the stubborn forelock that always fell over his brow. He stirred and she snatched back her hand, appalled at how easily she had surrendered her newfound indifference. She resolutely turned her back on him, determined to leave him to his dreams, whatever they might be.

She was halfway to the door when she heard something behind her.

She slowly turned. Julian's eyes were still closed, his striking face in sweet repose. But Valentine's contemptuous voice seemed to echo through the cozy silence: *How could I not know who you are, what with Julian here constantly murmuring your name in his sleep?*

Portia hesitated, knowing she would be the worst sort of fool to linger. Julian stirred again, his lips moving soundlessly. Her resistance crumbling beneath the weight of her curiosity, she tiptoed back to the couch.

A faint smile now curved his lips. "Oh, darling," he murmured. "Your lips are sweeter than wine. Give me another sip, won't you?"

Portia gasped. She should have known his dreams wouldn't contain anything as tame as a romantic stroll through a sunlit meadow. She stole a guilty look at the door. She knew she ought to back away and slip silently from the room, but instead she found herself leaning closer to the couch so she wouldn't risk missing a word.

A husky chuckle escaped his lips, sending a

delicious shiver down her spine. "You wicked little minx, you know it always tickles when you kiss me there."

She swept her speculative gaze down the length of his lean, well-muscled frame, wondering just where *there* might be.

"Oh, that's it, angel . . . just a little lower . . . lower . . . Ahhhhhhhh . . ." His sigh melted into a deep-throated groan.

Portia's mouth went dry. She fanned her flushed cheeks, wondering how it could be so warm in the room when the hearth was stone cold. Even worse, the heat seemed to be spreading like molten honey to her breasts and her belly.

Julian's voice had faded back to a murmur. Forgetting all about her lovely gown, Portia dropped to her knees and leaned over him, straining to make out his words.

His lips were nearly touching her ear when he whispered, "My angel . . . my sweet . . . my darling . . ."

She held her breath, bracing herself for the moment when he would blurt out Valentine's name.

". . . my shamelessly inquisitive Portia."

She jerked back her head to find Julian gazing up at her, his dark eyes sparkling with both triumph and mischief.

"Why, you miserable devil! You were awake the entire time, weren't you?" Scrambling to her feet, she snatched up one of the couch's tasseled bolsters and began to pummel him with it.

He lifted his arms to ward off her blows, laughing aloud. "I do hope you're not armed. Adrian loaned me this shirt and I'd hate to return it with a nasty hole over the heart."

"You ought to be shot for making sport of me in such an unchivalrous manner!"

"And I suppose it's chivalrous for a lady to eavesdrop on a gentleman, especially in his sleep?"

As he swung his long legs over the edge of the couch and sat up, Portia realized what a fool she'd been to believe him defenseless. His faint pallor only deepened the striking hollows beneath his cheekbones and sharpened the obsidian glitter of his eyes. With his hair rumpled and a pair of roguish dimples slashing his cheeks, he looked like temptation itself, a nearly irresistible invitation to sin.

Backing away from him, she clutched the

bolster to her breast like a shield. "You weren't sleeping and I wasn't eavesdropping. I was simply . . ." she paused, frantically scrambling for an alibi ". . . searching for a book I thought I'd left on the couch."

"Were you under the impression that I'd swallowed it?"

She gave him a reproachful glance. "I should have known you were mocking me. No woman with so much as an ounce of moral character would allow herself to be seduced by such hackneyed piffle. Lips sweeter than wine indeed!"

He clapped a hand to his heart, wincing in mock pain. "You wound me, Portia. It's one thing to shoot a man, quite another to cast aspersions upon his lovemaking skills." To her alarm, he rose and began to pad toward her. "Are you insinuating that you wouldn't be moved at all if I told you that your skin was as smooth and sweet as fresh cream?" He lowered his sultry gaze to her mouth. "That I couldn't tempt you to let me steal a kiss by whispering that your lips were like plump, ripe cherries just begging to be . . . plucked?"

Ignoring the treacherous tingling of those

lips, she forced herself to stand her ground, even when he halted less than a foot away from her. "No, but I might develop a sudden and uncontrollable craving for fresh fruit."

He cupped her cheek in his hand, gently tracing the ripe curve of her lower lip with the pad of his thumb. The teasing sparkle had vanished from his eyes, leaving them curiously somber. "What about forbidden fruit? Would you find that equally enticing?"

"Not if it were being offered to me by an unscrupulous snake." Pulling away from his caress to hide its unsettling effect on her, she said, "If all you have to offer a woman is such overwrought drivel, then perhaps it's just as well that you have your supernatural skills to fall back on."

Despite the dim light, she would have almost sworn she saw a flash of genuine hurt in his eyes. "Is that what you believe? That the only way I can hope to lure a woman into my bed these days is to work some sort of unholy enchantment upon her?"

She shrugged, so flustered by his touch that she was no longer entirely sure what she believed. "And why not? You confessed on that rooftop that Duvalier had encouraged you to embrace your dark gifts. If a vampire can truly work his will on the mortal mind as legend has long suggested, then what's to stop you from using that gift on poor unsuspecting women?"

She was caught off guard when he abruptly turned on his heel and paced back to the hearth. His retreat was the last thing she had expected and she could not quite squelch a treacherous flare of disappointment.

He stood with his back to her for a long moment before slowly pivoting to face her. "Come here, Portia."

"Pardon?"

He crooked his finger at her, the motion both lazy and deliberate. "Come here. To me."

She frowned, taking a step toward him without realizing it. "What do you think you're doing?"

He arched one devilish brow. "Embracing my dark gifts. Come to me, Portia. *Now.*"

Startled to realize his words were not an invitation but a command, Portia gazed into his eyes. A hypnotic flame seemed to be burning in their smoky depths, mesmerizing her like a moth helplessly drawn to the one thing that was destined to destroy it.

The bolster slipped from her fingers to the floor. She felt an irresistible tug as if he'd somehow bound her to him with an invisible but unbreakable cord. Then she was gliding toward him, putting one foot in front of the other until she stood directly in front of him.

"Touch me," he commanded, his smoldering eyes devoid of both conscience and mercy.

A tremor wracked her, but she couldn't tell if it was born from fear . . . or anticipation. "Please, Julian," she whispered. "Don't do this."

He leaned down to her ear, returning her whisper with one of his own. "Put your hands on me."

Almost as if they had a will of their own, her hands drifted to his chest. She touched him, spreading her fingers to stroke the firm, muscled planes of his chest through the thin lawn of his shirt. He made no move to touch her in return but stood as rigid as a marble statue beneath the loving caress of its sculptor. Her right hand wandered shyly to the open throat of his shirt, bringing them skin to skin, flesh to flesh.

She gently sifted her fingers through the crisp curls of his chest hair before twining her hand around the broad column of his throat. To her sensitive fingertips, his skin felt like heated satin stretched taut over bronze.

She gazed deep into his eyes, a helpless captive to his will. In that moment she would have offered him whatever he asked of her, including her throat. But she knew before he spoke that it wasn't her throat he wanted.

"Kiss me." His words were little more than the echo of a whisper in her mind, but she could no more resist them than the tide could resist the inexorable tug of the moon.

Drawing his head down to hers, she touched her lips ever so gently to the corner of his mouth. Forbidden fruit had never tasted so tempting . . . or so sweet. Perhaps if she closed her eyes, she thought, she could somehow break the wicked spell he had cast over her.

But the darkness only made it easier to surrender to him, to press feather-soft kisses along the firm, full curve of his lower lip, to breathe out his name on a sigh before deepening the delicious friction of her lips against his.

Still he made no move to return the caress,

forcing her to bear all the burden of pleasuring him. His purported indifference only made her more determined to coax a response from him. Remembering how he had claimed her mouth with such boldness on that snowy rooftop, she parted her lips and stole a taste of him with her tongue.

As Portia offered him the tender sweetness of her open mouth, Julian groaned his own surrender. He wrapped his arms around her, nearly dragging her off her feet in his desperation to mold her enticing curves to the hard, hungry planes of his body.

He didn't know what had possessed him to make the first move in a game he had no hope of winning, but he could not stop the dizzying rush of triumph that burned through his veins as she melted into his arms.

He had thought to enchant her but he was the one bewitched by the silken breath of her sighs, the warm velvet of her skin, the honeyed delights of her mouth. She cast her spell without need of a single word, beguiling him with the promise of pleasures no man could resist. He wanted her more than any woman he'd ever tasted, more than blood, more than life itself.

He'd spent over five long years trying to break the bond forged between them in that crypt only to discover it had been forged with unbreakable chains. No longer able to bear up under their weight, he sank back on the fainting couch, dragging her down on top of him. Still devouring her mouth, he raked a hand through her hair, scattering the pins until the dark strands came tumbling down around them in a silken cloud.

As their tongues tangled in a song older than words, his hands wandered over the slender contours of her back. He desperately wanted to unlace the built-in corset of her bodice, to free the plump softness of her breasts so he could touch and taste them as well. His deft fingers possessed the skill to do so, but some ghost of conscience stayed his hand. He consoled himself by allowing his hands to dance lower, to skate lightly over the small of her back before claiming the generous swell of her rump for his own.

Undone by his possessive grasp and the slippery silk of her dress, her thighs slid apart, leaving her straddling him. As she writhed against the throbbing ridge of his arousal, driven by raw instinct, Julian feared he was in danger of bursting into flame without the threat of torch or pyre. But if such a fire could destroy him, he would willingly cast himself into its flames and welcome his doom.

He lifted his hips, deepening that exquisite friction until he felt the vibration of Portia's own moan deep in his throat. He knew in that moment that he was one decadent kiss away from rolling her beneath him and ravishing her right there on the fainting couch in his brother's library.

Oddly enough, it was the dark and primal power of that image that gentled both his kiss and his embrace. He slid his hands to her back and dragged his lips from her mouth to her temple, nuzzling the downy skin he found there. She collapsed on top of him, resting her cheek against his chest.

He held her close, reluctant to surrender the warmth of her skin, the shuddering whisper of her breath against his throat, the blessed beat of her heart—all gifts he had surrendered when he lost his soul.

Toying tenderly with the silky strands of hair at her nape, he whispered, "Portia?"

"Hmmmmm?" she murmured.

"I have a confession to make."

She lifted her head to gaze at him, her eyes still shining with desire and her lips glistening with the dew of their kiss.

Swallowing back a sharp pang of regret, he smoothed a stray curl from her cheek and said quietly, "I don't possess any powers of mind control."

Ten

Portia blinked down at him, the mist in her eyes slowly evaporating. "What ever do you mean?"

He gently stroked her hair. "I didn't bewitch you, darling. Vampires can't mold mortals to their will. It's nothing but a silly myth."

She shoved herself to a sitting position, taking all of that precious warmth and life with her. "Don't be ridiculous. Of course you bewitched me! If you hadn't, I never would have behaved in such a shameless and wanton manner."

He shook his head. "I'm afraid it was nothing more than the power of suggestion."

She stared at him for several seconds, then rose stiffly to her feet, shaking the wrinkles from her skirt. With her hair tumbled, her lips swollen from his kisses, and the color high in her throat and cheeks, she looked as if he *had* ravished her. Instead of shaming him as it should have, her disheveled appearance only made him want to tug her back into his lap and finish what he'd started.

If you hadn't confessed your duplicity, you fool, she could have been yours. Recognizing that smooth, oily voice, Julian wondered if he would ever truly be free of Duvalier.

He watched through wary eyes as Portia wound her tumbled hair into a tight coil and secured it with the remaining hairpins, stabbing them into place with enough force to make him wince. "I can't believe you would play such a cruel trick on me."

He rose to his feet. "I wasn't trying to be cruel, Portia. Too clever for my own good perhaps, but not cruel."

Avoiding his eyes, she tucked a wisp of lace that had wiggled its way out of her bodice back into place. "I'm sure there's a perfectly sound explanation. It must have been some primitive form of hypnotism you learned in your travels. I've often heard of rogues and charlatans employing such practices for their own selfish gain."

He captured her wrist and tugged her around to face him, refusing to allow her to dismiss him—and those wild, tender moments of passion they'd shared—so easily. "Perhaps there is a perfectly sound explanation. Perhaps I simply offered you the freedom to do what you've never stopped wanting to do."

She gazed up at him, the hurt in her eyes warring with longing. He could see that she still wanted to touch him. Still craved the taste of his kiss, the feel of his hands against her skin.

"If this is nothing but a cruel trick," he said softly, touching a hand to the downy softness of her cheek, "then I fear it has been played upon the both of us."

Her eyes fluttered shut as if to deny the truth of his words even as her lips parted to confess them. He was lowering his mouth to hers to accept that confession when a knock sounded on the door.

Portia sprang away from him, blushing as if they'd been caught rolling around on the couch in *flagrante delicto* instead of just stealing a kiss.

"Come in," she called out, smoothing her skirts and giving her hair one last shaky pat.

Wilbury slunk into the library, his thin lips pursed in a sullen pout. "You have a caller, Miss Cabot. Will you be receiving this afternoon?"

She frowned. "Who is it?"

"The marquess of Wallingford," the butler drawled with the same enthusiasm he might have given to announcing Genghis Khan and his invading hordes. "He claims he wanted to make sure you hadn't suffered any distressing repercussions after your unfortunate 'adventure' the other night."

"How very kind of him," she murmured, stealing a thoughtful look at Julian's scowl. "Why don't you show him into the drawing room and ring for Gracie to bring us some tea? Perhaps Caroline will be kind enough to pour for us."

"Why don't you show him in here and I'll pour?" Julian suggested, parting his lips just enough to reveal a teasing threat of fang.

"On second thought, Wilbury, why don't you show our guest into the music room? The windows all face west and we wouldn't want to squander a moment of this lovely winter sunshine." Portia offered Julian a dimpled smile. "I should hope the sunlight would show me off to my best advantage."

He glowered at her. "Oh, I don't know. I rather like the way you look in the dark." *And the way you feel,* his smoldering glance plainly added.

As Wilbury took his leave, Portia hastened toward the door, turning back to face Julian only when she was well out of his reach. "It has occurred to me that if we're both going to be residing beneath your brother's roof while we decide what's to be done about your mistress—"

"*Former* mistress," he bit off, folding his arms over his chest.

"—then perhaps it would be best if you tried to think of me as your sister."

Julian shuddered. "I'd much rather think of you as the comely upstairs maid who stole my . . . *heart* when I was thirteen."

"Well, at least that explains what happened to it," she replied briskly. "Now if you'll be kind enough to excuse me, sir, I'll leave you to your dreams."

She ducked quickly out the door, knowing full well that the only thing that could follow her into the sunshine-dappled entrance hall was his frustrated growl.

"Would you care for another kiss, my lord?" Portia extended the elegant Sevres tea tray, a vapid smile frozen on her lips.

The marquess of Wallingford choked on his tea, his rather prominent Adam's apple bobbing in his throat. "Pardon me?"

As Caroline gave her ankle a sharp kick, Portia felt heat flood her cheeks. "A crumpet, my lord. Can I tempt you to try another crumpet?"

"Oh . . . well, in that case . . ." Still looking doubtful, he plucked a crumpet from the tray.

Resting the tray back on its wheeled cart, Portia glanced at the window. The sun's ruthless rays were streaming through the broad bay, illuminating every flaw in the beautifully appointed music room, including the marquess's receding hairline and the sneer of derision that haunted his lips even when he smiled.

"I'm relieved to see that you haven't suffered any ill effects after your little escapade the other night, Miss Cabot. I shudder to think of the fate that might have befallen you while you were searching for that—" the marquess stopped and attempted to clear the snarl from his voice. "Forgive me—I had a bit of crumpet caught in my throat—while you were searching for the viscount's brother."

Caroline shot Portia a knowing look. "Our Portia has always had a tender heart. You can't fault her for trying to bring our black sheep back to the fold."

"I have nothing but admiration for your Christian charity, my dear." Wallingford graced Portia with a thin-lipped smile. "But some lost souls are beyond redemption and best left to the devil's dubious mercies."

After her encounter with Julian in the library, Portia should have been in hearty agreement with him. Which didn't explain why her hands were suddenly trembling with anger.

Before she could slosh her tea into her lap, she lifted the cup to her lips and took a delicate sip. "Then I can only assume you haven't heard the wonderful news?"

His smile wavered. "What news?"

"Julian has come home," she said, affecting an ingenuous smile of her own. "After all these years, he's finally returned to the loving bosom of his family!"

Looking as if he had the tea tray itself lodged in his throat, Wallingford rose halfway to his feet, his gaze flicking ever so briefly to *her* bosom. "Kane is here? In this house? At this very moment?"

"You needn't whistle for the nearest constable, my lord." Portia returned her cup to its saucer. "We're all well aware that you bought up all of his gambling vowels."

"And I'm sure my husband will be more than happy to settle any debts his brother incurred while he was away," Caroline added, helping herself to another tea cake.

The marquess sank back down on the sofa, looking none too pleased by the notion. "Far be it for me to sully this lovely occasion with crass talk of commerce. I just can't help but question the wisdom of allowing a . . . a man with Kane's reputation to reside beneath the same roof as an unmarried and impressionable young woman."

Portia arched one eyebrow. "And I can't help but wonder if your fiancée would have embraced such a cynical viewpoint?"

Even in the poor light, she could see Wallingford's face darken. "Since Miss Englewood and I are currently estranged, her opinions are no longer any concern of mine. It's just been my experience that the best use for the black sheep of most families is to make mutton."

Portia abruptly rose to her feet. "I'm afraid I must leave you to my sister's care, my lord. I'm feeling a bit flushed and fear I might be taking a fever of some sort."

"Nothing contagious, I hope?" he ventured, jerking a scented handkerchief from the pocket of his waistcoat and holding it over his nose.

Keenly aware of Caroline's suspicious gaze, Portia offered him a cool smile. "It's nothing you need trouble yourself about, my lord. I appear to be the only one susceptible to this particular ailment."

Bobbing him a graceful curtsy, she hastened from the music room, hoping she could find a cure for the malady she suffered before it proved fatal to her heart.

The winter night fell hard and early, taking the temperature with it and leaving sparkling kisses of frost on the windowpanes of Portia's bedchamber. Although she knew the darkness would free Julian to prowl the house, she had no intention of remaining a prisoner in her own room. As soon as Adrian sent word that Larkin had arrived, she would join them all to discuss Valentine's future. Or lack thereof, she thought grimly.

Her restlessness growing, she tossed aside the book of Byron's poems she'd been trying to read and wandered to the window. After only one encounter, Julian had her craving the shadows, craving the night, craving his touch. It was hardly the first time his kiss—or his touch—had ignited this strange yearning, this nagging restlessness. She glanced at the ormolu clock on the mantel. The delicate brass hour hand was already creeping toward the seven.

She went to the door, peering toward the stairs. It was then that she detected the faint bass rumble of men's voices drifting up from the first floor of the town house.

Her suspicions growing, she hurried down the stairs, pausing to steal a look from the window on the second story landing. Larkin's curricle was already parked in the alley behind the town house, its matched pair of bays snorting out puffs of steam in the frosty air.

Her determined strides carried her past a pair of startled footmen and directly to the door of Adrian's study. She threw it open without bothering to knock.

Adrian was perched on the corner of his desk while Larkin and Julian sprawled in the leather chairs flanking it. Each of the men had a cigar in one hand and a tumbler of port in the other. At least Adrian and Larkin had enough sense to look gratifyingly guilty.

Portia closed the door behind her with a decisive thump, batting at the haze of smoke that hung over the lamplit room. Although Larkin and Adrian immediately put out their cigars in deference to her presence, Julian simply took a long, lazy drag on his slender cheroot, then blew out a ribbon of smoke that curled around him like a lover's hand. His fashionable pallor had given way to a healthy glow, which made her suspect Wilbury had made a late run to the butcher shop.

"Forgive me for being late," she said frigidly. "My invitation must have been lost in the post."

Adrian winced. "Please don't take offense, Portia. We simply saw no point in causing you any more distress."

"How very thoughtful of you to consider

my delicate sensibilities. Perhaps I should retire to my bedchamber to press some flowers or stitch a sampler with some inspiring homily on it."

"I'm not trying to dismiss you. Given what you endured last night, I just thought it would be best if you allowed us to handle—"

"Let her stay." Resting the side of his boot on his opposite knee, Julian stubbed out the cheroot on the boot's sole before flicking it toward the fire on the hearth. "She's earned the right."

As Larkin scrambled out of his chair and ushered her into it, Portia gave Julian a grudging nod of thanks. Larkin settled his lanky form against the windowsill, his shrewd gaze traveling between the two of them.

Adrian rested his tumbler on the desk and rubbed his jaw, looking as if he wished he were anywhere else in the world. "Julian here was just explaining to us how he came to make this . . . um . . . woman's acquaintance."

"She's not a woman," Portia said firmly. "She's a monster."

Julian hiked one eyebrow in her direction, giving her no choice but to tar him with the same brush. She lowered her gaze to her lap, but refused to blush.

Still eyeing her, he took a generous sip of his port. "As I was saying before we were interrupted, when I first went to Paris to seek the vampire who had sired Duvalier, I'm afraid I wasn't particularly subtle in my inquiries. The overlord of their nest was a rather nasty-tempered fellow who hated Brits even more than he hated mortals. When he discovered that I was seeking to destroy one of my own kind so that I could retrieve my mortality, he didn't take it very well. He had me bound to a stake, doused in oil, and was about to take a torch to me when Valentine stepped in to plead for my life."

Portia sniffed. "How very charitable of her."

"I rather thought so at the time since my hair was starting to smolder," Julian said dryly. "Because she intervened on my behalf, they ended up exiling her from the nest and we both had to flee Paris."

"At least you had each other." Portia leaned toward him in wide-eyed interest. "So did you find out she had your soul before or after the two of you became lovers?"

"Portia!" Adrian dropped his head into his hands with a groan while Larkin downed his port in a single gulp and turned to give the window a yearning look.

But Julian met her gaze squarely. "After, I'm afraid. When it would have seemed the height of hypocrisy to repay her for saving me by destroying her."

"I forgot that you're a man who always pays your debts," she said softly. "Although Wallingford might disagree."

"Enough about the past," Adrian said, earning a relieved look from Larkin. "We're here tonight to make certain that Portia has a future. If this Valentine is such a ferocious adversary, then why did she run away last night?"

Julian snorted. "She hasn't survived this long by being a fool. She's well aware of your reputation as a vampire hunter."

"Then perhaps she's already left London," Larkin offered.

"She won't leave him," Portia said dully but with utter conviction.

"And she won't leave Portia now that she knows where to find her . . . at least not alive," Julian added grimly. "Even if I could find her and somehow convince her to come away with me, she'd only leave behind one of her minions to finish Portia off. We have to capture her *before* she can give those orders."

"What if I send Portia away?" Adrian suggested. "I could send her and Caroline and Eloisa to the castle until we settle this matter."

Portia stiffened. "I won't give her the satisfaction of running from her! It's humiliating enough that I let her get the best of me last night."

"She'd only follow anyway," Julian pointed out.

Larkin stroked his narrow chin. "If we know she's going to come for Portia, then why can't we just sit back and wait for her to make her move?"

Julian shook his head. "Because she's clever enough to bide her time. For an impulsive creature, she can be extraordinarily patient. She'll wait until we relax our guard. And then it will be too late."

"Besides," Portia said, "we have to draw her out of hiding before she murders any more innocent women."

She rose to pace in front of the hearth, keenly aware of Julian's heavy-lidded gaze following her every step. "She seems to be operating under the delusion that Julian still harbors some sort of sentimental attachment to me, which we all know to be blatantly untrue."

Although Julian's jaw tightened, he wisely kept his thoughts to himself and took another sip of the port.

"If we could only find some way to use her jealousy as a weapon against her . . ." Portia tapped one finger against her bottom lip. "I keep thinking about something Duvalier said right before he locked me and Julian in that crypt together."

Adrian exchanged a worried glance with Larkin. "You almost died in that crypt, pet. There's no need for you to relive such painful memories."

"Your brother almost died, too," she reminded him before turning to Julian. "Do you remember what Duvalier said right before he shoved me into your arms? He said that if you took my soul, you could 'enjoy my company for all eternity.' "

"How could I forget? He was suggesting that I make you my eternal bride." Julian swirled the port around in the bottom of the tumbler, his expression bitter. "For such a bloodthirsty bastard, he was quite the romantic."

"What if we made Valentine believe that you've done just that?" Portia touched a hand to the white scarf encircling her throat. "She already knows that you've left your mark on me. So why not make her think that you returned to London to finish what you started all those years ago? Is there anything that would infuriate her more? Why, it would be as if we'd dashed holy water in her face!" Although she made a valiant effort, Portia couldn't completely hide her delight at the prospect.

"I thought we were trying to save your life, not goad her into killing you more quickly," Larkin pointed out. "Won't infuriating her just make her *more* dangerous?"

"Perhaps. But it will also make her more rash and apt to make mistakes. If she truly believes Julian has chosen me over her, she won't be willing to bide her time any longer. Her patience will have come to an end."

"As will your life if you make a single misstep," Adrian reminded her, his scowl deepening.

Julian eyed her with equal skepticism. "Do

you truly believe you could masquerade as a vampire with enough conviction to fool Valentine?"

Portia shrugged. "Why not? Your kind walks among us mortals with the setting of every sun. You eat our food. You drink our wine. You dance to our music. You mimic our breathing." She met his challenging gaze with one of her own, her voice deepening on a husky note. "Why, you even make love to us."

This time Adrian groped for the bottle of port instead of his glass. He took a long swig before handing it to a grateful Larkin.

"But mortals are more easily deceived," Julian replied softly, refusing to free her from the hypnotic tug of his gaze. "They're quite adept at seeing only what they want to see."

For a heartbeat of time, Portia was back in the library again. Back in his arms. "Perhaps that's because we're taught to believe in mermaids and leprechauns and noble princes on white horses before we grow up and have to put such foolish fancies behind us."

"Valentine is no fool. You won't just have to convince her that I've turned you into a vampire.

You'll have to make her believe that you're in love with me."

"That shouldn't be too difficult." Portia's voice sounded a shade too bright and brittle, even to her own ears. "You've said yourself that I'm an accomplished actress."

Adrian sighed, visibly running out of arguments. "Do you think this scheme stands a chance of working, Jules? You know this . . . *woman* better than anyone."

"In every sense of the word," Portia could not resist adding.

Julian slanted her a look that would have quailed any stranger he happened to encounter in a dark alley. "There's a chance it might work."

Larkin cleared his throat. "And just how is Valentine to learn that this momentous event has taken place? Should we take out an ad in the *Undead Gazette*?"

Julian glanced toward the fire, the set of his jaw one Portia was coming to know only too well. "I just might know a way."

They all gazed at him expectantly.

"Adrian may have driven all of the vampires

out of London, but he hasn't driven them out of England. There's a flourishing nest of them living in a country house in Colney, less than an hour's ride from the city."

"I've heard rumors about the existence of such a place," Adrian admitted. "I suppose I should have paid them a visit before now but ever since Eloisa was born . . ." He shrugged, plainly reluctant to admit that the birth of his daughter had encouraged him to guard his own life with more care.

"I took shelter there briefly after Cuthbert moved back into his father's house," Julian said. "Their overlord won the manor in a wager from some poor drunken sot who'd already gambled away the rest of his family's fortune. Vampires are worse gossips than mortals, you know. If we make an appearance there, I can promise you that Valentine will hear all about it before dawn of the next day."

"Oh, goody!" Portia exclaimed dryly. "I do so love a country house party! When do we leave?"

"Don't start planning your ensemble yet," Adrian warned her. "If you think I'm going to allow you to march into that nest of monsters all alone—"

"She won't be alone." Julian rose from his chair to join Portia, the note of authority in his voice quelling even Adrian. "I'll be right there by her side."

Adrian eyed him disbelievingly. "Weren't you the one who kept me up until dawn blistering my ears because I let her coax me into using her for bait?"

"She won't be the bait this time. I will. Once Valentine finds out that I've 'betrayed' her, she'll be too hellbent on my destruction to worry about anyone else." He took Portia's hand, drawing her even closer to him. "And I can promise you that I'd drive a stake through my own heart before I'd let anyone, living or undead, harm a single hair on Portia's head."

Before Portia could react to that impressive vow or the disarmingly natural feel of having his fingers laced through hers, Adrian said, "If you expect me to give this unholy little alliance my blessing, you're going to have to tell me exactly what you intend to do with our quarry once our trap springs shut."

Portia held her breath, trying to pretend her entire future didn't hinge on Julian's answer.

He was silent for a long moment before finally

saying, "I'll take her away from here. So far away she'll never again be able to hurt anyone I—" He stopped, his grip on Portia's hand tightening until it was almost painful. "Anyone at all."

Feeling as brittle as one of the Dresden shepherdesses she had coveted as a child, Portia dragged her hand from his. "If you'll excuse me, gentlemen, I should probably go inform my sister that I'll be attending a country house party tomorrow night hosted by a nest of bloodthirsty vampires."

After the study door had closed behind her, Adrian shook his head, his handsome features clouded by both bewilderment and anger. "What in the bloody hell are you doing, Jules? I don't understand your reluctance to destroy this creature."

Julian turned on him, his dark eyes blazing. "Well, maybe I've never understood your reluctance to destroy me!" Pivoting on his heel, he started for the door.

"Where do you think you're going?" Adrian demanded, moving to block his path.

"Out," Julian replied shortly, refusing to yield so much as an inch to his older brother.

Once Adrian might have cowed him with little more than a disapproving look, but now they stood toe to toe, equal in both stature and determination.

"Do you really think that's wise?"

"I don't know. That depends on whether I'm here as your guest . . . or your prisoner?"

When Julian's resolute expression did not waver, Adrian reluctantly stepped aside, freeing him to stride from the study and the house.

Eleven

Julian walked the bustling London streets as if he owned both the city and the night, sending everyone who dared to look upon his face scurrying out of his path. Some of them instinctively recognized a monster when they saw one while others had simply learned that it was wiser not to provoke a man who had been born to both privilege and power, but who still stalked the night with the dangerous grace of a predator.

When a pasty-faced clerk unwittingly bumped his shoulder as he ducked out of his Threadneedle Street office, it was all Julian could do to bite back a growl. He knew he ought to be relieved when the crowds slowly began to thin, but the thought of them all rushing home to their cozy fires and the welcoming arms of their loved ones only sharpened the edge of his temper. He didn't even have Cuthbert's stolid company to give him cheer. The note he'd had a footman deliver to his friend's house earlier in the day had been returned to him with its wax seal unbroken.

Although he walked the streets unfettered, he felt as if he was still dragging the chains from the crypt behind him. Duvalier's taunts had never stopped haunting him.

You disappoint me, Jules. I had expected so much more from you. You're not willing to be a vampire, but you're not a man, either.

Duvalier had been wrong. He was both man and vampire and cursed with the hungers of both. Hungers that gnawed at the aching hole where his soul had once resided every time he looked at Portia, caressed the milky softness of her skin, tasted the forbidden sweetness of her lips.

Duvalier would have been gratified to know that after all these years he still hungered for both her flesh and her blood.

Someone jostled him from behind and he whirled around, his lips parting in an involuntary snarl.

A woman was standing there, her pretty, freckled face wreathed in a halo of auburn curls. "Sorry, guv'nor. Me mum always said I was clumsy enough to trip over me own feet."

Although her cloak was threadbare, she'd taken some care with her appearance. Bright spots of rouge stained her cheeks and she'd tucked a wilted pansy behind one ear.

"No harm done, miss," he assured her stiffly. "I'm sure the fault was mine."

Before he could dismiss her, she boldly wrapped one gloved hand around his forearm. " 'Tis a bitter cold night, sir. I thought perhaps ye might be lookin' for somethin' softer than a heated brick to warm yer bed."

She was his for the taking. Julian could see that in the inquisitive tilt of her head, the appreciative gleam in her eye. She believed him to be a gentleman, not a beast.

There was nothing to stop him from accepting her offer and escorting her to some nearby inn with worn but clean sheets. He could court her with the same pretty words Portia had mocked, then feast on her in whatever manner he chose. By the time his practiced caresses had banished the memory of the fumbling hands and sweating, heaving men who had come before him, he doubted she would cost him a single coin.

But he couldn't shake the notion that she might cost him something much dearer.

Ignoring a savage stab of regret, he dug a coin out of his coat pocket and pressed it into her hand. "Why don't you take this and warm yourself by your own fire tonight?"

Tipping his hat to her, he started across the street, where a butcher was just stepping out to lock the door of his shop for the night.

Portia was back in the crypt.

The dank smell of crumbling earth and ancient decay filled her nostrils. She would have been paralyzed with terror if Julian hadn't been there. If he hadn't wrapped his strong arms around her to still her trembling. He had already torn away the gag and ropes Duvalier had used to silence and restrain her, chafing the feeling back into her numb wrists with his own unsteady hands.

"Why did Duvalier say those terrible things?" A

sob caught in her throat as she wrapped her arms around his waist and pressed her cheek to his chest. "Why did he say you were going to kill me?"

Julian shoved her out of his arms and staggered toward the corner, ducking his head and lifting a hand to shield his face from the torchlight. "Duvalier was right," he growled. "You need to stay the bloody hell away from me!"

Despite his warning, she took an instinctive step toward him. "But why? Why should I listen to anything that miserable monster has to say?"

"He may be a monster, Portia. But so am I." Julian slowly lifted his head and lowered his hand, baring his face to the torchlight and her anguished gaze.

She clapped a hand to her mouth, but it was too late to smother her horrified gasp. His skin was stretched taut over the striking bones of his face, his eyes hollow but glowing with a primitive hunger. It was as if everything he was had been pared down to its very essence, leaving something that was both beautiful and terrible to behold. As she watched, mesmerized by his feral grace, his eyeteeth sharpened and lengthened, curving into a pair of gleaming fangs designed by the devil for only one deadly purpose.

"Adrian was never a vampire, was he?" she asked softly, already knowing the answer.

Julian slowly shook his head.

"It's always been you."

He nodded.

She was distracted from the unlikely sight of his fangs by an even more impossible one. The rags of his shirt hung open halfway to his waist, revealing the familiar shape burned into the flesh of his chest.

With a broken cry, Portia ran to him. She traced the outline of the crucifix seared into his flesh as if she could somehow absorb his pain through her fingertips, then lifted her tear-filled eyes to his face. "Dear God, what did he do to you?"

Julian swallowed, his tongue sweeping over his parched lips in a vain attempt to moisten them. His voice had deepened to a raspy croak. "He drained me of my strength with the crucifix. Starved me. Refused to let me drink."

He struggled to pull away from her, but he lost his balance and stumbled to his knees, his body wracked by uncontrollable shivers.

Portia dropped to her knees beside him. "You're dying," she whispered, no longer able to deny the staggering evidence before her.

He nodded. "I don't have much . . . time left. You'll be safe once it's done. Duvalier will make sure we're discovered." A bitter smile curved his lips.

"The bastard never could resist . . . showing off his handiwork. Do you see those manacles over there?" he asked, pointing to the rusty chains dangling from hooks embedded deeply in the stone wall. "I need you to use them to chain me to the wall."

She recoiled, unable to hide her distaste. "Like some sort of animal?"

"I am an animal, Portia. The sooner you accept it, the safer you'll be."

She shook her head, her voice steady despite the tears trickling down her cheeks. "I won't do it. I won't leave you chained up to starve like some sort of rabid dog."

He closed his hands over her upper arms, his fingers biting into her tender flesh with bruising force. "Damn it, girl, you have to listen to me! I don't know how much longer I can trust myself not to . . . hurt you."

"You can drink from me," she urged. "Just enough to keep you alive until someone comes for us."

He made a strangled sound deep in his throat and she understood for the first time that this was about more than just bloodlust. "Don't you understand? If I allow myself to take that first taste of you, I won't be able to stop. Not until it's too late for the both of us." He shifted one hand to her face, his unsteady fingers stroking a sooty curl from her cheek with devastating tenderness. "Please, Bright Eyes, I'm begging you . . ."

Portia closed her eyes to block out his pleading gaze, knowing what she had to do. When she opened them, she was able to offer him a smile through her tears. "Why, Julian, you know I'd do anything for you. Anything at all."

Ignoring the threat of those deadly fangs, she cupped his face in her hands and pressed the softness of her lips to his . . .

Portia opened her eyes to gaze up at the canopy of her bed, both her body and her heart consumed by a wistful ache. As strange as it seemed, she wanted to summon back the dream. To return to that crypt and the ghost of her former self. That girl had been so sure of herself, willing to sacrifice everything—even her life—for the beautiful boy she had loved with such innocence and passion.

The dream had only served to remind her that Julian had once been willing to do the same. That he would have ended his existence as a soulless husk with no hope of salvation rather than risk hurting her. She rolled to her side, hugging her pillow to her breast in a vain attempt to dull the ache in her heart, and wondered what had changed. Just what hold did this Valentine have over him?

She squeezed her eyes shut, knowing it would be far wiser to wish for a dreamless sleep. But before her wish could be granted, the notes of a distant melody came drifting to her ears. Still hugging the pillow, she sat up, blinking in bewilderment. Had her dream somehow conjured up another ghost from her past?

Drawing her silk dressing gown over her night rail, she climbed down from the bed and padded to the door. She eased it open, half expecting to discover the music existed only in her overwrought imagination. But it grew a whisper louder—a bittersweet lullaby being played for the dreaming occupants of the mansion.

Knotting the sash of her dressing gown, she hurried down the stairs. Instead of discouraging her, the shadows that draped the deserted corridors of the house seemed to welcome her, drawing her deeper into their embrace with each step. The next thing she knew she was easing open the door of the music room, her thirsty senses drinking in the notes pouring out of the grand pianoforte beneath the window.

Julian sat at the instrument, his fingers dancing over the keys with a lover's grace, coaxing forth a response that was both tender and passionate. The sunlight might be his mortal enemy, but the moonlight streaming through the broad bay window clearly adored him. Her silvery rays kissed the glossy silk of his hair and caressed his strong masculine profile, limning it in silver.

It took Portia a puzzled moment to identify the piece he was playing as the first movement of Mozart's "Requiem," the only section the composer had completed before his tragic death at the age of thirty-five. She had heard the piece played on the towering pipe organs of more than one cathedral but never on the piano and never with such haunting depth of feeling. As rendered by Julian's ardent hands, it wasn't difficult to believe the requiem had been commissioned, as both gossip and legend claimed, by a mysterious stranger who had turned out to be a harbinger of Mozart's own death. Julian played it as both triumphal march and lamentation—the song of a man celebrating and mourning his own mortality before his voice was forever silenced.

He poured all of his hunger and passion into the piece, bringing it to a close with a dramatic flourish. The final note hung in the air like the tolling of a cathedral bell on a crisp, cold midnight.

When even its echo had faded, Portia said softly, "For a man who claims his soul belongs to the devil, you still play like an angel."

He didn't look the least bit startled to find her standing in the doorway. "It's one of my favorite pieces. Do you remember the words they found written in the margins of the score—*Fac eas, Domine, de morte transire ad vitam*?" he recited, the Latin rolling effortlessly off of his tongue.

Portia wasn't nearly as fluent in the language. She'd always been too busy reading about leprechauns and fairies to bother with such dry subjects. "Let, oh Lord, souls," she murmured, "enter through death . . . into eternal life."

"It's a pity I couldn't have warned the poor bloke that eternal life isn't everything it's reputed to be. So have you come to turn the pages of my music, Bright Eyes?" he asked, his crooked smile reminding her of the many happy hours she'd spent doing just that at Trevelyan Castle before she'd discovered he was a vampire.

"I would have sworn you were playing from memory."

"So I was." He nodded toward the sheet music opened on the stand. "But I'm not nearly as familiar with this next piece. I could use an extra hand . . . or two." He slid over on the mahogany bench to make room for her. When she hesitated, he added, "As my eternal bride-to-be, there's really no need for you to cling to your maidenly modesty."

Unable to resist the challenging sparkle in his eye, Portia marched across the room and slid onto the bench next to him. She reached across him to open the first page of the piece, refusing to shy away from the press of his muscular thigh against hers or the fleeting brush of his elbow against the softness of her breast.

As she watched his deft hands stroke the achingly tender Beethoven melody from the keys, it was only too easy to imagine them dancing over her own flesh with equal skill. She could not help but wonder what breathless song he might coax from her lips with those long, aristocratic fingers. Feeling a flush creep into her cheeks, she stole a look at his face only to find him watching her instead of the music.

Plagued by a niggling suspicion, she reached over and flipped the sheet of music a full measure before he reached the end of the page. He kept playing without missing a single note.

She cleared her throat with enough force to be heard over the rippling passage.

Julian's fingers froze on the keys, bringing the piece to a discordant halt. "Oh, dear. I've been found out, haven't I?" His nose brushed her unbound curls as he leaned over and whispered, "If you must know, I've always played from memory—even at the castle. I just never could resist the way you leaned across me to turn the pages or the scent of your hair."

This time she leaned away from him. "Why, Julian Kane, you really are an incorrigible rogue!" She struggled to keep her lips pressed together in stern disapproval, but could not stop them from tilting up at the corners.

He tweaked the tip of her nose. "Only when it comes to you, Portia Cabot."

She wanted to believe him so badly that she didn't even protest when his gaze drifted from her nose to her mouth. When he gently tipped up her chin with one finger to expose the softness of her lips. When he lowered his head, his own lips parting as they brushed over hers with the fluid grace of a butterfly's wing.

"Unca Jules! Unca Jules!"

They sprang apart and swiveled around as one to find Eloisa standing in the doorway. With her bare feet and treacle-and-jam stained nightdress, she looked like a grubby little angel. Although Portia knew she should be grateful for the timely interruption, she wanted to kick herself for leaving the door ajar.

Before either of them could react, Eloisa flew across the room, scrambling right over Portia's knees to bound into Julian's lap.

At first he appeared at a complete loss to find a strange toddler bouncing up and down on his lap, but then a delighted grin slowly spread across his face. "Why, you must be Eloisa! I'd know those eyes anywhere." He glanced at Portia, plainly baffled. "But how on earth does she know who I am?"

Portia attempted a cavalier shrug, realizing it might be too late to avoid a confession of her own. "I can't possibly hazard a guess. Although

I suppose there's a chance that I might have shown her your miniature one or two . . . thousand times."

To her keen relief, Eloisa jerked on his shirtfront at precisely that moment, demanding his attention. She was scowling up into his face with unnerving concentration, her nose wrinkled.

"Does she bite?" he asked, eyeing her nervously.

"Only buttons, cushion tassels, pearls, and the occasional kitten. But the kittens tend to bite back so that discourages her."

Eloisa reached up to stroke his cheek with her chubby little fingers. "Pretty," she crooned, a smile dimpling her plump cheeks.

Portia burst out laughing. "You needn't look so horrified. It only proves that no female can resist your charms."

"Except for you," he retorted, slanting her a wry glance over his niece's honey gold curls.

"Eloisa!"

This time it was a white-faced Caroline standing in the doorway with Eloisa's nurse hovering behind her, wringing her apron. When Caroline saw her daughter in Julian's lap, she went a shade paler.

She strode across the room, the unfastened sash of her dressing gown sailing behind her, and whisked Eloisa out of his arms. "You're a very naughty girl, Ellie," she scolded, burying her face in her daughter's curls. "You gave both Nurse and Mummy a terrible fright."

"Unca Jules!" Eloisa crowed, wriggling her arms free of her mother's stranglehold so she could reach for Julian. "Pretty!"

"It's all right, sweeting." He gave her a reassuring smile. "You'd best let Nurse tuck you back into bed before your little toes freeze clean off."

While Julian watched, his expression guarded, Caroline reluctantly surrendered Eloisa to the waiting nurse.

As the woman carried away the sniffling child, Portia said, "The music probably woke her. It was my fault, not Julian's. I shouldn't have left the door ajar."

"And I should have found a quieter pastime to amuse myself. It's just that the hours between dusk and dawn can be very long and lonely." Julian slid off the piano bench and rose to face her sister, a mocking smile playing around his mouth. "There's really no need for you to fret,

Caro. A wee morsel like that would hardly be enough to whet my appetite."

After giving them both a stiff bow, he strode from the room.

Caroline stood there in the moonlight, her face stricken. "I'm sorry, Portia. When I saw her empty bed, I thought . . ."

"I know what you thought. And so did he."

Without another word, Portia slipped past her sister and out of the room, already dreading the long, lonely hours she would spend in her own empty bed.

Twelve

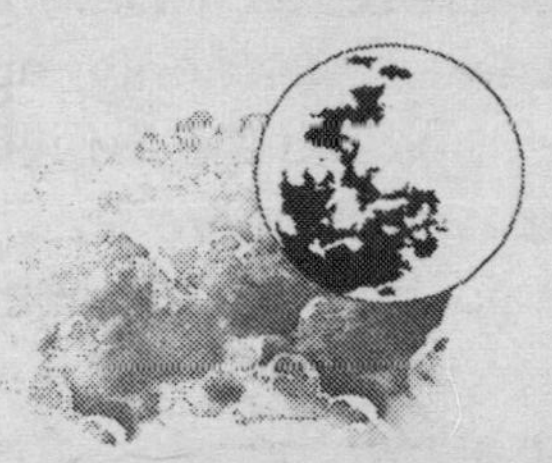

Portia stood in the entrance hall of the mansion the following night, gazing at her reflection in the looking glass with the same horrified fascination one might give to a particularly beautiful garden spider.

She was almost glad that Adrian had taken Caroline and Eloisa and retreated to Larkin and Vivienne's town house to spare his wife from having to watch her little sister depart on such a dangerous mission. She wasn't sure she wanted any of her family to witness her startling transformation.

She'd smothered the natural roses in her

cheeks beneath a layer of ivory face powder. The flawless mask only made the rouged scarlet of her lips and the dark graceful arch of her brows that much more striking. She'd instructed her maid to sleek her hair up and away from her face with a pair of mother-of-pearl combs, then to allow the glossy ringlets to tumble freely down her back. The unfamiliar style revealed a hint of a widow's peak and sculpted cheekbones that were normally hidden by a soft fringe of curls, making her look both older and more worldly.

The startling whiteness of her face and powdered bosom only made the glossy black satin of her gown seem more decadent. Its artfully ruched bodice was cut deep and off the shoulder, imbuing her neck with a swanlike grace accentuated by her black velvet choker.

Her eyes were glittering with a fevered excitement, making her look like a stranger even to herself. Oddly enough, she had never looked—or felt—more alive.

"Death becomes you, my dear."

At that smoky masculine murmur, Portia whirled around to find Julian standing just behind her, the gleam of appreciation in his eye unmistakable. She could not resist sneaking a look back at the mirror only to be rewarded by the unsettling vision of herself standing all alone.

She returned her attention to Julian, trying not to notice how dashing *he* looked with the crisp white of his ruffled shirt peeking out from the elegant lines of his black silk waistcoat and cutaway tailcoat. A pair of ivory trousers hugged his lean hips, tapering down over black leather Wellingtons polished to a dazzling sheen.

She tweaked his flawlessly tied cravat in what she hoped was a sisterly manner. "I don't suppose you've been giving Wilbury pointers on how to creep up on people and frighten them half out of their wits?"

"Don't be ridiculous. The shameless old sneak taught me everything I know."

"I heard that!" The quavery voice drifted to their ears from a nearby room.

Shaking her head, Portia turned back to the mirror. "I rather think this look suits me. Perhaps I have a natural affinity for evil."

"Something I've long suspected," he said, an unmistakable ripple of amusement in his voice.

She twined a curl around her finger. "You're

just jealous because you can't admire your own reflection. With a face that pretty, I'm sure you used to spend hours in front of the mirror before you became a vampire."

"Once I met you, I never needed a mirror. Every time I looked in your eyes, I saw everything about myself that I needed to know."

Portia's startled gaze shot to where his reflection should have been. By the time she had gathered enough of her scattered wits to turn around, he was already reaching into the pocket of his coat and withdrawing a glass scent bottle.

"I'm guessing that's not holy water," she ventured as he withdrew the delicate stopper. The musky floral scent of wild orchids assailed her nose, the fragrance so rich and sensual it made her feel slightly drunk just to inhale it.

"This should help to mask your scent." He tilted the bottle to wet the tip of his forefinger. "If there's anything a vampire can smell, it's fresh human."

"What do I smell like to you?" she asked, genuinely curious.

He dabbed some of the cologne in the delicate hollow of her throat, his lashes sweeping down to veil his eyes. "You smell like blackberry scones fresh from the oven, so sweet and crumbly you can't wait to sink your teeth into them." His touch still brisk and impersonal, he dabbed another drop behind each of her ears. "You smell like sunlight warming the petals of a rose at the very peak of its bloom." He used one finger to boldly anoint the cleft between her breasts, his nostrils flaring as if not even the overpowering scent of the cologne could completely mask her scent. "You smell like a woman . . ." he lifted his gaze to hers ". . . who needs a man."

What Portia needed at that moment was a way to draw breath into her suddenly starved lungs. But before she could find it, he had moved away to accept her mink-lined mantle from a waiting footman. She supposed it was fortunate that the servants in Adrian's household were well compensated for both their service and their discretion.

Julian swept the sleeveless cape around her shoulders, his deft hands fastening the frog beneath her chin as if she were no older than Eloisa. "If we're going to be convincing tonight, you'll have to gaze adoringly at me." His mocking gaze flicked to her face. "As I recall, you used to be quite adept at it."

"I suppose I can pretend you're a particularly succulent syllabub." She sighed wistfully. "I do so love a nice creamy custard."

"Does that mean you might try to take a nip out of me before the night is done?"

She bared her pearly white teeth at him.

He studied them with a critical eye. "I know it doesn't come naturally but do try to keep your mouth shut tonight."

She bared her teeth again, adding a hiss.

"Now *that* was more convincing." He offered her his arm. "Shall we go, my lady? The first thing a vampire must learn is to never squander a moment of the night."

Portia tucked her hands deeper into her muff and stole a furtive look at Julian. His good humor had vanished. He seemed to be growing more distant with each revolution of the carriage's wheels. Although their knees brushed every time the vehicle jolted through a fresh rut, he could just as easily have been half a world away instead of sharing the plush squabs of the carriage seat with her. He gazed out the window at the frost-draped fields sparkling in the moonlight, his forbidding profile reminding her that the night was his domain and she was entering it at her own peril.

By the time the carriage rolled to a halt, the tension between them had grown so thick Portia was almost grateful when one of the grooms appeared to swing open the carriage door.

"Leave us," Julian commanded, jerking the door shut in the man's startled face.

He turned to her, the carriage lamp casting an ominous shadow over his features. "I'm afraid I haven't been completely honest with you."

"Surely you jest!" she exclaimed, clapping a hand to her breast in mock horror. Beneath her palm, she could feel her heart double its rhythm.

He ignored her sarcasm. "There's something you should know before we go in. Despite their love of inflicting chaos on mortals, vampires delight in adhering to a very rigid hierarchy when among their own kind." He captured her hand in his, the broad pad of his thumb caressing her sensitive palm as if to soften the impact of his words. "If we're to make them believe that you surrendered your soul to me willingly, I won't just be your lover tonight. I'll be your master."

His primal words sent an unexpected shiver down her spine. She was besieged by a provocative vision of herself on her knees at his feet, breathlessly eager to surrender her will and obey his every command because she knew instinctively that pleasing him would only result in unspeakable delights for herself.

Appalled by her rioting imagination, she said, "Does this mean I should address you as 'His Majesty' or as the 'Great Most Munificent Ruler of My Universe?' "

His lips twitched against their will. " 'My lord' should suffice. But I'm afraid the vampires will require more visible evidence of your . . . submission." Freeing her hand, he reached into his coat and withdrew a broad gold circlet attached to a length of dangling chain.

She frowned. "I do believe that's a bit large for my finger."

"That's because it was designed to fit your throat."

She blinked at him in disbelief. "You expect me to wear a collar? Like one of the king's pugs?"

"Try not to think of it as a collar. Think of it as a—a—"

She arched one eyebrow. "—ball and chain?"

His patience plainly waning, he snapped, "If so, it's hardly any different from the one that binds most mortal couples."

"It's gratifying to know you have such a sentimental view of matrimony."

He raked a hand through his hair in frustration. "Why don't you think of it as sort of a vampire chastity belt? As long as you're wearing it and I have the only key, no other vampire can nibble on your neck."

"I'm sure that will be a tremendous comfort to me." She folded her arms over her chest. "Weren't you the one who so glibly informed me that there were other places that a vampire might drink from? What about that juicy little artery on a woman's thigh, just below—"

Julian stilled her lips with two of his fingers, his narrowed gaze encouraging her to proceed only at her own risk. She glared at him for a moment, then reached up and tugged off her velvet choker. Flouncing around on the seat, she lifted her hair to expose her neck.

Julian's stillness was so absolute she briefly entertained the notion that he had slipped out of the carriage while her back was turned. She glanced over her shoulder to find him eyeing the naked curve of her throat, his face hard but his eyes softened by an inexpressible longing. She realized in that moment that as challenging as this was for her, it must be doubly difficult for him.

As she averted her face, drawing in a shaky breath, she half expected to feel the warm velvet of his lips brush her skin . . . right before his fangs sank deep into her tender flesh. But he simply slipped the circlet of gold around her throat and secured it.

When she lowered her hair and turned, he was dropping the tiny gold key into his waistcoat pocket. "Do you always keep one of those on hand," she asked, "just in case you run across a woman you'd like to enslave?"

He gave her a dark look. "I procured it this evening as soon as the sun went down. You'd be amazed at what you can purchase from the Chinese vendors down at the docks."

She touched a hand to her new piece of jewelry. Although the gold had been beaten until it was as thin and delicate as a piece of parchment, it felt as heavy as iron to her. Especially when

Julian took up the end of the chain and looped it around his wrist.

"Are you ready?" he asked gently.

"Yes, master," she replied, shooting him a sullen glance.

He peered into her face. "You don't look the least bit adoring at the moment."

She fluttered her lashes and made calf's eyes at him.

"Now you look as if you're going to be sick."

"I think I am," she muttered as he swept open the carriage door and offered her his hand.

She slipped her hand into his, knowing she couldn't very well confess that the collar and chain felt like visible evidence of the invisible chain that had bound her heart to his from the first moment she had laid eyes on him quoting Byron in his brother's drawing room. As all-consuming as a young girl's fancies were, she was quickly discovering that a woman's desires could be twice as dangerous.

The aptly named Chillingsworth Manor loomed up out of the night, a crumbling heap of slate and stone. Judging from the air of decay hanging over the formerly imposing estate, its family's fortunes had been collapsing long before some reckless second cousin had gambled the house away in a drunken wager with a vampire.

A tattered veil of clouds dashed across the moon, parting just long enough to reveal a row of chimneys silhouetted against the night sky like an old man's crooked teeth. Every window in the house, even the cracked ones, had been draped in black crepe, making it look as if the house itself was mourning its lost grandeur and reproaching those who had been foolish enough to squander it. It seemed only fitting that it had been abandoned by the living and claimed by the undead.

As Julian escorted Portia up the walk, the hem of her mantle snagged on the frost-encrusted weeds that had been allowed to grow up through the paving stones.

"I should warn you," he said, "that vampires don't always communicate in the same manner as humans. Growling, hissing and nipping are perfectly acceptable ways of expressing affection for one's mate."

"How sweet," she murmured, clutching his

arm even tighter. "Just like a litter of baby badgers."

They were nearly to the door when he tugged her to a halt. "From this point on," he suggested, "it would probably be best if you walked a few paces behind me."

She gazed at him flatly for a few seconds before sweetly intoning, "As you wish, my lord."

A devilish grin crooked the corner of his mouth. "I could get used to that."

"Don't," she warned.

He took a few steps, but she remained frozen in place until he gave the chain a gentle tug. Sighing, she fell into step behind him.

The front door of the house creaked open beneath the urging of his hand. As its murky interior swallowed him whole, she hastened to follow, keenly missing his imposing presence beside her. Matching him step for step, she peered through the shadows, waiting for her eyes to adjust to the gloom.

She nearly screamed aloud when a hollow-eyed chap popped out of nowhere to take her mantle and muff.

"I didn't know vampires had footmen," she whispered as he carried the garments away, his pale hands stroking her mink muff as if it were a cherished cat.

"They don't," Julian whispered back.

Portia opened her mouth to protest but the fellow had already whisked her mantle around his bony shoulders, darted out the door and disappeared into the night.

As Julian led her through an archway and into a long, deep hall that must have once served as the manor's ballroom, she hugged herself, praying the dim light would hide the only too human gooseflesh prickling her arms.

She inched closer to Julian, whispering, "For creatures who can be destroyed by fire, vampires seem to be extraordinarily fond of candles."

Wax tapers burned throughout the cavernous room in every manner of stick and branched candelabrum. Their flames danced in the invisible drafts and cast a flickering web of light and shadow over the ballroom's three dozen or so occupants. Portia was surprised to find most of the vampires simply standing around chatting or gathered around tables playing cards. Many of them appeared rather bored with both the night and themselves. At the far end of the ballroom, a set of broad marble stairs swept upward to the second-floor gallery that ringed the chamber.

A ragged quartet of vampires sprawled on chairs in the corner, fitfully tuning their instruments, while a particularly pale fellow with an aquiline nose, artfully curled forelock, and boldly cleft chin stood with one foot on the dusty marble hearth, regaling his companions with some sort of recitation. His sonorous voice carried throughout the ballroom:

"Though the night was made for loving,
And the day returns too soon,
Yet we'll go no more a-roving
By the light of the moon."

Portia stumbled right into Julian's back, gaping. "But isn't that Lord B-B-B- . . ."

"Hello, Georgie," Julian called out.

As the vampire returned the greeting with a slightly effeminate wiggle of his fingers, Portia's eyes widened. "Do you mean to tell me that the rumors were true? Lord Byron really is a v-v-v-"

"—vapid narcissistic hack? Yes, I'm afraid so.

And although I would have thought it impossible, he's even more boring in death than he was in life. Try to imagine the horror of listening to him blather on like that for all eternity. It's enough to make one want to drive a stake through one's own heart. Or through his."

Shaking his head in disgust, Julian shouldered his way through Byron's rapt audience. Portia stood gawking at the legendary poet until Julian gave the chain a pointed tug.

Hurrying to catch up with him, she murmured, "I have to confess that this gathering isn't at all what I expected. I pictured more of a Bacchanalian revel of debauchery with virgins and kittens being sacrificed on some blood-soaked altar."

He swung around to face her, his voice low but ripe with emotion. "You needn't sound so disappointed. Vampires hardly have a monopoly on evil, you know. If you want to see acts truly worthy of eternal damnation, you should join His Majesty's army or visit one of the hellfire clubs in Pall Mall where screaming virgins are routinely sacrificed to the lusts of unscrupulous noblemen with too much money and too little mercy. Vampires only destroy and kill so they can survive. Mortals do it for the sheer giddy pleasure of it."

She took a wary step backward, thrown off balance by the force of his passion.

"Lover's quarrel?" The melodic voice poured over them both like liquid silk.

A vampire had materialized out of the shadows. He was dressed in the style of a century ago in knee-breeches and a dark blue *habit à la française* with gleaming gold frog-and-button fastenings and a flared skirt. Extravagant falls of lace cascaded from the collar and cuffs of the elegant coat. Although he wasn't wearing a powdered wig, his long, sleek golden hair had been gathered at his nape in a velvet queue. His angelic features and bright blue eyes would have looked equally at home painted on the ceiling of some Florentine cathedral.

Julian executed a deep bow. "My dear, this is Raphael—our host for the evening. He was kind enough to extend his hospitality to me when I first returned from the Continent."

"Lovely place you've got here," she murmured awkwardly, trying not to look directly at Raphael or at the silk hangings peeling in ribbons from the walls, the cascades of melted wax dripping from the candelabrums, the cobwebs festooning the crystal chandeliers, the dead leaves drifting about the floor, the sparrows darting among the exposed ceiling beams, or the shattered mirrors that hung between each window.

"Even more lovely now that it has been graced with your presence, my lady." Raphael captured her hand and brought it to his mouth. Instead of kissing her knuckles, his moist lips flowered over the sensitive skin on the inside of her wrist. From the corner of her eye, Portia saw Julian's mouth tighten with displeasure.

"Why, thank you," she replied shortly, offering him a thin-lipped smile. As she felt one of his fangs graze her flesh, she jerked her hand out of his grip, terrified he would feel her racing pulse.

He peered into her face, a moue of concern softening the sensual cut of his lips. "You look a trifle bit pale, my dear. Can I offer you someone to eat?"

She swallowed, but before she could choke out a reply, Julian slipped an arm around her waist. "That won't be necessary. We dined before we came."

Raphael was still staring at her, his narrowed gaze slightly less benevolent than before. "I never forget a beautiful face, you know, and I would almost swear I'd seen yours before."

Julian cast a furtive look about them as if to make sure that no one was eavesdropping on their conversation, then leaned down and whispered something in Raphael's ear.

"No!" the vampire exclaimed, his eyes widening to shocked pools of blue.

"Indeed," Julian said in a voice just loud enough to carry to the vampires lounging around the baize-covered card table in the corner. "And you can imagine my brother's chagrin when she willingly surrendered both her body and her soul to me."

Raphael clapped his beautifully manicured hands, all but chortling with delight. "Stole her right out from under the vampire hunter's nose, did you? What an amazing coup! Why, you're sure to be the talk of every nest in England!"

Julian ducked his head modestly.

Raphael's gaze lingered on the creamy swell of her breasts as revealed by the low-cut décolletage of her gown. "Given her history, how can you be sure she's not still hiding a stake or a crucifix in there?"

"Oh, I can promise you she's been *thoroughly* searched. I'll be the only one doing the staking tonight." As Julian stroked her nape just above the collar, Portia could only hope that the heavy layer of powder would mask her scalding blush.

Raphael smiled and chucked her under the chin as if she were a particularly delightful puppy. "She's very quiet, isn't she? I do so love a woman who knows how to keep her mouth shut and her legs open."

Portia lunged at him, her snapping teeth barely missing his fingers. He recoiled in surprise.

Wrapping the chain around his fist, Julian jerked her around until they were nose to nose. "Mind your manners," he hissed, baring his own fangs. "I'd hate to have to discipline you in front of the others."

Portia had forgotten what it was like to be at the mercy of all of that tightly coiled power. Before she could stop it, a growl had escaped her own lips. Something more primal than lightning arced between them, jolting every pulse in her body to throbbing life. Suddenly it was as if they were the only two creatures in the room, perhaps in the entire world.

She didn't know what might have happened if the musicians hadn't chosen that precise moment to strike up their instruments.

As several couples eagerly took to the floor, Julian slowly released the tension on the chain. "Shall we dance?"

"As you wish, my lord," she replied, lowering her lashes to veil her mutinous expression.

Splaying his hand at the small of her back, he swept her away from Raphael and into the waltz, leaving their host and everyone else within earshot watching with open-mouthed fascination.

As they whirled around the floor to the soaring strains of one of Mozart's more joyous pieces, Portia held herself as stiff as his possessive embrace would allow. "How could you allow him to say such horrid things to me?"

"What did you expect me to do? Challenge him to a duel to the death?"

"How could *you* say such horrid things? I hadn't realized you'd be playing your role as villain with such conviction."

"*Me?* What about you? I *am* a villain. You've only been pretending to be one for a few minutes and you're already snapping and snarling like some sort of rabid wolverine."

She tossed her head, sending her mane of curls rippling down her back. "I thought you vampires liked that in a woman."

He urged her closer—so close that there was no escaping the hard, hungry press of his hips against hers—before growling in her ear, "We do."

He swept her into a dizzying turn, leaving her with no choice but to surrender to his mastery. On the very night Duvalier had abducted her, she had dreamed of dancing in his arms exactly like this. In her innocence, she had believed such a dance might lead to a whispered exchange of endearments or perhaps a chaste kiss in a moonlit garden. She had never anticipated this wild abandon coursing through her veins, this irresistible temptation to succumb to an even more dangerous dance—one that had been luring women to both rapture and ruin since the beginning of time.

She lifted her chin and met his gaze boldly, gaining in confidence with each step. Perhaps they were more alike than either of them would care to admit. They both lived for the thrill of the game, the exhilarating rush that came when the fragile sphere of their fates was precariously balanced in their own hands.

"We shouldn't have to remain much longer," he murmured beneath the guise of nuzzling her ear. "Raphael is a shameless gossip without an ounce of discretion. It's been whispered that he was the one who informed Henry VIII that Anne Boleyn was dallying with four lovers who were plotting to dethrone him. It wasn't true, of course, but the rumor still cost poor Anne her head."

As he straightened, Portia followed the direction of his gaze. Their host was wending his way among the various groups, recounting what he'd just learned with a relish that left the men smirking and the women whispering behind their fans. Apparently, vampires loved a juicy morsel of scandal every bit as much as mortals did. Soon every gaze in the ballroom was riveted on them. Portia didn't need a mirror to know what a striking couple they must make.

Julian's eyes glittered with triumph. "I do believe our mission has been a rousing success. I predict that before the sun rises tomorrow Valentine will have heard all about our unholy little union."

A gust of wind suddenly ripped through the ballroom, driving a shivering heap of dead leaves before it. Portia lifted her gaze to a spot just over Julian's shoulder, thankful that the powder caked on her cheeks would also hide the sight of every last drop of blood draining from her face. "Something tells me you might not have to wait that long."

As both the musicians and the dancers stumbled to an awkward halt, Julian turned to find his former mistress standing at the top of the stairs.

Thirteen

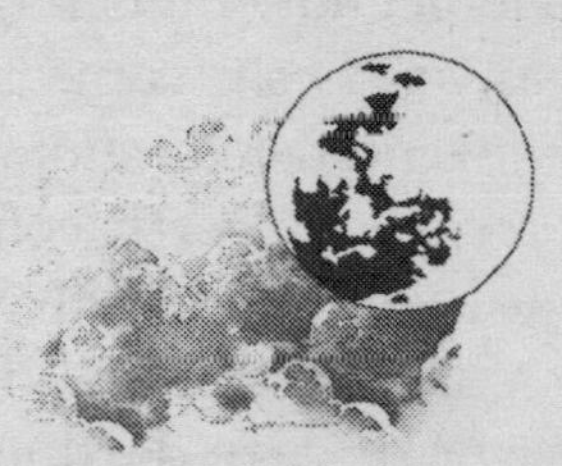

"Bloody hell," Julian breathed as Valentine came sweeping down the stairs, looking like an angel with her silvery-blond hair piled high on her head and the train of her snow white gown flowing behind her.

"Well, we wanted to find her, didn't we?" Portia whispered weakly.

"Not when we're outnumbered and on her turf." He glanced behind them, measuring the number of steps to the door. "I have to get you out of here."

Valentine's regal presence parted the other dancers like an arctic ice floe. Portia had tried to forget how ravishingly beautiful the woman was, but as she came gliding toward them, her jewel-encrusted slippers barely grazing the marble floor, Portia could feel herself shrinking into a squat homely troll.

Valentine stopped directly in front of them, her feline gaze darting between the chain and collar. "And what's this, *mon cher*?" she asked, her contemptuous gaze raking over Portia. "A peace offering? Have you grown bored with the kitten's charms already and decided to let me have her after all?"

"I'm afraid not," Julian replied, coiling the chain around his fist and tugging Portia into his side. "On the contrary, I've decided to keep her for myself."

Valentine pursed her lush red lips in a becoming pout. "You needn't be so greedy. If I caught such a pretty pet, I'd share her with you."

He snorted. "If you caught such a pretty pet, there wouldn't be anything left of her to share once you were through with her."

Valentine's low ripple of laughter raised the gooseflesh on Portia's nape. "You know me too well, don't you, darling? So why did you come here tonight? To beg my forgiveness for behaving so abominably the last time we met?"

"To be perfectly honest, I didn't expect to find you here. I thought you'd always considered yourself above all . . . *this.*" Julian's elegant shrug somehow managed to encompass Raphael and his motley group of guests, most of whom were watching their exchange with a disturbing combination of malevolence and delight.

She sighed. "If you must know, the nights have been very long and I've been very bored and lonely without you. Raphael keeps a pair of strapping young minions chained upstairs who were only too happy to *alleviate* my boredom for a few hours."

Portia couldn't resist stealing a glance at Julian's face, but it remained as impassive as a piece of sculpted marble.

"If you'd like," Valentine continued, "they can keep your kitten here occupied for the rest of the night while you and I get *reacquainted.*"

Portia edged even closer to Julian, his sidelong glance reminding her to hold her tongue.

"My 'kitten' has a name. Or have you forgotten it?"

Valentine tapped her lips with one pale, slender forefinger. "Let me see . . . was it Penelope? Prudence? Prunella?"

"Why don't you try Portia?" Julian gently prodded.

"Ah yes—Portia." Her upper lip curled in a sneer. "Its name is Portia. And she's a sentimental relic from your misspent youth. I do hope you've had your fill of the little chit by now. Judging from her pallor, you're in danger of drinking the poor creature dry." She reached over and gave Portia's arm a sisterly pat. "You have my heartfelt sympathy, my dear. I'm well aware of how insatiable Julian's appetites can be. *All* of his appetites."

As her barbed words struck a tender nerve, Portia bit her lip so hard she was afraid she was going to spoil their ruse by making it bleed.

Julian only laughed. "You needn't worry about her. I can assure you that she now shares those appetites. *All* of them."

It was Valentine's turn to look horrified. "Surely you didn't . . . You can't mean that she's . . ."

"That's right." His smile was so cold Portia wouldn't have been surprised to see frost forming on his lips. "She's one of us now." He wrapped a possessive arm around her waist, drawing her into his arms. "And all mine."

She wasn't prepared for the primal thrill that coursed through her soul at hearing him claim her so boldly. For a dangerous moment, it was only too easy to pretend he was speaking from the heart.

Valentine shook her head, plainly aghast. "Why would you do such a foolish thing? You've never even killed a human before, much less stolen a soul."

Julian reached up to draw the backs of his fingers down Portia's cheek in a lover's caress. "Maybe I never before found one worth stealing. One so bold and tender and irresistibly sweet. What man—or vampire—wouldn't want to spend an eternity in her arms?" He eased aside her hair and pressed his lips to the exquisitely sensitive spot just behind her ear, sending a shudder of melting delight deep into her belly. She did not have to feign her gasp of pleasure. "Or her bed?"

Valentine began to sputter, deserted by her oily composure. For a brief moment, Portia almost pitied her. When she finally found her voice, there was an ugly hiss to it that hadn't been there before. "She may be tender and sweet but she'll *never* please you as I did. Has she been the lover of both emperors and kings? Has she spent a year of her life in a sultan's harem, studying a thousand different techniques for pleasuring a man?"

"I'm the only man she'll ever have to pleasure. And I can assure you that she's more than equal to the task." He gave the chain a gentle tug, turning her away from Valentine. "Come, darling. Let's leave this place while the night is still young."

They were halfway to the door when a terrible shriek echoed through the ballroom. "She can't have you! I'm the one who rescued you from the stake in Paris! *You belong to me!*"

Portia stopped, turning so quickly that she whipped the end of the chain right out of Julian's hand. Before he could make a grab for it, she had gone striding back across the ballroom, trailing the length of chain behind her. As she came to a halt in front of Valentine, several of the gawking vampires began to back away from the two of them.

"You know, Mademoiselle Cardew," she said.

"I don't really care how many sultans you've serviced or which king's harlot you've been. You may know a thousand different techniques for pleasuring a man, but I can still give Julian something you never can."

Valentine sneered down her patrician nose at her. "And just what would that be?"

Portia took a deep breath. "My love. You may have saved him from the stake, but it was my love that kept him alive when Duvalier tried to destroy him all those years ago. So that means he was mine first. And he's still mine. You may very well have his soul." She leaned closer, tossing the woman's own words back in her livid face. "But *I* will always have his heart."

Although Portia would have thought it impossible for Valentine's alabaster skin to go a shade whiter, it did. With a howl of rage, she wrenched a small glass bottle from her belt. Clawing the stopper free with her crimson nails, she flung its contents into Portia's face.

Portia cried out and clapped her hands to her face. From the horrified gasps and keening wails that arose from the vampires, she half expected her flesh to start sizzling and melting from the bone. But when she didn't feel so much as a sting, she slowly lowered her hands, blinking the stuff from her eyes.

She gave Valentine a disbelieving look, her relief so keen she could not hold back a startled burst of laughter. "I don't know why they're all making such a fuss. It's only water!"

As Portia realized what she'd done, the phrase "dead silence" had never seemed so apt. She stole a look around her and all she could see were eyes narrowing to hostile slits and lips parting to reveal the deadly gleam of fangs. She gave Raphael a beseeching look, but her formerly amiable host's only response was a serpentine hiss.

Then the real outcry began.

"He tricked us!"

"She's a mortal!"

"I thought I smelled something sweet!"

"I can't wait to sink my teeth into that!"

"You'll have to wait your turn just like the rest of us!"

The vampires closed in around her, forming a circle even Julian couldn't penetrate. And at their head was Valentine, her green eyes glowing and her ripe ruby lips curved in a triumphant smile.

"Portia! The water!"

Julian's deep voice held a commanding note that was impossible to ignore. She glanced down at her dripping hands in bewilderment. Then inspiration dawned and she shook herself like a wet dog, flinging drops of holy water everywhere.

Valentine and the other vampires shrieked and recoiled, shielding their eyes and faces with their hands. The stench of sizzling flesh filled the air.

That was all the distraction Julian needed. He cleared the thrashing vampires in a single leap, sweeping Portia clean off her feet and into the cradle of his arms. She shrieked and instinctively threw her arms around his neck as he flexed his knees and jumped, sending them soaring toward the gallery.

He landed in a crouch on the balls of his feet, absorbing the shock of the impact before it could rip through her. Furious shouts rang through the ballroom below.

Julian sprang to his feet, his frantic gaze searching for any means of escape.

Following the direction of his gaze to the stained-glass window at the far end of the gallery, Portia's mouth fell open. "Surely you don't intend to . . ." She swiveled back around to blink at him. "You do know I can't turn into a bat, don't you?"

"I'm hoping you won't have to," he said grimly. "Just hang on to me as if your life depended upon it. For it very well might."

Giving her little choice in the matter, he took off at a dead run. They went barreling toward the window, his long strides eating up the length of the gallery. Her whimper rising to a wail, Portia squeezed her eyes shut and buried her face against his throat at the precise moment he leapt and the window exploded in a moonlit rainbow of shattering glass.

Fourteen

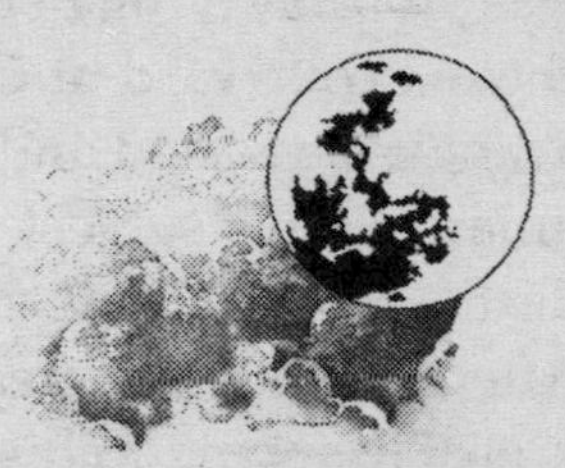

Portia opened her eyes to find a heavenly choir of cherubs beaming down at her. They perched on downy white clouds in a sky of celestial blue, their chubby little fingers plucking the strings of golden lyres.

"Oh, dear Lord," she whispered. "I'm dead."

She clapped a hand to her mouth. Perhaps this wouldn't be the wisest time to start blaspheming.

The cherubs smirked down at her, deepening the dimples in their rosy cheeks. Her spirit might be residing on a cloud of its own in this glowing little corner of paradise, but her body was probably lying in the middle of some weed-choked courtyard at Chillingsworth Manor in a tangle of twisted and shattered limbs. At least Julian wasn't subject to the grim finality of death, she thought with a wistful little sigh. After sending her crashing to her doom, he'd probably sprang to his feet, dusted off his coat, and headed back to London for a fresh bottle of port and another game of brag.

Unaccountably annoyed with the cherubs' good cheer, she jerked her gaze away from them.

"Oh, dear Lord!" she said again, this time with an entirely different inflection.

The vision that greeted her eyes was decidedly more pagan in nature. A most curious creature—half-man and half swan—appeared to be forcing his romantic advances on a voluptuous and nearly naked young woman. Despite the maidenly way she clasped the scraps of her ruined gown to her breasts, her parted lips and dazed expression left one with the indelicate hint that she might actually be enjoying his rapacious attentions.

"Oh my," Portia murmured, forced to turn her head sideways to absorb the full impact of their coupling. As heat flooded her cheeks and other less respectable parts of her body, she almost wished she hadn't.

The heat seemed to burn away the last wisps of fog drifting through her head. She realized in that moment that she wasn't floating on a cloud gazing up at the heavens but lying on a feather tick blinking up at a faded mural painted on a domed ceiling by some artist who was probably long dead. The innocent cherubs were perched next to various far less innocent characters from Greek mythology, including the cunning god Zeus who had transformed himself into a swan to ravish the unsuspecting—but not entirely unwilling—Leda.

Portia sat up in the sagging four-poster, shocked to realize she was wearing only her thin silk chemise. The drooping neckline of the garment revealed an alarming expanse of creamy bosom and shoulder. Her hand flew to her throat only to find the gold collar gone as well. It seemed she'd been liberated from both her clothing and her chains.

Someone had also freed her hair from its combs and wiped the mask of powder from her face. Oddly enough, it was more stirring to imagine Julian's hands tenderly mopping the powder from her cheeks than unlacing the whalebone corset of her gown.

A branch of candles stood near the foot of the bed, their flickering glow doing little to brighten the gloom of the chamber. Although the candles were molded from fragrant beeswax instead of tallow, most of them were little more than salvaged stubs. A fall of cobwebs draped the tarnished brass of the chandelier, drifting like tattered lace before the breath of some unseen draft. The frozen pearl of the moon peeped through the mullioned window tucked beneath the eaves on the far side of the room.

She jumped as the door swung open and Julian ducked into the bedchamber, a woolen blanket draped over his arm.

"I suppose that answers one of my questions," she said, tightening her grip on the neckline of the chemise. "I'm definitely not in heaven or *you* wouldn't be here."

He swept her a mocking bow. "The Prince of Darkness at your service, my lady."

His wind-tossed hair and sparkling dark eyes made him appear only too well-suited to the role. The mischievous sprite who had stolen her gown also seemed to have made off with his coat, waistcoat, and boots, leaving him garbed in his white lawn shirt and ivory trousers. His cravat hung loose around the broad column of his throat.

He tossed her the blanket with an apologetic shrug. "I would have laid a fire in the hearth but I'm afraid it's not one of my talents."

Portia could well understand that. Especially when a single stray spark could incinerate him.

As she wrapped the blanket around her shoulders, he settled himself into a gilded chair with padded arms that sat a few feet from the bed. If the gilt hadn't been peeling and the padding spilling from the arms, it would have made a fitting throne.

"Where are we?" she asked, nervously eyeing the shadowy corners of the room.

"I thought it best that we lay low for a few hours and fortunately, Chillingsworth Manor isn't the only abandoned house in this parish. Judging from the sheets draping the furniture, the occupants of this house may very well plan to return someday. I'm just hoping it won't be tonight."

"How did we get in?"

"Through a freshly broken window." He smiled at her expression. "You needn't look so shocked. I can assure you that burgling a deserted house is the least of my sins."

"Well, I certainly won't argue with that." Their eyes met for a long moment, but it was Portia who had to look away first. "I thought vampires couldn't enter a house without an invitation?"

He wiggled his eyebrows at her. "That's only when there's someone at home."

She frowned. "Why don't I remember coming here?"

"If you don't recall stealing a horse from Raphael's stables and boldly eluding our pursuers, it's probably because you were draped across my lap like a sack of potatoes. You fainted."

She groaned. "How embarrassing! I've faked any number of swoons in my life, but never succumbed to a genuine one." She opened the blanket to peer down at her unconventional attire. "It's very odd but I also can't seem to recall how my gown came to be missing? Did it by any chance *fall off* as we were galloping across the moors?"

"No, but it was sprinkled with holy water

and I got tired of burning myself every time I touched you." He tugged up the cuffs of his shirt to reveal blackened scorch marks along the length of his muscled forearms.

"Oh," Portia breathed in genuine dismay. She had to fight an absurd desire to go to him, to press her lips against his wounded flesh and try to draw out the pain.

He lifted his shoulders in a diffident shrug. "They'll heal. Not as quickly as a gunshot wound, of course, but in time." He leaned back in the chair, crossing his long legs at the ankle. "So when you found your gown missing, did you fear my intentions toward you might be less than honorable?"

Portia matched his mocking tone with one of her own. "Usually when a man sweeps a woman up into his arms and carries her off, it's for some nefarious purpose."

"I was trying to save your life, not force you to elope with me to Gretna Green."

She tilted her head, studying him from beneath her lashes. "I thought perhaps you really had decided to set up housekeeping with me as your kitten."

"If I wanted a pet, I'd get a dog. Their claws

aren't nearly as sharp and their affections are more easily engaged."

"That was an unfair jibe, don't you think? Especially since I spent the earliest part of our acquaintance scampering after your heels like an overeager pup." She touched a hand to her throat. "Perhaps you should have left on the collar and chain so you would have a way to bring me to heel."

"Don't think I wasn't tempted. I briefly considered telling you I'd lost the key during our mad dash for freedom."

"Well, I could have hardly berated you for your carelessness when I'm the one who managed to whip an entire nest of vampires into a murderous rage."

Julian's jaw tightened. "If you were trying to create a diversion, your plan was a smashing success. I briefly wanted to murder you myself."

Portia lowered her eyes. She might not recall their dramatic escape, but she remembered only too well the moment when she had marched across that ballroom to confront his former mistress. "That was quite the royal snit Valentine threw along with that holy water, wasn't it?"

"Capturing her shouldn't prove to be much

of a challenge now. She'll probably be waiting for me on Adrian's doorstep when we get home. You were quite magnificent tonight," Julian added softly. "You're an even more accomplished actress than I realized. Were I not such a heartless cynic, I would have believed every word you said to her."

She lifted her head to look him straight in the eye. "Perhaps that's because they were true."

Fifteen

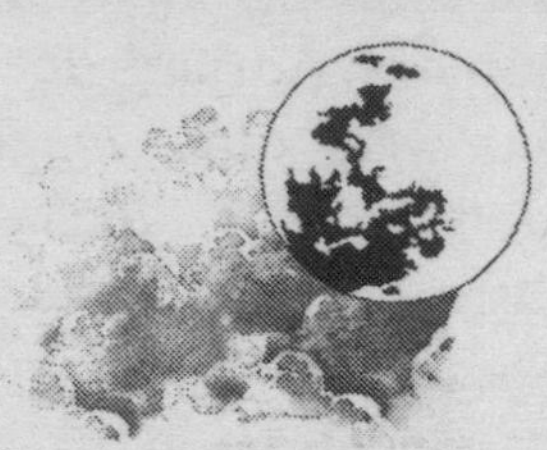

Julian gripped the arms of the chair, every muscle in his body going rigid.

Portia lifted one delicate shoulder in a shrug, sending the blanket spilling to the tick. "Oh, I've tried not to love you, truly I have. I disliked you quite passionately for nearly a week after you went off the first time and I've even been moderately successful at hating you ever since I found out about Valentine. But I'm afraid old habits die hard, especially those ingrained in the tender heart of a young girl. When Valentine laid claim to you tonight, I decided I wasn't going to surrender so easily. If she was willing to fight for you, then so was I."

Uncurling her long, slender legs from beneath her, she slid off the bed and to her feet. As she glided toward him like a vision out of one of his sweetest and darkest fantasies, the candlelight played over the translucent folds of the chemise, stroking to life a rosy hint of nipple and an enticing web of shadow between her shapely thighs.

He came to his own feet, scooting around the chair and backing away from her as if she was the one who had the power to destroy him. "What do you think you're doing, Portia? You were supposed to drive Valentine insane with jealousy, not drive me insane."

"Have you forgotten that I'm supposed to be your eternal bride? And every bride deserves a wedding night, doesn't she?"

He pointed a finger at her, surprised to find it none too steady. "If I lay so much as a finger on you tonight, I won't have to worry about Valentine destroying me. Adrian will do it for her."

She smiled and took another step toward him, bringing herself within his reach. "It just might be worth it."

He backed right into the wall, clenching his teeth against a savage rush of longing. "That's what I'm afraid of."

Resting her hands lightly on his shoulders, she rose up on her tiptoes and pressed a kiss to the underside of his jaw, the enchanting softness of her breasts brushing his chest. "I saved you in that crypt," she whispered. "You owe me."

"I know I do," he growled. "That's why I've stayed away from you for all these years. To repay you for your kindness."

She gazed up at him, her eyes soft and luminous. "Do you remember what happened?"

"How could I forget? I almost killed you."

"That's not how I remember it at all."

Desperate to erase the tender expression from her face, he seized her by the shoulders and reversed their positions, pinning her against the wall with the hardness of his hands, the hardness of his body. "Then let me refresh your memory, angel. You kissed me. Then you chained me to the wall just as I had begged you to do. But you didn't do it to protect yourself. You did it so you'd have me at *your* mercy. So you could force me to do the unthinkable."

"I didn't have any choice. You were dying."

"Then you should have let me die!" As the echo of his shout faded, he pushed himself away from the wall and her, raking his hair out of his face. "With or without my soul, how could I ever be anything less than a monster after what I did to you?"

She caught his arm, tugging him back around to face her. "You did everything within your power to save me. *I* was the one who seduced you. *I* was the one who sat on your lap while you were in chains and kissed you and touched you and used all of the pathetic skills at my naïve disposal that I'd learned from reading lurid Gothic novels to entice you into burying your fangs in my throat."

"You were an innocent! You didn't realize what manner of beast you were about to unleash."

"I may have been an innocent, but I wasn't stupid. I knew exactly what saving you would cost me. And I was only too willing to pay the price." She shook her head helplessly. "You were never a beast, Julian. Don't you remember? You broke those chains. You ripped them right out of the wall and came after me. But you didn't kill me." Despite the tears sparkling in her eyes, both her voice and her gaze were steady. "And you didn't rape me."

"Only because you gave yourself to me willingly. If you hadn't . . ." He let the brutal thought go unfinished, still remembering the taste of her blood on his lips, the horror that had washed over him when both the lust and the bloodlust had passed and he had found her pale, still body sprawled beneath his.

"You would have taken me anyway? Is that what you believe?"

"Don't you?" he asked, refusing to let her flinch from his uncompromising gaze. "My only comfort was knowing you wouldn't suffer the shame of bearing my child." A bitter laugh escaped him. "Who ever thought I would be grateful that I couldn't create life, only death?"

She lifted her chin. "I did what I had to do and so did you. I've never regretted it. Not for a single minute."

"Well, I've regretted it every minute of every day and night since then. And my curse is to go on regretting it for all eternity." He caught her by the shoulders and gave her a harsh shake.

"Do you really think getting my soul back now would cleanse me of all my sins? Have you any idea of the things I've had to do just to survive? Even with my soul, I'd be no more fit for a woman like you than some filthy rag that's been lying in the gutter for all these years!"

She blinked up at him, wonder slowly dawning in her eyes. "You didn't let Valentine keep your soul because you were in love with her, did you?"

Although he looked even more desperate than before, both his voice and his grip softened. "No, God help me, I let her keep my soul because I was in love with you. I knew I could never be worthy of you and I believed that as long as I remained a vampire, I wouldn't even have to try." He touched a hand to her throat, gently caressing the scars he had left there. "When you opened your arms to me in that crypt, it was the greatest gift anyone had ever given me. But you deserved so much more from your first lover. So much patience and tenderness . . . and pleasure . . ."

She covered his hand with her own. "It's not too late, Julian. You can still give me what I deserve."

"I don't know if I can," he confessed hoarsely. "I don't trust myself with you, Portia. I never have. With any other woman, I can control my . . . my more *unnatural* hungers. But with you . . ." He shook his head, his body already beginning to burn with a wild, sweet fever.

"You don't have to trust yourself. I trust you enough for the both of us."

With that promise, she cupped his face in her hands just as she had done in the crypt all those years ago and pressed her lips to his. Growling his surrender, Julian wrapped his arms around her and dragged her into his embrace, knowing it would take an eternity to completely slake his desperate craving for her kiss. He tried to temper his hunger with tenderness, but she welcomed the bold thrust of his tongue, twining her arms around his neck and kissing him back with a ferocious need that matched his own.

There was still a savage part of him that wanted to bear her back against the door, shove the gossamer silk of the chemise up over her hips, and take her with just as much passion but no more finesse than he had shown the first time.

But she stroked her fingers through his hair, gentling him with nothing more than her touch and the whisper of her sigh against his lips. In her arms he didn't feel like a monster. She made him feel like a man.

Still savoring the melting sweetness of her mouth, he slipped one arm beneath her hips, lifting her as if she weighed no more than a child. As he carried her toward the bed, she wrapped her legs around his waist, coaxing a strangled sound from deep in his throat.

He laid her back on the feather tick, reluctant to surrender her warmth but eager to devour her with his eyes. As he drew back to tug off his cravat and shirt, she watched him, her eyes misty in the candlelight, the dew of their kiss shimmering on her parted lips. He was dismayed to find a tear clinging to her feathery, dark lashes.

"Don't cry, Bright Eyes," he said fiercely, dropping down on the bed next to her and brushing the crystalline drop away with his thumb. "Shoot me, burn me, drive a stake through my heart if you must, but please don't cry. I can bear anything but your tears."

"It's just that I've been waiting so long for you," she whispered.

"An eternity," he agreed softly.

Yet still he hesitated. He was so much bigger than she was, so much stronger. He had hurt her once and if his nature drove him to do it again, there was no power on hell or earth that could stop him. But he didn't want to cause her pain. He wanted to give her pleasure. He wanted to use every precious minute of the night and every skill at his disposal to bring her to shuddering ecstasy again and again. He wanted to make love to her until she cried out his name and forgot her own. Until there was no past and no tomorrow, only the endless hours between midnight and dawn.

His mouth hovered over hers, his raw senses overwhelmed by the warmth of her body, the richness of her scent . . . her very *aliveness.* He could hear her heart beating, taste the sweetness of her breath, smell her arousal. He'd wandered the world over only to find the most potent aphrodisiac right here in his arms. If she turned him out of her bed before he could so much as steal another kiss, she would have already ruined him for any other woman.

She stroked the hair at his nape, curling it around her fingers. "When you used to murmur my name in your sleep, what were you dreaming about?"

"This." He lowered his mouth to hers, kissing her with all of the aching tenderness he had once denied her.

Portia moaned as Julian's tongue swirled over her parted lips before delving deep into her mouth. He kissed her as if she were an innocent, a cherished bride who would require wooing and coaxing before surrendering herself to the pleasures of his touch. His mouth slanted over hers again and again, drugging her with a thick, sweet delight that flowed like honey through her veins and made her nipples swell and harden before surging between her thighs.

"Why, Mr. Kane," she blurted out when he allowed her to steal a breath, "are you trying to seduce me?"

"You told me to give you what you deserve," he murmured, the rich, hypnotic timbre of his voice a seduction all its own. "And a woman as beautiful as you deserves to be *seduced* at least three times a night, perhaps more often."

As that clever mouth of his worked its way from the corner of her mouth to the curve of her jaw to the tiny pulse that beat at the base of her throat, she closed her eyes and breathed out a shaky sigh. She had never dreamed she would be so thankful he was a nocturnal creature.

As his lips grazed her throat, a shudder wracked his powerful body. But he held it in check, nuzzling the sensitive shell of her ear and filling his hands with her breasts. She gasped at his boldness, arching off the bed into his masterful hands. The room was cold but his body was burning, its feverish warmth kindling an answering fire in her own flesh.

His mouth closed over one of her breasts, licking the flames even higher. He teased the taut nubbin of her nipple with his tongue until the silk of her chemise was damp and clinging, then drew back to blow softly on the fabric. She'd never known such exquisite torment. But instead of begging him to stop, she tangled her hands in the raw silk of his hair, urging him on. He drew her other nipple into the lush heat of his mouth, suckling her deep and hard until delicious little shivers of need wracked her womb.

A husky moan of protest escaped her lips as

he sat up on his knees, straddling her thighs. She opened her eyes just as his hands caught in the silk of her chemise. The delicate fabric parted like parchment beneath the supernatural strength of his hands, leaving her naked and vulnerable beneath his gaze.

Julian's eyes feasted upon the wonder that was Portia's body bathed in candlelight. He'd been half blind with starvation and lust in that torchlit crypt. He'd fallen upon her like the ravening beast he'd been at that moment, barely taking the time to shove up her skirt and jerk open his trousers before driving both his fangs and himself deep into her tender young body. Only in his imagination and in the countless dreams that had haunted him since that day had he seen her like this.

She was more beautiful than even his most feverish imagining. Her dark curls spilled across the feather tick, framing her flushed cheeks and moist, parted lips. Her full breasts were ripe and rosy from his lavish attentions. His gaze swept down her body, past her slender waist and the delicious little dimple of her navel to her generous hips and the nest of glossy curls between her thighs.

No longer able to resist the temptation, he stretched his long, lean body out beside her and touched her there, parting those silky curls and the delicate petals beneath with just one finger.

Portia trembled beneath his touch. In that moment she *was* his kitten, purring and writhing beneath the masterful stroke of his hand. She pressed her eyes shut as his long, aristocratic fingers played her even more deftly than they had the pianoforte keys, coaxing forth a melody of gasps, moans, and shuddering sighs of delight. When he stopped touching her, leaving her perched at the very peak of some extraordinary precipice, she'd never been so aware of her own mortality. She thought she was going to die.

She opened her eyes, gasping aloud when she saw his face.

Julian didn't need a reflection to know that his fangs were fully extended, his eyes glowing with an unholy light. He lifted them to her face, no longer able to hide what he was or his all-consuming hunger for her.

Instead of recoiling in horror as he feared she would do, she simply whispered, "Do you need to feed?"

A lazy smile curved his lips. "Oh, I intend to."

Then he was sliding down, down, down on her in the flickering shadows cast by the candles.

As his mouth followed the path his fingers had forged, taking exquisite care not to graze her delicate flesh with his fangs, Portia arched off the bed and into his keeping. The nimble flick of his tongue transported her to some dark and dangerous Eden where the two of them could feast on forbidden fruit without being banished from the garden. He was both serpent and angel, temptation and salvation, and she knew he wouldn't be satisfied until she'd surrendered herself to him, body and soul.

She clutched at his hair as pleasure pulsed through her in molten waves. Just as those waves engulfed her in a shuddering spasm of ecstasy, he used his longest finger and the thick, creamy nectar of her surrender to stroke his way deep into the very heart of her, prolonging her rapture for an exquisite eternity.

When her eyes finally fluttered open, Julian was looming over her, peering into her face.

"You frightened me for a moment. I thought you might have fainted again."

She gave him a dazed and drowsy smile, her body still quaking with little aftershocks of delight. "I wouldn't miss a moment of this night. No matter what wicked manner of carnal mischief you work on my body, I refuse to swoon."

He arched one devilish eyebrow. "Is that a challenge?"

"I suppose I can't stop you if you choose to take it as such," she replied primly.

"Good," he said, sitting back on his haunches and reaching for the front placket of his trousers. As it was, they were barely able to contain him.

Portia closed her hand over his, her courage faltering. "Is it too late for me to behave like a blushing virgin and beg you to blow out the candles?"

His eyes heavy with both longing and regret, he brought her hand to his lips, pressing the tenderest of kisses to the back of it. "For you, my lady, I'd blow out the moon itself."

Portia almost regretted her request as he slipped out of the bed and padded to the candelabrum, stealing one last look at her over his shoulder. As he extinguished the candles one by one, she drank in the fluid grace of his movements, the sculpted muscles of his chest and the rippling planes of his abdomen, her mouth going dry with longing. Then the last candle flickered out and the night enfolded them in its sheltering embrace. She was surprised to find that the darkness only emboldened her. When Julian returned to the bed and her arms, she was the one who reached for the front of his trousers.

He shuddered as she set him free from the straining fabric, her fingers shyly tracing the length and breadth of him. In the darkness, he seemed to go on forever.

She managed a shaky little laugh. "No wonder it hurt the first time. If it hadn't happened once before, I'd almost swear it was impossible."

He rested his brow against hers. "It hurt because I behaved like a barbarian who had just laid eyes on his first woman. Had I been in my right mind, there were things I could have done to make it more . . . tolerable for you."

Her hand enfolded him, gently squeezing a guttural groan from the depths of his throat. "Show me."

She didn't have to ask twice. Before Portia could catch her breath, he had shed his trousers and they were naked in each other's arms.

"Julian?"

"Mmmmm?" he murmured, using his nimble tongue to tease one of her nipples to a rigid peak.

"Before we proceed, I have a shocking confession to make."

"I thought I was the only one allowed to make shocking confessions."

She sat up and hugged one knee to her chest, her cheeks burning in the darkness. He followed, gently brushing the veil of hair from her face. "What is it, Bright Eyes? You're as pink as a rose."

She sighed, cursing herself for forgetting that vampires had exceptional night vision. "It's about the crypt."

He grew very still. So still it was possible to tell he wasn't breathing for the first time that night. After a long moment, he said, "If you can't go through with this because of what I did to you before, I understand. I won't force you. I'm not that much of a monster."

"I'm not going to lie. You hurt me. But there

was more. That . . . *thing* you did to me earlier with your mouth and your hands? That thing that made me feel as if I was going to die of pleasure?" She hesitated. "I felt it then, too. When you bit me . . . when you . . ." She turned to look at him, knowing it was impossible to hide from him, even in the dark. "I was frightened out of my wits, afraid you might very well kill me. But for just a few seconds there, I wasn't sure I cared."

He was silent for even longer this time. "I have an even more shocking confession to make."

Portia closed her eyes, her throat thickening with dread.

"I love you, Portia Cabot." Cupping her face in his hands, he laid his lips against hers, kissing her with a wrenching tenderness that took her breath away. "And whether I'm a vampire or a mortal, I will love you for all eternity."

She opened her arms and he went into them, covering her as he had on that cold stone floor a lifetime ago. As they sank into the feather tick, it was as if they'd never truly left that crypt, as if there had never been any other woman in his arms or in his bed during all of those long, lonely nights.

Feeling the heavy weight of him against her thigh, Portia shuddered with dark anticipation, expecting him to roughly drive himself home in her as he'd done before. But instead he reached between them with his hand, petting and stroking her as if he had all night to prepare her for what was to come. Those delicious little frissons of delight began to shiver through her again and soon she was panting with need and whispering his name over and over in a breathless plea for deliverance. As his thumb gently flicked over the live ember nestled at the crux of her nether curls, she was afraid she was the one who was going to burst into flames. Especially when his other fingers began to have their way with her at the same time, dipping into her one, then two at a time.

She bloomed beneath the rhythmic stroke of his hand, her body weeping tears of desire for what only he could give her. She wanted to draw him so deep inside of her she'd never have to let him go.

"Please, Julian," she moaned, his fingers no longer enough to satisfy her. "Oh, please . . ."

He shifted his weight, kneeing her thighs apart so that she was utterly vulnerable to him.

Only then did he bring himself to bear against her. She gasped as he rubbed his smooth, hard length between her sleek petals, laving himself in the molten nectar he'd teased from the very heart of her. This was an even more exquisite torture, one that made her writhe and whimper beneath him.

"Are you ready for me, angel?" he whispered hoarsely, dipping into her with the thick head of his shaft.

In reply, she wrapped both her arms and her legs around him and arched off the bed, impaling herself on his rigid length.

Julian shuddered, his body battered by a wave of pure sensation. Portia might not be a virgin, but she was every bit as tight as one. And as unfair as it was, knowing that he was the only man she had ever given herself to sent a savage thrill of satisfaction through him.

He had thought he'd been lost before, but now he was lost in the slick velvet heat of her, in the intoxicating scent of her arousal, in the wild, sweet abandon of her surrender. He would have gladly risked eternal damnation for a taste of this heaven. He withdrew, then rocked back up into her, hard and deep.

As Julian began to glide in and out of her in a hypnotic rhythm older than time, Portia clutched at his back, exultation roaring through her veins. This was how it was always meant to be between them. No more genteel conventions of society to restrain them. Just this primal passion, as powerful and undying as he was.

Her eyes drifted open and she gazed up over his shoulder at the mural on the ceiling. Now that she was being ravished by her own beloved beast, she understood the dazed expression in Leda's eyes, the mindless rapture on her face. With each powerful thrust of his hips, Julian drove her to the very brink of some sweet madness she was powerless to resist. She didn't know if she would ever again feel complete without him moving deep inside of her.

Which was why it was such a shock when he went utterly still, buried so deep between her legs that her heart began to throb in time to the pulse that beat there.

"What is it?" she whispered.

He gazed down at her. Even in the dark, she could see the gleam of his fangs, the faint reddish glow of his eyes. "I'm afraid of what I'll do to you if . . . *when* I lose control."

Taking a deep breath, she said, "Don't be. I want you to give me what you gave those other women when you were fighting to survive. And I want you to take from me what you took from them."

A shudder rocked his body. "I won't do that to you again! You can't ask that of me."

"Oh, no?" Lifting her head, she caught his bottom lip between her teeth and gave it a sharp little nip.

He recoiled. "You bit me!"

She blinked up at him innocently. "Didn't you tell me that nipping was a perfectly acceptable expression of affection?"

"Among vampires!"

"Which you just happen to be." She tangled her hands in his hair, her grip as fierce as her voice. "If I'd have wanted a perfect gentleman, I can promise you that there would have been no shortage of them willing to bed me. But I wanted you. And I'm not going to ask you to be anything less than what you are. Not even for me. *Especially* not for me."

With that, she turned her face away from him, baring the pale curve of her throat to his hungry gaze.

Growling, he came for her. But instead of burying his fangs in her throat, he wrapped his arms around her and bore her back against the headboard of the bed, pounding into her with a driving rhythm that sent shock waves of pleasure all the way to her womb. All she could do was hold on as he rode her hard and fast and deep until her body was slick with sweat and she was nearly insensible with delight.

But not so insensible that she didn't feel the feverish heat of his open mouth graze her throat or the scrape of his fangs as he claimed the kiss he had denied himself earlier. His mouth settled over her throbbing pulse, his tongue flicking out to taste the salty sweetness of her skin.

Portia shivered, although she could not have said whether it was out of fear or anticipation. She only knew that her hunger was as deep and primal as his own. That she craved his surrender just as much as he craved hers.

She didn't have long to wait. Without missing a stroke, he reached between them to gently flick that smoldering ember between her thighs with his thumb and the entire world burst into flames.

At the exact moment those flames engulfed

her, his fangs pierced her tender flesh. The pain was fleeting but the pleasure rolled on and on, crashing over her in blinding waves. She felt him surge deep within her and knew that he was in just as much danger of drowning as she was.

Sixteen

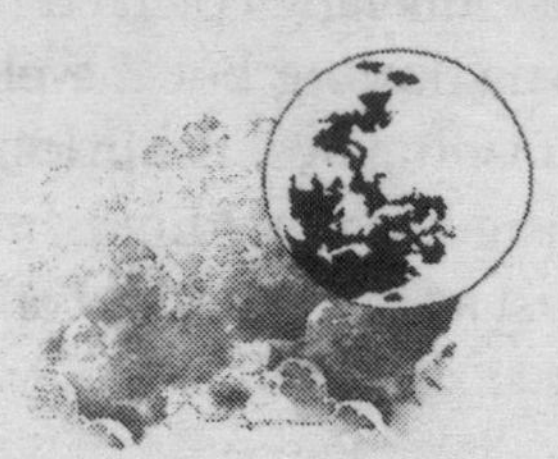

"*Well, that was certainly tolerable*," Portia murmured a short while later, snuggling deeper into Julian's arms and resting her cheek against his chest. Moonlight spilled over the bed, bathing their entwined limbs in a silver haze.

"You might find it even more tolerable if you'd stop bullying me into biting you." She could hear the scowl in his voice as he gently stroked his fingertips over the fresh puncture marks on her throat. "The next time I'm going to put *you* in manacles."

"I shudder to think what wicked things you'd

do to me if you had me at your mercy," she said, knowing full well that he already did.

"Oh, you'd shudder all right," he vowed, his husky chuckle sending a delicious ripple of gooseflesh dancing over her bare skin. "All night long."

"I don't know why you're so concerned. I don't even feel weak, just a little drunk."

"That's because I took just enough blood to keep me going until we can get back to London and I can find a butcher shop." He paused. "Or a nice plump puppy."

She sat up on one elbow, gaping at him in open-mouthed horror.

"I was only jesting! I haven't eaten a single puppy." He waited until she was nestled back in his arms before adding, "Kittens are so much more tender and delicious."

She gave a coil of his chest hair a punishing tweak. "You know, you really shouldn't blame yourself for succumbing to temptation. Haven't you heard the old legends? Mortals have always had supernatural powers of persuasion over vampires." She rolled over onto his chest, batting her eyelashes at him. "Only weak-willed vampires, of course."

He smoothed a tousled curl from her cheek, his gaze still heavy-lidded with desire. "When it comes to you, I'm as weak-willed as a newborn babe."

"Indeed? Well, perhaps we should put that claim to the test."

Ignoring his protest, she wiggled out of his embrace and scooted to the opposite side of the bed.

Keenly aware of his appreciative gaze drinking in the moonlit curves of her naked body, she lay back among the pillows and stretched like a cat before crooking one finger at him. "Come to me, Julian."

"Did you want me to come *to* you?" He prowled over to her like a marauding jungle cat, bringing his mouth close to her ear before whispering, "Or *in* you?"

She covered her shudder of desire with a haughty wave of one hand. "Put your hands on me."

She expected him to cup the softness of her breasts in his palms. Instead he began to trail his fingertips over every inch of her alabaster skin, deliberately avoiding the heavy globes of her breasts and the damp nest of curls between her legs. He stroked and caressed her until her every nerve ending was tingling and aching for more. She turned her face away from him and bit her lip, struggling to pretend indifference.

"Kiss me," she commanded when she could no longer endure another second of such sweet torture.

His hands gently parted her thighs and she gasped as he pressed that sweetest and most unholy of kisses to her throbbing flesh. She arched off the bed, her fingernails digging into the tick as he brought her to a climax so swift and fierce it left her trembling like a leaf in the wind.

Only then did he cover her mouth with his own, feeding her an intoxicating taste of her own pleasure.

She shoved at his shoulders, rolling him to his back, then straddled him, shaking her tousled mane of hair out of her eyes. "You're a very wicked and rebellious vampire, Julian Kane. I can see it's going to take more than just my powers of persuasion to enslave you."

He folded his hands behind his head, his grin as wicked as a pirate's. "Ready to break out the manacles, are we?"

She lifted her chin, a temptress's smile curving her lips. "I don't believe I'll require them."

As she ducked her head to touch the very tip of her tongue to one of his rigid nipples, he eyed her warily. "Have we been reading lurid Gothic novels again?"

She stole an impish glance at his face. "I'm afraid I've moved on to some naughty etchings I found stashed between the pages of one of the books in Adrian's library. I'm sure he'd be mortified if he knew I'd stumbled upon them. But you always did accuse me of being shamelessly inquisitive, didn't you?"

She lowered her head, the moist heat of her lips grazing the twitching muscles of his abdomen. He swallowed, his voice suddenly unsteady. "I'm beginning to believe it's one of your more endearing traits."

As she enfolded him in the softness of her lips, he arched off the bed with a guttural groan, his powerful body a slave to her will. Portia only took him deeper, determined to prove once and for all that her appetites could be just as insatiable as his.

* * *

Portia lay as limp as a rag doll in Julian's arms, her every muscle sated with pleasure. She was nearly asleep when she felt something hard and persistent nudging the softness of her rump.

She moaned softly without opening her eyes, her body instinctively wiggling even closer to his. "I thought you were only going to *seduce* me three times a night. Wouldn't this make . . . oh, I don't know . . . seven? Nineteen?"

His smoky whisper tickled her ear. "Six and a half. But who's counting? Perhaps I should have warned you that there is one advantage to being turned into a vampire as a young man."

"Mmmmmm? And just what would that be?"

He cupped the softness of her breasts in his hands, gently rubbing his thumbs over her nipples as he slid into her from behind. "Stamina."

For the first time in a very long while, Julian allowed himself to dream.

He stood in a church, no longer banished from the presence of God. Sunlight streamed through the stained-glass windows, warming his face and glinting off the glossy silk of Portia's curls. She smiled up at him, her bright blue eyes sparkling with love and tenderness. She wore a snow white choker around her throat and a halo of white rosebuds in her hair, making her look like the angel she was.

His loving gaze drifted downward, lingering on the gentle swell of her belly. Joy flooded his heart as he realized she was carrying a child—a child he had given her.

He lifted his head to find Adrian there, too, beaming at him proudly. Caroline stood beside her husband with little Eloisa nestled in the crook of her arm.

As Julian winked at the toddler, she clapped her plump hands and crowed, "Unca Jules! Unca Jules!"

Portia's merry ripple of laughter rang like bells through his soul. He tugged her into his arms, drinking in the radiance of his bride's beauty before claiming her with a tender kiss.

When Portia's eyes first fluttered open, she thought she must surely be dreaming. Surely this was no different from a thousand other dawns when she had imagined waking in Julian's bed.

He sprawled next to her on the feather tick, his eyes closed and one long leg thrown possessively over hers. With the pearly light of dawn glazing his body, he was truly a work of pure masculine beauty—long and lean and perfectly muscled, rough where she was smooth, hard where she was soft. She rolled to her side and studied him with drowsy delight, content to make this dream last for as long as she could.

The usual boyish forelock tumbled over his brow. Although her fingers ached to brush it back, she stayed her hand, not wanting to risk disturbing him in this rare moment of peace. A faint smile curved his sculpted lips, drawing the lines carved on either side of them into striking relief. Her gaze strayed lower, drinking in the impressive breadth of his chest, his lean hips, the tendrils of smoke rising from his skin.

Portia shot straight up in the bed, suddenly wide awake. Her panicked gaze flew to the window to discover the first rays of sunlight already creeping across the foot of the bed.

Acting purely on instinct, she gave Julian a violent shove, rolling him clean off the bed.

He landed in the floor with a painful thud. *"What in the hell . . . ?!"*

It took her several seconds of frantic fumbling to locate the blanket. Despite the stars of frost sprinkled across the windowpanes, they hadn't had much use for it last night. She finally found it balled up against the footboard of the bed along with the tattered scraps of her chemise. She shot the window another desperate glance. The sun was drifting higher on the horizon, its golden fingers coaxing a rosy blush from the sky. Ignoring Julian's muttered oaths, she tossed the blanket over him.

He sat up, but before he could cast away the blanket and expose himself to those ruthless rays, she threw herself on top of him, driving him back to the floor.

He went utterly still beneath her. It wasn't until she saw one lean foot protruding from the end of the blanket less than an inch from her nose that she realized she was straddling his head.

"You do know this would be a great deal more fun for the both of us without the blanket," he finally said, his voice muffled but dry.

She crawled off of him, switched ends, and poked her head beneath the blanket. He was eyeing her balefully, like a large, ill-tempered cat who resented being stirred from its nap.

"We slept through the dawn! The sun is coming up. You were starting to smoke!"

This time his oath was both more profane and more succinct. Without any warning, he rolled away from her, disappearing beneath the bed and dragging the blanket with him.

She hesitated for a moment, not sure how to proceed, then slowly dipped her head to peer under the bed. Julian was still glaring at her, his tousled hair furred with dust. Fortunately the bed was high enough for there to be a dark and cozy little cave beneath it.

"It will be hours before the sun goes down and we're able to travel," she said, feeling quite miserable on his behalf. "What should I do?"

He caught one of her wrists in his hand and tugged, his scowl melting into a winsome smile. "Keep me company."

Portia perched on the edge of the bed, drawing on one of her silk stockings by the light of the rising moon. "You might have told me earlier that those were *your* naughty etchings I found, not Adrian's."

Julian lifted her hair and bent to brush a kiss

over her nape, sending a shiver of fresh desire down her spine. "Why tell you when it was so much more fun to show you? I purchased them from an upperclassman when I first arrived at Oxford. I was studying them one day, trying to figure out which end was up, when I heard Adrian coming up the stairs. I stashed them between the pages of the first book I could put my hands on and forgot all about them. Until you so generously reminded me of their existence."

"You may have forgotten where you stashed them, but you obviously didn't forget what you saw. Or which end was up." She rose and stepped into her delicate kid slippers before turning into his embrace. "Why, I didn't even know that . . ." Blushing furiously, she stood on tiptoe and whispered something in his ear before finishing with ". . . was humanly possible!"

Lifting a hand to caress one of her rosy cheeks, he grinned down at her. "I'm not a human, remember?"

With Julian to share it, the day hadn't been nearly as long as Portia feared. As soon as the fiery orb of the sun had slipped beneath the horizon, he had gone out and foraged some wood so she could build a fire in the bedchamber's stone hearth. He'd also found a few forgotten potatoes in the house's vegetable cellar. While he had drawn fresh water from the well outside, she had roasted the potatoes in their steaming jackets to appease her growling stomach. Oddly enough, sitting cross-legged and barefoot in front of the fire wearing nothing but Julian's shirt while he fed her tender bits of potato had made her feel as pampered as a queen. She had also used the fire to warm water for an impromptu bath for the both of them.

Of course once they were both all wet and slick and naked . . .

Portia sighed wistfully and stroked the wayward strand of hair she loved so well from his brow, reluctant to admit that their moonlit idyll was coming to an end. She'd already donned her gown, smoothing out the wrinkles as best she could. The holy water had dried without leaving so much as a spot.

Julian draped his cravat around her neck. He used it to pull her into him for a lingering kiss before gently knotting it into an impromptu scarf that would cover the fresh marks on her throat. "Adrian and Caroline are probably frantic with worry by now. If I don't get you home soon, my own brother may very well challenge me to pistols at dawn. And we both know how disastrous that would be."

"Once he realizes we're safe, he'll probably just demand to know if your intentions toward me are honorable." Although Portia kept her tone light so as not to betray the cost of the question, she could not hide the shadow of doubt in her eyes. "Are they?"

His somber expression reminded her all over again of what had passed between them in the crypt. And in the night. He caressed her shoulders, gazing deep into her eyes. "When we return to London, I have every intention of swallowing my stubborn pride and begging my brother to help me capture Valentine and retrieve the only gift worthy of a woman like you."

"Your soul?" she whispered, hardly daring to speak the words aloud.

He shook his head, a rueful smile curving his lips. "Not *my* soul, angel. Because as soon as I wrest it away from Valentine, I plan to surrender it into your keeping, along with my heart and the rest of what remains of my mortal life."

Blinded by a sweet rush of tears, Portia threw her arms around his neck. "For a man without a soul, you're quite the romantic, Julian Kane."

He buried his face in her hair and gently rubbed her back. "Then I guess you won't object when I insist that we name our first daughter after you."

"You want to name our first daughter Portia?"

He drew back, blinking down at her in mock confusion. "Portia? Why, I would have sworn your name was Prunella!"

Portia was still chiding him for teasing her as they crunched their way across the frozen fields toward the lights of the nearest manor house. Although Julian had wrapped her in his coat and draped his arm over her shoulders, Portia was beginning to sorely miss her mink-lined mantle and muff.

As he disappeared into the manor's low-slung stone stable, she crouched behind a bush, her teeth clenched to still their chattering. He emerged from beneath the stable's thatched roof a short while later, leading a jaunty little bay mare harnessed to an equally jaunty little cabriolet. The elegant two-wheeled cart had just enough room for two.

As he closed his hands around her waist and lifted her effortlessly to its padded seat, she whispered, "Did you leave a note explaining that we were only borrowing the horse and cart and would be returning them on the morrow?"

He gave her a narrow look. "Why do I need a soul when I have you to be my conscience?"

"I'd just hate to see you get your soul back only to be hanged for horse thievery. Wallingford would be beside himself with delight."

"Ever practical, aren't we, my love?" He climbed aboard the cabriolet, settling into the seat next to her. "As soon as we arrive at Adrian's, we'll roust one of his grooms out of his warm bed and order the poor fellow to return both horse and carriage to our anonymous benefactor."

Despite the need for both stealth and haste, he refused to proceed until he'd tucked several soft woolen blankets around her, creating a cozy nest. He walked the mare all the way to the road, then gently tapped the whip on the horse's flanks to coax her into a trot.

Portia laughed with delight when frosty feathers of snow began to spill from the luminous night sky. Julian wrapped an arm around her, tugging her close. She rested her head against his shoulder, unable to remember a time when she had felt so happy and full of hope for the future. She knew there were dangers ahead to face, but at the moment she felt utterly safe in the arms of the man she loved.

Everything sounded like music to her ears—the crisp clip-clop of the horse's hooves, the jingle of the harness bells in the frosty air, the whisper of the falling snow. A part of her wished they would never reach London, but could simply continue on this road forever.

Despite her determination to savor every second, the steady rocking of the cart and the sheer delight of being cocooned in Julian's arms soon lulled her exhausted body into a doze.

The next time Portia stirred and opened her eyes, Julian was turning the cabriolet down a cobbled street lined with elegant town houses.

She yawned and stretched like a drowsy little

cat. "I don't suppose we're going to find Adrian in a very amiable temper."

He slowed the horse to a walk. "I just hope he gives me a chance to explain before he whips out that infernal crossbow of his."

"Don't be silly." She gave his knee an encouraging pat. "He wouldn't dare shoot you without asking me first."

He slanted her an amused glance. "Remind me to stay on your good side, you bloodthirsty little minx."

"You can start right now," she said, tipping her face up to his for a long, lingering kiss.

When they broke apart, it was snowing even harder. Portia frowned up at the sky. "Those are some of the biggest snowflakes I've ever seen."

Julian brushed a flake from her cheek, then rubbed his fingers together, creating a black, sooty smear. He slowly lifted his eyes to hers. "It's not snow. It's ash."

His face going grim, he withdrew his arm from her and slapped the reins on the mare's back, doubling her pace. Portia clung to the side of the cabriolet as they raced the final block to Adrian's mansion. As they approached the house, they both realized that something was wrong.

Terribly wrong.

Because there was no house—only a burned-out hulk silhouetted against the night sky.

Seventeen

Gray clouds of ash and cinders drifted through the air, tainting the falling snow. The stench of charred wood hung over the smoldering ruins of the mansion. Here and there plumes of smoke were still rising like ghosts from the fallen beams and blackened walls. A rocking horse lay on its side among the rubble, its brightly colored paint blistered and peeled. As Portia watched in numb horror, the entire second story stairwell collapsed in a shower of sparks, burying the grand pianoforte beneath it.

Overturned buckets littered the small square of scorched lawn in front of the house. A cart with an abandoned hand pump slumped near the corner of the street, its leather hose curled up like a defeated snake—damning evidence that the fire brigade had either arrived too late or given up too soon.

Adrian's neighbors and several weeping servants huddled together on the opposite side of the street, some still in dressing gowns and nightcaps. As Portia climbed down from the cabriolet, mired in the slow motion haze of a nightmare, she could feel the sting of their pitying glances.

She drifted toward the house with Julian moving like a shadow behind her.

"Portia!"

The joyful cry startled her so badly she nearly shrieked. She could only stand frozen in place as Vivienne came sprinting toward her. She had been so mesmerized by the sight of the house that she hadn't even seen Larkin's carriage parked beneath the gaunt branches of a nearby oak.

Throwing her arms around Portia's neck, Vivienne burst into tears. "Oh, Portia, I'm so glad you're all right! We were so terrified for you!"

"We?" Portia whispered, equally terrified of giving too much weight to the word.

Vivienne grabbed her hand and tried to tug her toward the carriage but Portia's feet remained rooted to the walk.

Oblivious to her agony, Vivienne kept up her steady stream of chatter. "When there was no word from you or Julian today, we feared the worst. I tried to tell them all that things would work out for the best because they almost always do, but then one of Adrian's servants came banging on our door shortly before midnight to tell us the house was on fire. I have to confess that when we arrived and I realized how dire things were, I nearly lost faith myself. But now that *you're* here, I just know everything will . . ." She trailed off, finally realizing that she was still tugging but Portia wasn't moving.

"It's Portia!" she called over her shoulder. "She's come home!"

Several figures slowly emerged from behind the carriage, their faces dappled with shadows from the branches above.

There was Larkin, his eyes even more soulful and wary than usual. Wilbury, his nightshirt billowing around his bony body like a shroud.

And finally Adrian, holding on to Caroline as if he never intended to let her go.

Portia's relief was so keen she felt her knees give way. Julian caught her before she could fall, holding her upright until she could find the strength to stand.

Gently disengaging herself from his arms, she moved toward her family, her vision blurred by grateful tears. She was almost upon them before she realized that their faces were so haunted they looked like shades of themselves. It was as if both a day and a lifetime had passed since she'd last seen them.

Caroline was garbed in her flowing white nightdress with Larkin's greatcoat draped over her shoulders while Adrian wore only trousers, boots, and a soot-streaked shirt that hung open over his powerful chest. As Portia approached, neither one of them made a move toward her. She gave Larkin a bewildered glance, but he simply folded his arms over his chest and lowered his gaze, studying the scuffed toes of his boots.

She glanced at Wilbury and found a sight even more chilling than the desecrated ruins of the house. The old man's chin was quivering and tearstains streaked his papery cheeks.

Despite the gentleness in Adrian's hands as he stroked his wife's tangled hair, there was a wild look in his eyes that Portia had never seen before. Caroline's face was devoid of any expression at all. It was as blank as the painted face of one of Eloisa's dolls.

Portia gently touched her sister's sleeve, her hand already beginning to tremble. "Where's Ellie, Caro? Is she asleep in the carriage?"

Caroline drew in a shuddering breath before lifting her lifeless eyes to Portia's. "She's gone. They took Eloisa with them. They took my baby."

At first Portia thought the inhuman sound of grief and rage had come from her own throat. But it was Julian who stumbled a few feet away from them and stood gazing up at the house as if it was the tomb of his every dream.

"Your plan must have been a spectacular success," Adrian said, his voice still raw from the smoke he'd inhaled. "You obviously succeeded in driving Valentine into a murderous frenzy. As you well know, vampires hate fire so she sent her minions to do her dirty work for her. If Wilbury hadn't smelled smoke and sounded the alarm, we'd have all burned to death in our beds. By the time Caroline rushed into the nursery, it was too late. Eloisa was gone. The bastards had taken her."

Julian shook his head, his own voice nearly as hoarse as Adrian's. "I never dreamed she'd come after you. It was me she wanted. I should have been here . . . waiting for her. Or destroyed her when I had the chance."

Vivienne clutched at Portia's arm through the sleeve of Julian's coat. "Where have the two of you been? We feared Valentine had taken you as well."

Portia gazed into her sister's guileless blue eyes, at a loss for words. How could she explain that it wasn't Valentine who had taken her but Julian? And not just once, but numerous times. While little Eloisa was being wrenched from her bed by brutal strangers as the only home she'd ever known collapsed around her in flames, she and Julian had been huddled together in the cabriolet, still drunk on the pleasure of each other's kisses.

She was fumbling for an answer when Adrian gently handed Caroline off to Wilbury and walked over to her. Before she realized what he meant to do, he tugged at the end of

Julian's cravat, unwinding it from her throat and revealing the fresh puncture marks for all of them to see.

Larkin swore and Vivienne gasped. Wilbury simply bowed his head, his rheumy eyes brimming with sorrow. Caroline didn't even blink.

There was a moment when even the snow seemed to stop. Then Adrian lunged for Julian, closing the distance between them in three long strides. Before any of them could react, his powerful fist had smashed into his brother's jaw.

Julian staggered but did not fall. Nor did he fight back. He simply spread his arms as if to make himself an even larger target for his brother's wrath. Portia doubted he would have lifted a hand to defend himself if Adrian had picked up one of the charred scraps of wood scattered across the yard and driven it through his heart.

Before Adrian could do just that, both she and Larkin made a grab for him, each of them seizing one of his arms. He could have shaken her off as if she were no more bothersome than a gnat, but Portia knew he would never deliberately hurt her.

"You bastard!" he spat at Julian, straining against their grip. "I should have known you

couldn't keep your greedy fan
greedy hands—off of her!"

"No, Adrian!" Portia cried, still tug
tically at his arm. "It wasn't like that a
didn't want to do it. I was the one who
that he drink from me."

Adrian wheeled on her, shaking himself free of Larkin's grasp. "Why, Portia? Was he dying again? Or had he simply run out of the port he swills as if it were water?" He swung back toward Julian, shaking his head in disgust. "Didn't you hurt her enough in the crypt? Did you have to make her a victim of your accursed appetites again? Does your greed and lust and selfishness know no bounds?"

Julian simply gazed at him, his face nearly as expressionless as Caroline's.

Adrian's own face crumpled. His fists were no longer clenched with rage but helplessness. "You're my little brother, Jules. I've loved you since you were old enough to crawl out of your crib and toddle after my heels. And I've done everything within my power to protect you and save you. But at what cost? Portia's innocence? My daughter's life?"

"Don't blame yourself, Adrian," Julian said

"Mercy was your only sin and I'm sure God will forgive you for that."

Portia watched in disbelief as he turned and began to walk away from them all.

"This wasn't your fault, Julian," she said fiercely, hastening after him. "And Valentine won't dare harm a hair on Eloisa's head as long as she believes there's a chance you'll come back to her. We'll find her. We'll bring her home together!" Growing more frantic with each step, she caught the back of his shirtsleeve, trying to tug him to a halt.

He wheeled on her, his fangs in full bloom, his eyes burning like live coals in the savage mask of his face. She recoiled before she could stop herself.

"Don't you see, Portia? Adrian's right! This is exactly what I was trying to warn you about. It's why I stayed away from you for all those years."

Hot tears began to spill down her cheeks. "But you admitted that in all that time you never stopped loving me!"

"My love poisons everything I touch! If I let it destroy you, I'll be even more damned than I already am!" Despite the violence in his voice, he reached to tenderly brush a tear from her cheek with the pad of his thumb. "You should have let me die in that crypt."

As he turned to walk away from her, Portia was surprised to feel a scalding rush of fury. "You know, you're absolutely right. I'm sorry I kept you alive. And I'm sorry I ever laid eyes on you. Because there hasn't been a moment since then when I've been free of the burden of loving you. And I haven't drawn a single breath that hasn't been poisoned with that love!"

He just kept walking.

"If you walk out of my life this time, Julian Kane, don't bother coming back! Ever!"

He stopped in his tracks, then turned and strode back to her. Snatching her up by the shoulders, he gave her a savage kiss that was both bitter and sweet, laced with a lifetime of longing and an eternity of regrets.

Then he was striding away from her again, leaving her with nothing but the taste of his kiss on her lips and the ghost of a passion she might never feel again.

She took a stumbling step after him, but was halted by Caroline's impassioned cry. "Let him go, Portia! He can't change what he is and he's brought nothing but heartbreak and disaster to this house. I wish to God he'd never come home!" Her voice breaking on a wail of agony, she crumpled to her knees, clutching her stomach.

"Get a doctor, Larkin!" Adrian shouted, scrambling to his wife's side.

Portia stood frozen on the walk, torn between her sister's suffering and the man she loved. With one final look at Julian's receding back, she snatched up her skirts and ran to Caroline.

Dropping to her knees, she squeezed her sister's icy hand to her breast. "Everything will be all right, Caro. We'll find Ellie and bring her home. I swear it on my life."

When she glanced back over her shoulder again, the snow and ash was falling on an empty walk. Julian was gone.

Eighteen

Cuthbert nestled deeper into his bed, sighing with contentment. With a heated brick wrapped in flannel to warm his toes and the flaming plum pudding he'd eaten at supper still warming his belly, he was looking forward to a long cozy nap on this cold winter night.

He was nearly asleep when something began to tap on his bedchamber window. The snow must have turned to sleet, he thought drowsily, rolling over and drawing the blankets up to his chin. The tapping continued, not only persistent, but oddly rhythmic.

He abruptly sat up in the bed, the tassel of

his nightcap flopping over one eye. Perhaps the weight of the snow had simply snapped a branch and set it to smacking against his windowpane. Knowing there was only one way to find out, he parted the bed curtains and reluctantly slid his feet to the cold wooden floor.

His heart settling into an uneasy rhythm, he crept toward the window. The waning firelight cast peculiar shadows on the wall, making even the familiar shapes of wardrobe and washstand look strange and forbidding. He was nearly to the window when he caught a glimpse of a winged shadow out of the corner of his eye. He whirled around, but everything in the room looked exactly as it had.

Shaking his head at his own fancy, he turned back to the window. Julian was perched on the narrow ledge outside, peering directly at him.

Letting out a high-pitched shriek, Cuthbert stumbled backward. He fumbled inside the ruffled neck of his nightshirt, wrapping his shaking hand around the piece of jewelry he'd obtained for just such an eventuality. Snapping the chain with a desperate twist, he whipped out the silver crucifix and thrust it toward the window.

Julian recoiled, letting out a disgusted hiss. "Oh, for God's sake, Cubby," he said just loudly enough to be heard through the window, "put that thing in a drawer and open the bloody window. I'm freezing my ass off out here." When Cuthbert only added a theatrical flourish, he sighed and rolled his eyes. "You don't need the crucifix anyway. I can't come into the room unless you invite me."

"Oh," Cuthbert said, mildly disappointed that both his dramatic gesture and the two pounds he'd spent on the bauble had been wasted.

He obediently went over and dropped it into a drawer of the wardrobe before returning to edge open the window a crack. "So why have you come here? Did your master send you?"

Julian frowned. "My master?"

"You know—the Dark Prince. Lucifer. Beelzebub."

Julian glared at him. "Although I suspect I'll be making the gentleman's acquaintance sooner than I'd like, we're not on the friendliest of terms right now."

"Then why have you come?"

"If you'll invite me in, I'll tell you."

Cuthbert eyed him suspiciously. "How do I

know this isn't just a trick so you can sink your fangs into my throat and suck every drop of blood from my poor, helpless body?"

Julian's hand shot through the narrow opening, catching him by the ruffled collar of his nightshirt and jerking him back through the window until they were nose to nose. "Because it would be much quicker to just drag you out this window and drop you three stories to the ground below. With all your bones broken, I doubt you'd be able to struggle very hard when I was sucking the life out of you."

As Julian released the choking pressure on his nightshirt, Cuthbert said with withering politeness, "Very well. Please *do* come in."

"How on earth did you get up here?" he inquired, backing away as Julian came clambering over the ledge.

"Trust me—you'd rather not know," Julian replied, dusting the snow off of the shoulders of his shirt.

"What happened to your coat?"

"I gave it to a pretty girl. Would you have expected anything less of me?"

"I suppose not."

Cuthbert leaned out the window and peered

both ways down the empty street before drawing it closed. "You're lucky no one saw you arrive. Wallingford and his hired guns have been following me everywhere for the past few days."

"Why is that?"

"From what I can gather, he's hoping you'll lure me back into your snare and he can catch us at something that would warrant a trip to either prison or the gallows. Rumor has it that he's absolutely furious because your brother paid off all your gambling debts. He's also obsessed with the notion that you're intent upon some new lechery now that you're living beneath the same roof as the lovely and chaste Miss Portia Cabot."

Julian averted his eyes, his lean face grim. "Well, he doesn't have to worry about that anymore."

"Because she's no longer chaste or you're no longer living beneath the same roof?"

In lieu of replying, Julian simply gave the rumpled cuffs of his shirt a practiced flick.

"Oh, dear," Cuthbert said, sinking down against the windowsill. "She's no longer chaste and that's *why* you're no longer living beneath the same roof. Why am I not surprised?"

Still avoiding his eyes, Julian began to prowl restlessly around the room. When he neared the bed, he recoiled, his nostrils flaring with distaste. "Christ, Cubby, what is that awful stench?" When Cuthbert didn't answer, he drew back the bed curtains to reveal a string of garlic bulbs dangling from the canopy.

Beneath Julian's reproachful gaze, Cuthbert retrieved them and tossed them out the window to the snow below.

He returned to find Julian gazing down at the glass of water on the table next to the bed. "Please tell me that's not—"

"Oh, no," Cuthbert said hastily. "That's just water. Sometimes I get thirsty in the middle of the night and I hate to trot all the way down to the kitchen in my dressing gown."

"You know, if I was going to eat you," Julian said pleasantly, "I'd have probably done it the time you drank too much wine at that little tavern in Florence and passed out in the opera dancer's lap. It would have been so much easier than throwing you over my shoulder and carrying you all the way back up the hill to our hotel."

Cuthbert blew out a sheepish sigh. "Truth be

told, Jules, I've missed you something terrible. My father keeps dragging me to afternoon musicales and high teas and excruciatingly long sermons on the physical and spiritual benefits of temperance."

Julian shuddered. "I'm surprised you haven't been praying for a swift death at the fangs of the nearest vampire."

"I read your letter, you know. About how you became a vampire and what that dreadful rascal Duvalier did to you."

Julian frowned at him in bewilderment. "How could you have read it? It was returned to me with the seal unbroken."

"I didn't want you to know I'd read it so I melted a candle and resealed it." He pulled off his nightcap and began to toy with its tassel, avoiding his friend's eyes. "If you must know, I was only sulking because it hurt my feelings when that brother of yours and his friend called me your 'minion.'"

"Don't be ridiculous! You're not a minion! A minion is a mortal who willingly serves a vampire by taking care of his business during the daylight hours. He runs errands and provides the vampire with funds when he doesn't have . . ." Julian trailed off as Cuthbert cocked one sandy eyebrow at him. "Never mind."

He paced a few feet away, then turned back, his soulful dark eyes as earnest and desperate as Cuthbert had ever seen them. "I didn't come here tonight because I needed your money, Cubby. I came because I need your help. A little girl's life and my entire future may very well be at stake."

"By any chance, will this help I provide you put me in dreadful danger?"

Julian nodded solemnly. "Of the very worst sort."

"Will I be risking both life and limb and possibly my own immortal soul?"

"I'm afraid so. We may even face a painful and gruesome destruction at the hands of my enemies."

Cuthbert shrugged. "Oh, well. Beats dying of gout or old age in my warm cozy bed. Or attending another temperance lecture with my father." He donned his nightcap, adjusting it to a cocky angle. "So when do we leave?"

It was shortly after dawn when the physician finally emerged from the bedchamber of Larkin and Vivienne's town house where Adrian had carried Caroline just a few short hours before.

Adrian pushed himself away from the wall he'd been slumped against, his eyes burning with hope despite his unshaven jaw and haggard face. Larkin slipped a steadying arm around Vivienne, who had just returned from one of her numerous trips to the nursery to make sure the twins were still tucked safely in their beds. Portia turned away from the window at the end of the corridor. She'd been watching the sun begin its slow creep over the horizon and wondering if Julian was safe from its deadly rays.

Adrian still wore his soot-streaked shirt and ash-covered boots. "How is she, doctor?"

Dr. McKinley was a short, stout man with a snub nose and kind eyes that might very well twinkle in less grave circumstances. "I'm afraid your wife has suffered a severe shock. But I have reason to believe the baby she's carrying will be just fine."

"Thank God!" Adrian sagged against the wall, blowing out a shuddering sigh of relief. He ran a shaking hand through his disheveled hair. "Please tell me what I can do for her."

"I believe the baby is safe . . . at least for now.

But I fear what might happen if you don't find the villains who abducted your little girl."

"Oh, we'll find them," Adrian vowed, the look in his eye making the doctor take an uneasy step backward.

"Have you contacted the authorities?" the physician asked.

Exchanging a look with Adrian, Larkin cleared his throat. "I was once a constable myself, Dr. McKinley. I can assure you that all of the proper authorities have been notified and that everything humanly possible will be done to return my niece to her mother's arms before the sun has set today."

"May I go to her?" Adrian asked, already starting forward.

The man held up a restraining hand, a rather brave move considering Adrian's imposing size. "Not just yet." He peered over his wire-rimmed spectacles at each of them in turn, his gaze finally settling on Portia. "Are you Portia?"

She stepped forward. "I am."

"Your sister wishes to see you first."

"Me? She wants to see me?" Portia could not hide her surprise. She had assumed that Caroline could only blame her for what had happened. Her older sister had forgiven her many faults and foibles throughout their lives, but surely even Caroline's grace couldn't cover up a sin this damning.

She exchanged a bewildered glance with Adrian, but he only gave her a weary nod, encouraging her to respect his wife's wishes.

Mustering her courage, she brushed past the doctor and slipped into the bedchamber, gently drawing the door shut behind her.

Caroline was lying on the bed in one of Vivienne's lavender dressing gowns, propped up on a nest of pillows. Her pale face was turned toward the window as if all of her hopes rested on the coming of the dawn.

She spoke before Portia could. "I'm afraid they'll keep her somewhere dark. She doesn't like the dark, you know. I've always told her not to be afraid, that monsters don't live in the dark." She turned her gaze from the window to Portia, her eyes as clear and gray as the dawn sky. "I shouldn't have lied to her, should I? It was wrong of me."

Portia crossed to the bed, sinking down next

to her. "You used to tell me the same thing when I was little. But I never believed you."

"That's because you wanted to believe that there were all sorts of monsters nesting beneath your bed—pixies and bogies and goblins, all looking for the right little girl to break their dark enchantment and set them free."

"Well, I'm obviously not the right little girl." Portia bowed her head, hoping to hide the tears misting her eyes.

Caroline rumpled her uncombed curls, reminding them both of a time when they had only each other to cling to. "I shouldn't have said those terrible things about Julian. He may be a monster but he's *your* monster and it wasn't fair of me."

Portia took her sister's hand, swallowing past the knot in her throat. "I need to tell you what happened in the crypt."

Caroline shook her head, a ghost of her old, familiar smile curving her lips. "No, you don't. There are secrets that should only be shared between a woman and the man she loves. As far as I'm concerned, there's only one thing you need to do for me."

Portia gave Caroline's hand a fierce squeeze.

"Anything. You know I'd do anything at all for you."

Caroline cupped Portia's cheek in her other hand, enunciating each word as if it was the last she would ever utter. *"Bring my baby home."*

Adrian and Larkin were sitting on their mounts atop the small rise overlooking Chillingsworth Manor when Portia came cantering up on the dappled filly Adrian had given her for her twenty-first birthday. She wore a dark blue riding habit of figured merino and a sturdy pair of calf-length boots. She'd drawn her hair back into a serviceable leather queue at the nape of her neck and draped a silk scarf around her throat to hide the fresh bruises.

Just as she had expected, Adrian didn't try to lecture or dissuade her. He'd been well aware that she'd been following them ever since they left the outskirts of London. If he'd have wanted to stop her from accompanying them on this mission, he would have done so long before now.

Instead, he simply slanted her a long look. "You know why we're here, don't you? If we destroy Valentine . . ."

He didn't have to finish. If they destroyed Valentine, then Julian's soul would revert to the vampire who had stolen *her* soul over two hundred years ago. Even if Julian was able to locate such a creature, the vampire would probably be so powerful that he—or she—would be nearly impossible to defeat.

Portia gazed straight ahead, her profile no less determined than theirs. "Julian made his own choice when he walked out on . . ." she swallowed, closing her eyes briefly ". . . on all of us. All that matters now is finding Eloisa and bringing her home."

Adrian nodded his approval before unstrapping a small but lethal crossbow and a quiver of wooden bolts from his saddle and handing them across to her. He and Larkin had spent most of the day trolling the armories, blacksmiths, and docks just to replace a handful of the ancient weapons they'd lost in the fire.

Portia slid the crossbow's strap over her shoulder and fastened the quiver of bolts to the belt of her riding habit, the motion she'd practiced so many times in the deserted ballroom of the mansion as natural to her as breathing.

The manor below looked even sadder and

more dilapidated washed by the golden hue of the late afternoon sun. Sunlight sparkled off the thin crust of snow that draped its sagging roof and crumbling chimneys, but still failed to brighten the shadow of gloom that hung over the place.

Before they could drive their horses down the hill, the crisp winter wind carried the sound of muffled hoofbeats to their ears. They turned to find another rider cresting the knoll behind them.

For one agonizing moment, Portia could barely breathe. Then she saw the startling shock of white hair that crowned the head of the approaching rider.

Larkin shook his head in disbelief. "Surely you jest."

Adrian shot Portia an accusing glance, but she could only shrug. "I had no idea he was following me."

Wilbury came riding up on one of Adrian's most spirited—and most expensive—stallions. The butler was hunched over the saddle, his bony body bowed nearly double beneath the weight of numerous weapons, including a bow and a quiver of arrows, a leather sash sporting several stakes of varying lengths, and a blade that looked suspiciously like a kitchen carving knife. He'd even jammed an ancient flintlock pistol into the waistband of his old-fashioned knee breeches. Despite his attempt at bravado, he still looked as if he'd be more comfortable riding in the back of a hearse.

He drew his mount up beside Portia's, drolly intoning, "You rang?"

"No, I most certainly did not ring," Adrian snapped. "Have you lost your wits, old man? You should be at home polishing the silver, not risking your fragile old bones cantering across the countryside on a horse that's barely been broken."

"In case you've forgotten, I don't have any silver to polish. Nor a home to polish it in. Which is why I've come to lend you my assistance. I've lived a long and full life, my lord. What's the worst that could happen to me?"

Eyeing his cadaverous form, Larkin bit back a grin. "They might mistake you for one of their own and try to make you their king?"

Wilbury gave him a withering look. "With a little good fortune and some excellent shooting on *your* part, Mr. Larkin, I might even live to see my sixty-fourth birthday."

Larkin's eyes widened in disbelief while Portia hid a sudden coughing fit behind her riding glove.

Adrian studied him through narrowed eyes. "Wilbury, you had to be at *least* sixty when I was in short pants."

"Nonsense," the butler said with a dignified sniff. "I just seemed older because you were younger. And you needn't worry that I'll get in your way. It's not as if I don't know how to handle myself in these situations. I can assure you that I saw my share of battle in my youth."

Larkin snorted. "Battled the Norman hordes when they invaded England, did you?"

Portia reached over and gave the old man's gnarled hand a squeeze. "I would consider it an honor to ride into battle at your side, Wilbury."

"Thank you, Miss Portia," he replied with equal earnestness. "I wouldn't have come, but I was worried about Miss Eloisa. You see, I'm the only one who's able to comfort her when she awakens from a nightmare. A nice cup of warm milk and a few verses of 'Sally in Our Alley' and she usually goes right back to sleep."

Portia blinked away the sting of tears, hoping Wilbury would blame them on the chill wind whipping across the hillside. "I'm sure you'll be a tremendous comfort to her when we find her."

Adrian glanced over his shoulder at the rapidly sinking sun. "If we're going to go, we'd best go now before the twins show up on a pair of ponies, waving wooden swords."

Following his lead, they spurred their mounts down the hill, determined not to waste another precious minute of daylight.

They stormed the manor as if it *were* a battlefield, ripping every scrap of crepe from every window and flooding its dusty rooms and deserted corridors with winter sunshine. Portia and Adrian searched the upstairs chambers and attics for any sign of secret stairwells or passages while Larkin and Wilbury combed the basement kitchens and cellars, crossbows at the ready.

Portia started into a spacious bedchamber on the third floor, then froze in her tracks. Two empty sets of iron manacles hung from iron hooks set deep in the wall. She shuddered, remembering how Valentine had offered to let Raphael's minions keep her *occupied* while she entertained Julian. Judging from the coppery tang still hanging in the air and the dark stains soaked into the wooden floor, she doubted they would be keeping anyone *occupied* ever again.

"What is it?" Adrian murmured, coming up behind her.

She shook her head. "Something I'd rather not remember."

He gave her shoulder a comforting squeeze before leading the way to the next room.

They returned to the ballroom just as Larkin and Wilbury were emerging from the lower reaches of the house, cobwebs draping their hair. Not surprisingly, Wilbury looked rather natural in them.

"Nothing," Larkin confirmed, his expression grim. "No vampires. No minions. And worst of all—no Eloisa. We didn't even find a single coffin where a vampire might be hiding."

Portia frowned. "Could there be a family crypt located somewhere on the grounds of the estate?"

Larkin shook his head. "I took the liberty of paying a visit to the former owner of the property today. He swore his ancestors were all buried in the village churchyard."

Shadows had begun to creep down the length of the long room, bruising the fading light. Portia stole a glance at the French windows at the far end of the ballroom. "The sun is setting, Adrian. What are we going to do?"

He swore an anguished oath. "What I'd like to do is burn this accursed place to the ground and leave nothing but a pile of ashes where it once stood."

"I know you would but we don't dare," Portia said. "Not until we're absolutely sure they haven't stashed Eloisa somewhere within its walls."

"There's a good chance that Valentine knew this would be the first place we'd come looking for her," Larkin said. "If she warned this Raphael chap, none of the vampires may ever darken this door again. Perhaps we should return to the town house," he reluctantly suggested. "She might have sent some sort of note while we've been away."

"A ransom note?" Adrian snorted. "What's

she going to say? Bring me your brother's head or you'll never see your little girl alive again?"

"Well, actually you couldn't bring her Julian's head because if you cut it off, he would crumble into dust," Larkin pointed out.

Adrian just glared at him. "I was speaking figuratively."

"It's not his head she wants anyway," Portia said grimly. "It's his heart."

Adrian raked a hand through his hair. "Perhaps I should take one last look at the cellars myself before we go. If only to ease my own mind."

"I'll stay here and keep a lookout," Portia volunteered as Larkin and Adrian went striding toward the archway. "The cellar is the last place we want to get trapped if the vampires should return."

"Shall I stay with you?" Wilbury asked, casting a longing look after the men.

Portia drew her crossbow over her shoulder and slotted a bolt before giving him a reassuring smile. "I'll be just fine, Wilbury. They might need a strapping young fellow like you to pry open a door or move a heavy stone."

Nodding gratefully, he hurried after the men,

a youthful spring in his shuffle. Portia sank down on the marble steps that led up to the second-floor gallery, secretly grateful for the moment of privacy.

She could hardly believe that only two nights ago she had been whirling around this very ballroom in Julian's arms. It was even more difficult to believe that she might never again taste the tender and intoxicating pleasure she had found there. She almost wished he had been able to get her with child. She would have gladly endured whatever disgrace society chose to heap upon her just to have something to remember him by. A little boy perhaps with dashing dark eyes and a devilish grin. The image sent a jolt of raw pain through her heart.

She surged to her feet, disgusted with herself for being so selfish as to dream of holding her own child when little Eloisa was still at the mercy of those fiends. She prowled restlessly around the ballroom, watching the last of the sunlight bleed from the air. Unable to bear the oppressiveness of the encroaching shadows, she drew a tinder box from the skirt of her riding habit and lit several of the candles scattered throughout the room.

As she retrieved her crossbow and surveyed her handiwork from the foot of the stairs, she once again saw Julian's eyes sparkling down at her in the candlelight, felt his powerful hand against the small of her back, urging her closer with each graceful shift of his hips, each dizzying revolution around the ballroom floor. The dead leaves had swirled beneath their feet with each step, a crisp counterpart to the soaring strains of the waltz.

As Portia closed her eyes, she would have almost sworn she heard those strains again, drifting to her ears in a ghostly echo. She cocked her head to the side, so beside herself with yearning that it took her a minute to realize that she wasn't hearing a waltz, but a lullaby. A lullaby crooned in a lilting soprano with just a trace of a French accent.

She slowly opened her eyes and turned, her hackles rising.

Valentine stood at the top of the stairs just as she had on that night. Portia instinctively lifted the crossbow, then lowered it just as quickly. Because cradled tenderly in Valentine's arms was a sleeping Eloisa.

Nineteen

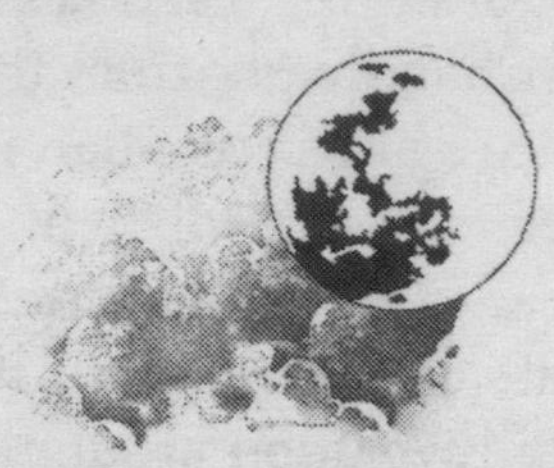

Portia frantically searched her niece's face beneath its tumbled cap of honey-colored curls, torn between horror and relief. Eloisa's little mouth was pursed into a perfect rosebud, her cheeks flushed a soft shade of pink. Her throat was unmarked and her chest rose and fell evenly beneath the ruffled bodice of her nightdress. She appeared to be both alive and unharmed.

Portia wanted to kick herself when she realized that Valentine must have come from the one room neither she nor Adrian had searched. The room with the nasty stains on the floor and the empty chains on the wall—chains that could be tugged or twisted to reveal a secret chamber or passageway.

Her finger caressed the trigger of the crossbow. She knew she had no hope of getting a clean shot at Valentine's heart—not as long as she was using Eloisa as a human shield.

Ellie was as sturdy as a little pony, but the vampire's pale, slender arms showed no sign of strain. Her supernatural strength would probably allow her to bear the child for hours without suffering so much as a pesky muscle twitch.

"I had a child of my own once, you know," Valentine said softly, gazing down into Eloisa's face with chilling fondness. "A little girl much like this one."

"What happened to her? Did you eat her?"

Valentine shot her a chiding glance. "Of course not. After I was attacked when I was strolling along the banks of the Seine and turned into a vampire, I never laid eyes on her again. I've often wondered what became of her." She sighed, her striking emerald eyes touched with a hint of sadness. "I suppose she would be long dead of old age by now."

Portia steeled herself against a pang of pity, knowing she could ill afford it. "If you were a mother once, then you must remember what it's like to suffer in fear for your child. My sister is suffering right now, her every moment a waking nightmare." She planted a foot on the bottom stair, bringing herself one step closer to Eloisa. "If there's even a scrap of humanity left in you, an ounce of mercy, please give me the baby and let me return her to her mother's arms."

"I really wish I could," Valentine said with a sigh of regret. "Especially since you asked so prettily. But I'm afraid your sister will just have to continue to suffer until Julian is back in my arms."

"That's the one thing I can't give you! I don't even know where he is."

"Surely he hasn't tired of you so quickly? Have you forgotten that I know exactly how insatiable his sexual appetites can be? Why, the first time we were together, it was an entire glorious week before he even let me out of his bed."

Portia's stomach clenched into an agonized knot as she desperately tried not to picture Julian doing to Valentine all of the same wild and tender things he'd done to her.

"Why would he abandon you when you can

give him the one thing I never could—your *love?"*

On Valentine's lips, the word sounded like an epithet. Eloisa stirred restlessly in her arms, her brow puckering in a frown.

"How could I expect you to understand the love of a mother for a child or the love of a woman for a man?" Portia demanded, inching up another step. "All you understand is greed and hunger and lust and violence. Love requires patience and tenderness and the willingness to sacrifice yourself for a greater good."

"Love does nothing but make you weak! It turns you into an object of pity and derision—a mewling pathetic creature no more fit to live than a worm squirming on the pavement after a hard summer rain."

Portia shook her head. "That's not love. That's obsession. True love doesn't make you weak. It makes you strong. It gives you the courage you need to get through even the loneliest night." Eloisa's lashes were beginning to flutter. Portia dared another step. "I used to think that falling in love meant being swept off your feet by a handsome prince who would never leave you.

But now I know that prince can love you so much that he feels he has no choice but to let you go."

A man's droll voice came from behind her, accompanied by a round of dry applause. "Bravo! I haven't heard such a touching performance since they coaxed Sarah Siddons out of retirement to trod the boards at the Drury Lane Theatre one final time."

Before Portia could even turn around, Eloisa opened her eyes, stretched out her chubby little arms toward the French doors and crowed, "Unca Jules! Unca Jules!"

Twenty

Portia slowly turned to find Julian standing just inside the French doors at the far end of the ballroom. He was garbed all in black. He wore a black shirt with an elegant fall of midnight lace at the collar and cuffs and black breeches tucked into a pair of tall leather boots. He had never looked more like a prince of the night.

"Had I known Miss Cabot was going to deliver one of her impassioned speeches on the sentimental nature of true love, I would have tucked an extra handkerchief in my pocket," he said, his cool, contemptuous gaze raking over her like a particularly beautiful but lethal blade.

Before Portia could assess just how much damage it had done to her heart, Valentine unleashed a bitter laugh. "I knew if *she* was here, you couldn't be far behind. It's quite tiresome the way you trot at her heels like a stag in rut."

"Don't flatter the chit, angel. You know I trot at every pretty girl's heels like a stag in rut . . . especially yours."

Eloisa was beginning to squirm in earnest now, her big gray eyes filling with frustrated tears. Whining and fretting, she arched her back, obviously wanting to be set down so she could run to her handsome uncle.

Valentine hissed at her, the tips of her fangs just beginning to show. "I knew I should have given you a few more drops of laudanum."

"Give her your necklace," Portia blurted out, terrified Valentine's legendary patience was about to run out.

Valentine shifted her glare to her. "What?"

"She likes to play with shiny baubles. If you give her your necklace, it may distract her for a little while."

Valentine lifted one haughty eyebrow. "The

sultan of Brunei gave me these sapphires. Do you have any idea how much they cost?"

"No," Portia replied, "but I'm sure you earned every penny of their price."

Valentine's eyes narrowed, but she drew the necklace over her neck and reluctantly surrendered it to Eloisa. Just as Portia had predicted, her niece was enchanted by the string of sparkling gems. Within seconds she was cocked back in the crook of Valentine's arm, happily sucking on the largest stone. Her eyelids began to droop again, obviously still beneath the spell of the laudanum.

Shuddering in disgust, Valentine returned her attention to Julian. "So have you come to plead for your niece's life? Because at the moment I would like nothing more than to see you on your knees before me."

Julian shrugged. "The brat's life is of little import to me. But I have brought you something I think you'll find much more filling."

He stepped outside the doors. He reappeared a brief moment later, driving a man ahead of him. Portia gasped as she recognized his friend from both the duel and the alley. Cuthbert's hands were bound behind him and a grubby cloth had been stuffed between his lips. One of his eyes was nearly swollen shut and ringed with an ugly bruise. Blood was still oozing from his split bottom lip. Valentine's patrician nostrils flared as if she'd scented a particularly juicy cut of meat.

Julian marched his captive across the ballroom. Without sparing Portia so much as a glance, he shoved Cuthbert roughly to the floor at the foot of the stairs. Resting one booted foot on the small of his back, he sketched Valentine a graceful bow. "For my lady's pleasure."

Valentine tilted her head to the side and studied his offering for several seconds. "He's a bit plump for my tastes, but I suppose it's the sentiment that counts."

"Ellie!" They all turned as Adrian's cry of mingled joy and anguish reverberated through the ballroom.

He came running into the room with Larkin and Wilbury just behind him, their weapons at the ready. While Julian looked mildly amused by their sudden appearance, Valentine didn't betray so much as a flinch of alarm. She didn't have to. Not as long as she was holding all of the cards—and Eloisa.

Adrian stumbled to a halt several feet from the stairs, his desperate gaze flicking from Eloisa to Portia and finally to Julian before returning to Valentine.

"Give me my daughter," he demanded, raising the crossbow in his hands and pointing it straight at her beautiful face. "Now."

"Or you'll what? Shoot me? If I were you, I wouldn't so much as startle me. You wouldn't want me to drop the child, would you? A tumble down these marble stairs would probably snap her fragile little neck right in two."

While Portia inched up one more step, Adrian made an inarticulate sound through teeth clenched with rage. He slowly lowered the crossbow. "What do you want from us?"

His foot still resting on Cuthbert's back, Julian spread his arms wide. "Isn't that obvious? She wants what every woman with an empty bed and a lonely heart wants. Me."

Adrian stared at his brother as if he'd never seen him before. "Have you lost your wits?"

"No, brother dear, I've finally come to them. Duvalier was right all along. Why should I spend a miserable eternity fighting my destiny when I could be embracing it? Which is why I brought Valentine this tasty little offering as proof of my sincerity." Cuthbert grunted as Julian stepped off of him and onto the first stair. "And my undying devotion."

Valentine looked even more skeptical than Adrian. "Why should I believe a word you say? You and your precious little Penelope have already tried to trick me twice."

He shook his head. "I was the one who was deceived by my ridiculous infatuation with the chit. After only one night in her arms, I realized she isn't half the woman you are. She could never please me the way you can."

Although he was now abreast with Portia, he was gazing up at Valentine, his dark eyes softened with a melting tenderness Portia recognized only too well. She turned her face away and bit her lip, not knowing whether to laugh or cry.

"Was she truly so tiresome?" Valentine asked, sounding intrigued in spite of herself.

Julian continued to climb. "I can assure you that you would have found her pathetic attempts to please me just as amusing as I did." When Valentine continued to eye him with open suspicion, he added, "I had her once before, you know.

When she was just a girl. I had hoped she would take a few lovers between then and now to improve her skills, but I'm afraid she wasted the whole time I was gone mooning over me like some besotted child. If you must know, I found her to be as clumsy and inept as ever."

Portia sucked in a breath, her lungs burning as if she'd inhaled ground glass.

"You son of a bitch," Adrian whispered, his worst fears about the crypt finally realized. His face going stark white, then red, he raised the crossbow again, pointing it not at Valentine but at his brother's back.

Although Portia wanted nothing more at the moment than to snatch the weapon from Adrian's hands and shoot Julian herself, she shouted, *"No!"* and lunged for Adrian.

Before she could even reach the foot of the stairs, he adjusted his aim and fired, sending the lethal bolt whizzing just past Julian's ear. It embedded itself in the gallery rail with a resounding thud.

Julian slowly pivoted. As he gazed down at his brother, an insolent smile touched his lips. "It's a bit late to be defending her honor, don't you think?"

Adrian's face was a mask of anguish and fury. "She saved your life in that crypt! And that's how you thanked her—by robbing her of her innocence? My God, you are a monster, aren't you?"

"So they tell me." Dismissing his brother with a snort of contempt, Julian climbed the last few steps to join Valentine at the top of the stairs. She was beginning to eye him with new appreciation.

Prowling behind her, he closed his hands over her shoulders. "What do you say, love? Why don't you give the brat back to my brother so you and I can finally be alone?"

Valentine glanced down at Eloisa, a petulant frown wrinkling her brow. "Oh, I don't know. I was rather hoping we could keep her. If you'd let me turn her, she could be our very own little daughter. Strangers on the street would stop to admire and adore her, which would only make it all the more thrilling when she sank her little fangs into their throats."

Julian grimaced. "What an appalling idea! Who wants to be saddled with a sniveling brat for all eternity?"

She sighed. "I suppose you're right. We'd

never be able to keep a nurse. I guess I could give her up," she said grudgingly. "But only on one condition."

Julian inclined his head to nuzzle her ear. "Anything for you, my love."

Her voice softened to a dangerous purr. "I want you to kill Prunella."

Julian's face went completely blank for the exact amount of time it took Portia's heart to start beating again, then he shrugged as if Valentine had asked for an inexpensive bottle of perfume bought from a street vendor or a bouquet of posies filched from someone's garden. "Very well. If I agree to kill *Portia,* will you give the brat back to her doting papa?"

"Only if you'll seal our bargain with a kiss."

He smiled. "It would be my pleasure."

As Julian turned Valentine in his arms and lowered his mouth to hers, Portia thought she might very well spare him the trouble of killing her. Judging from the pain lancing through her heart, she was already dying. All that remained now was to lie down on the ballroom floor and wait for the undertaker to arrive.

The kiss seemed to go on for an eternity and when Julian drew away from Valentine, Portia recognized the enraptured look on her face only too well.

"There. Are you satisfied?" he asked her.

"No, but I have the feeling that I will be very soon."

"Oh, I can promise you that." He gave her snow white cheek one last lingering caress before turning back to the ballroom. "Come here, Portia," he commanded, crooking one arrogant finger at her just as he had done in Adrian's library.

She stood frozen on the steps, finding it impossible to even contemplate putting herself at the mercy of this cruel, cutting stranger. But as her gaze fell on Eloisa, she edged forward.

"Don't," Adrian said hoarsely. "I won't let you do it."

"Don't dawdle, darling," Julian said. "I can remember a time when you would have gladly run into my arms, bleating like a lovestruck lamb."

Her gaze still fixed on the tender innocence of Ellie's sleeping face, Portia climbed another step, her feet feeling as if they were mired in quicksand.

Julian rolled his eyes. "She's always been a hopeless romantic. Perhaps she just needs to be wooed with some tender words and courtly verse." He folded his arms over his chest, looking directly at her for the very first time since entering the ballroom. "What is it my favorite poet once wrote? 'She walks in beauty like the night of cloudless climes and starry skies . . .' "

As she gazed into the fathomless depths of his sparkling dark eyes, Portia's heart swelled with emotion. She climbed the next step without hesitation, then the next. Still gazing into his eyes, she drew the scarf from her throat and let it drift from her fingers. Despite the tears blurring her vision, her voice rang out clear and true. " 'And all that's best of dark and bright meet in her aspect and her eyes.' "

Then she was at the top of the stairs and Julian was holding out his hand to her. She went to him, trusting her heart and her life into his hands just as she had done all those years before in the crypt.

He enfolded her in his arms, slipping them around her waist from behind. His body was already burning with fever, so hot she feared they might both go up in flames. He inclined his head, the very tips of his fangs grazing the softness of her throat.

"I'm prepared to carry out my end of the bargain," he informed Valentine, his voice a smoky growl in Portia's ear. "I expect you to do the same."

She blew out a beleaguered sigh. "If you insist." She surveyed the men watching helplessly from the ballroom floor below. Her gaze finally settled on Wilbury. "Send the old man."

With more haste than Portia would have thought possible, Wilbury leapt over Cuthbert's prostrate form and came dashing up the stairs. Before Valentine could even retrieve her sapphire necklace from the child's clutches, he had snatched Eloisa out of her arms and gone scampering back down the steps.

Adrian was waiting at the foot of the stairs to gather his daughter into his arms. She roused just long enough to give him a drowsy smile before resting her head on his shoulder. He squeezed his eyes shut and buried his lips in her tousled curls for a long moment before raising his anguished gaze to Portia.

She smiled down at him through her tears,

wishing he could know what was in her heart at that moment.

Then Julian's implacable hand was urging her head to the side, giving him unfettered access to the vulnerable curve of her throat. As his fangs descended, Valentine devoured them both with her gaze, her own fangs sharp and bright against her blood red lips, her fingers curled into talons.

Portia closed her eyes, praying that her faith had not been misplaced. Just as his fangs were on the verge of piercing her skin, Julian abruptly lifted his head to look at Valentine. "Why don't you do it?"

"Really?" Her eyes glowing with delight, she clapped her bejeweled hands. "I thought you didn't like to share."

"For you, I'm willing to make an exception. Here. She's all yours." He shoved her into Valentine's arms just as Duvalier had once shoved her into his own arms.

Valentine seized her, her hands brutal where Julian's had been achingly tender. Grabbing a handful of the hair tied at the nape of her neck, she yanked Portia's head to the side, so intent upon devouring her prey that she never even saw Julian slip around behind her.

One second Valentine was hissing in Portia's ear, the next she was letting out a furious wail as Julian's fangs sank deep into her own throat. Her limbs went rigid, sending Portia sprawling to her knees on the slick marble.

As Julian truly unleashed the beast within him for both the first and last time, Portia wanted to hide her face in her hands, but all she could do was gape in astonishment. His wrath was majestic, his power of destruction both terrible and irresistible. There wasn't even a trace of passion or desire in the act, only savagery and violence. He sucked what had passed for life right out of Valentine, seeking his own soul with a ravenous hunger that would no longer be denied.

As she stopped fighting, going limp in his embrace, his head snapped back as if he'd been struck by a jolt of lightning. Portia knew she would never forget the look on his face at that moment. It was both agony and rapture, despair and joy, death followed by the miraculous flush of new life. He gasped, his chest shuddering as his starved lungs demanded their first real breath in nearly a decade.

Portia slowly rose, so mesmerized by the sight that she wasn't even aware that all of the

French windows had flown open or that men were streaming into the ballroom through every archway and door.

She might have remained oblivious if Wallingford's booming shout hadn't penetrated her daze. "Unhand that woman, you monster! See! I told you you'd find him here with that Cuthbert fellow. First he burns his brother's house to the ground and now this! Give me that bloody pistol, man, before it's too late!"

At the exact moment Valentine crumbled to dust in Julian's arms, a pistol shot rang out.

A pall of silence fell over the ballroom. Julian glanced down at his black shirt. An even darker stain was blossoming across the front of it. He touched his hand to the stain, then held it up in front of his eyes, blinking in wonder at the blood dripping from his fingers.

"Well, I'll be damned," he whispered, slowly lifting his eyes to meet Portia's. A heart-wrenching smile broke across his face. "Or maybe I won't."

As his knees crumpled, Portia launched herself across the landing with an anguished cry, breaking his fall with her arms. They sank to the floor together, Julian's head cradled in her lap.

Chaos erupted on the ballroom floor below but for Portia there was nothing but this moment, this man. She pressed her hand to his chest, gazing at the blood welling between her fingers in helpless horror.

She shifted her gaze to his face, astonished by the changes that had taken place there. There were fresh crinkles around his eyes and the lines that bracketed his mouth had deepened. A few stray threads of silver streaked the dark hair at his temples. Those unmistakable signs of mortality only made him more beautiful in her eyes.

Her breath caught on a sob. "Damn you, Julian Kane! If you try to die on me now, Valentine's wrath will be *nothing* compared to mine. Why, I'll let them . . . I'll let them read Byron at your funeral!"

His grimace of pain deepened. "You know I loathe Byron."

"Yes, I do. Which is why I knew exactly what you were going to do when you said he was your favorite poet."

He smiled up at her, his eyes drinking in her face. "That's my clever girl." He drew in a ragged breath that escaped in a sigh. "This is very disappointing, you know. I was so looking forward to growing old with you."

"We *are* going to grow old together!" Portia said fiercely, her fingers tangling in his shirt. "I'm going to eat too much plum pudding and get as fat as I please and nag you about your smoking. And you're going to get gray and paunchy and crotchety and demand to know where I've hidden your pipe. And we're both going to dance at our grandchildren's weddings, even if it mortifies them."

Julian lifted a hand to her cheek, stroking it with trembling fingers. "I never should have left you. When I think of all the wasted time . . ."

"Then don't leave me now," she begged, her tears beginning to fall like rain. "Please . . ." Her voice breaking, she rested her brow against his.

"Don't cry, angel," he murmured, urging her head up so she could meet his gaze. "You did exactly what you set out to do in that crypt. You saved me." He pressed his other hand over hers, forcing her to feel each miraculous, shuddering beat of his heart. "Will you weep over my grave when I'm gone?" he asked hoarsely.

"Every day," she whispered, struggling to smile through her tears.

"And if one of your suitors should give you a cat, will you name it after me?"

She nodded, no longer able to speak at all.

He gave her the crooked smile she had always loved so well, the sparkle already fading from his eyes. "I had hoped to give you my soul but I'm afraid I may have need of it where I'm going. But don't worry, Bright Eyes. You'll always have my heart."

Portia buried her face against his breast, letting out a muffled wail of agony as she felt that heart stop beating beneath her hand.

Twenty-one

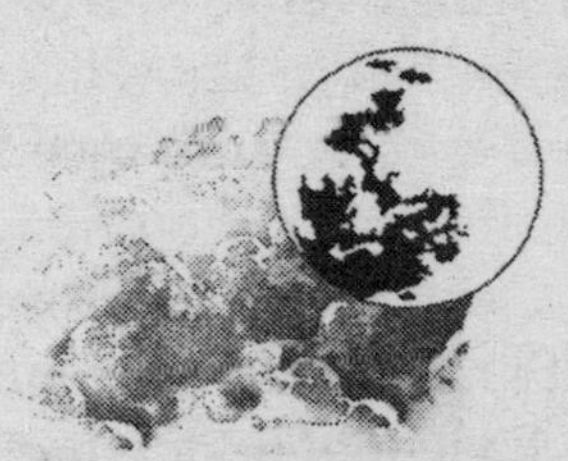

The women were weeping.

Caroline and Vivienne huddled together on the hard wooden pew with Eloisa perched between them, nibbling on a string of her mother's pearls. Larkin sat on the other side of Vivienne, squeezing her hand to offer what comfort he could.

"I never dreamed this day would come, did you?" Caroline asked her sister, dabbing at her pink nose with the monogrammed handkerchief she always carried in her bodice.

Vivienne shook her head, her big blue eyes

misting over with fresh tears. "My only consolation lies in knowing that we can be here for her, to offer guidance and advice and comfort during the difficult days to come."

Caroline reached over and patted her hand. "It's never easy to let go of someone you love."

Vivienne nodded. "Especially someone so dear."

Growing more restless by the minute, Eloisa wiggled around and climbed to a standing position on the pew. Spitting out the pearls, she studied the somber faces of the grown-ups lining the pews behind her with grave interest.

Until a man appeared in the doorway at the back of the church, his long, lean form silhouetted by the sunlight.

Chortling with delight, she held her plump little arms out to him. "Unca Jules!"

Julian came striding down the long aisle, a grin breaking over his face. He swept Eloisa up into his arms, planting a kiss on her rosy cheek. "Hello, pumpkin. Did you miss your dear old uncle?"

She nodded, resting her head on his shoulder with a contented sigh.

"Oh, for heaven's sake," Caroline said,

rolling her eyes. "She just saw you at breakfast."

Julian drew back in mock reproach. "Can I help it if I'm irresistible to the ladies? Once they've had a taste of my kisses, they're never the same."

"So I've been told," Caroline replied with a teasing smirk.

Larkin drew a pocket watch from his waistcoat, frowning down at it. "Aren't you running a bit late? We were beginning to think you'd run off to the Continent with some opera dancer."

"I had to stay and help Wilbury oversee the icing of the cake. In case you've forgotten, I owe the old rascal my life."

Larkin shook his head. "How could I ever forget? I had no idea what he was up to when he knocked Portia aside on that landing and started pounding on your chest. Turns out it was a trick he learned in battle when he was a young man. Thank God Wallingford had that surgeon on hand. If he hadn't been able to staunch the bleeding and stitch you back together . . ." Although he left the thought unfinished, a brief chill seemed to touch the sun-warmed air.

One of the men in the pew behind them leaned forward, no longer satisfied with simply eavesdropping on their conversation. "Ah, Wallingford! I hear he's gone quite mad, you know. Keeps babbling on and on about some sort of bloodsucking monsters prowling the streets of London. Had to lock the poor bloke away in Bedlam, they did, before he did anyone else any harm."

Larkin and Julian exchanged a hard-eyed glance, unable to completely hide their satisfaction.

The man went on. "He keeps swearing Kane here murdered some poor woman, although there was no trace of a body to be found. Wallingford can't even get the men who were with him that night to testify on his behalf. They all swear the light was poor and they didn't see anything until Wallingford jerked that constable's pistol out of his hand and started firing. I'm afraid he's going to be locked away for a very long time. But as I see it, he's lucky he wasn't hanged for shooting an innocent man."

As the fellow settled back in his pew, Julian murmured, "Well, no one's ever called me *that* before."

He glanced toward the altar at the front of the church, where Adrian and Cuthbert were patiently waiting for his arrival. He hadn't been able to choose between them, so he'd asked them both to stand up for him on this day.

Cubby was fidgeting nervously with his cravat while Adrian stood straight and tall, his hands linked at the small of his back. Julian handed Eloisa back to Caroline, giving the child's curls an affectionate rumple before moving toward the altar.

Cubby greeted him with a relieved sigh. "Thank heavens you're here, Jules! I've managed to get this blasted thing into a terrible tangle!"

Julian gently pushed Cubby's hands out of the way. It only took him two deft twists to work the cravat into a crisp knot. "There. You look quite the gentleman. Your father would be very proud of you."

Cuthbert beamed at him. His lip was healed, but a sallow yellow bruise still ringed one eye.

Julian shook his head ruefully. "Out of all the things I had to do when I was a vampire . . ."

Cubby waved away the apology. "You don't have to say it. Why, I'd let you hit me again if it meant I didn't have to attend any more of those godawful temperance lectures!"

Giving his friend one last clap on the shoulder, Julian took his place at Adrian's side.

Without looking at him, Adrian asked, "Have I told you lately how very proud I am of you?"

Julian slanted him a disbelieving glance. "It wasn't so long ago that you wanted to put a crossbow bolt through my heart."

"I missed, didn't I?"

"On purpose?"

Adrian continued to stare straight ahead, the smile flirting with his lips reminding Julian that even though they would always be brothers, there were still some secrets neither one of them would ever confess.

"I should have shot you for keeping Wilbury stationed outside of Portia's bedchamber every night for the past three weeks while our banns were being read." Julian sighed. "I thought I knew what an eternity was before . . ."

"I'm surprised you didn't try to sneak through her bedchamber window."

Julian shot him a glare. "I did. But without wings, it's not quite as easy as it looks. Especially not with a big fat rosebush planted right beneath her window." He gave his hip a rub, his flesh stinging from the memory.

"Aren't you the one who's always said that anything worth having is worth waiting for?"

Julian might not have been inclined to agree with his brother if the door at the back of the church hadn't swung open at precisely that moment. He caught his breath, an act that was still a miracle to him.

But not as much of a miracle as the woman in the doorway, the woman who had made his every dream come true.

He stood in a church, no longer banished from the presence of his family or God. Sunlight streamed through the stained-glass windows, warming his face and glinting off the glossy silk of Portia's curls and the exquisite Brussels lace of her gown.

Because of her, he could sleep through the night and rise to greet the dawn. He could turn up his nose at blood pudding and order his beefsteaks charred to the bone. He could sit with his niece in his lap and teach her how to bang out the first few bars of Mozart's "Requiem" on the piano. The only thing that remained from his lonely years as a vampire was his insatiable hunger for this woman.

She smiled at him, her bright blue eyes

sparkling with love and tenderness. She wore a snow white choker around her throat and a halo of white rosebuds in her hair, making her look like the angel she was.

His loving gaze drifted downward. She wasn't yet carrying his child as she had been in his dream, but starting tonight he planned to devote his every effort to the task.

He knew he was supposed to wait for the bishop to bless their union, but he already felt so blessed that he couldn't wait another minute to claim his bride. Leaving Adrian and Cuthbert to exchange a bemused glance, he strode back down the aisle, ignoring the shocked gasps that followed him.

As he swept Portia into his arms, her merry ripple of laughter rang like bells through his soul. "Why, Mr. Kane, I don't believe you're supposed to kiss your bride until *after* you promise to love and cherish her for a lifetime."

He gazed down at her, lovingly tracing every dear and familiar curve of her face. He had thought she was beautiful by candlelight and moonlight, but it had taken the sunlight to reveal her true radiance. "A lifetime won't be long enough to love you. I told you once before that whether I was a vampire or a man, I would love you for all eternity." He touched his lips to her brow. "My sweet . . . my darling . . . my angel . . ."

She drew back, scowling up at him through narrowed eyes. "If you say Prunella, we may be together for a lifetime but I can promise you I'll make it feel like an eternity."

"My sweet . . . my darling . . . my angel . . ." He tweaked the very tip of her nose, then pressed a meltingly tender kiss to her lips. ". . . my Bright Eyes."

NEW YORK TIMES **BESTSELLING AUTHOR**

TERESA MEDEIROS

After Midnight

0-06-076299-3/$6.99 US/$9.99 Can

Most of the *ton* firmly believe Lord Trevelyan, the enigmatic nobleman is...a *vampire*. Surely, it is nonsense. And yet the brooding gentleman inhabits a dark castle and is never seen in the daylight. And when Caroline Cabot encounters the hypnotically handome viscount, she is shaken by a fevered desire that borders on the unnatural.

YOURS UNTIL DAWN

0-06-051365-9/$7.50 US/$9.99 Can

Gabriel Fairchild's valor during battle costs him his sight and hope for the future. And he claims his prim nurse Samantha Wickersham doesn't possess an ounce of womanly softness, yet she can feel his heart racing at her slightest touch.

ONE NIGHT OF SCANDAL

0-06-051364-0/$7.50 US/$9.99 Can

Carlotta Anne Fairleigh's latest impetuous "adventure" ends in disaster, thoroughly compromising her reputation and leaving her betrothed to the handsome, mysterious marquess Hayden St. Clair. Yet there is something thrilling—and surprisingly tender—about her dark, unreachable groom.

Visit www.AuthorTracker.com for exclusive information on your favorite HarperCollins authors.

Available wherever books are sold or please call 1-800-331-3761 to order.

TEM 0706